Mary Ellen

D0661093

"A tense romantic suspense thriller . . . an exhilarating tale." —Harriet Klausner

"Fast-paced enough to appeal to fans of mystery thrillers, but contains enough sizzle to satisfy those who lean to-ward the romance aspect of romantic suspense."
—The Romance Readers Connection

Are You Afraid?

"Cassidy's sharp new thriller boasts an easy, masterful balance that's rare and ambitious for a suspense novel. Quiet details make Cassidy's novel work. . . . Smooth, simple prose tells a full story that's equal parts romance, family drama, and sheer terror." —*Publishers Weekly*

The Perfect Family

"[An] exciting thriller." —The Best Reviews

"Gritty and gripping psychological suspense is rapidly becoming Cassidy's hallmark. *The Perfect Family* is creepy and frightening—but really intense, fun reading."
—*Romantic Times*

continued . . .

Also by Carla Cassidy

Promise Him Anything
The Perfect Family
Are You Afraid?
Without A Sound

PAINT IT
RED

Carla Cassidy

A SIGNET ECLIPSE BOOK

SIGNET ECLIPSE
Published by New American Library, a division of
Penguin Group (USA) Inc., 375 Hudson Street,
New York, New York 10014, USA
Penguin Group (Canada), 90 Eglinton Avenue East, Suite 700, Toronto,
Ontario M4P 2Y3, Canada (a division of Pearson Penguin Canada Inc.)
Penguin Books Ltd., 80 Strand, London WC2R 0RL, England
Penguin Ireland, 25 St. Stephen's Green, Dublin 2,
Ireland (a division of Penguin Books Ltd.)
Penguin Group (Australia), 250 Camberwell Road, Camberwell, Victoria 3124,
Australia (a division of Pearson Australia Group Pty. Ltd.)
Penguin Books India Pvt. Ltd., 11 Community Centre, Panchsheel Park,
New Delhi—110 017, India
Penguin Group (NZ), 67 Apollo Drive, Rosedale, North Shore 0745,
Auckland, New Zealand (a division of Pearson New Zealand Ltd.)
Penguin Books (South Africa) (Pty.) Ltd., 24 Sturdee Avenue,
Rosebank, Johannesburg 2196, South Africa

Penguin Books Ltd., Registered Offices:
80 Strand, London WC2R 0RL, England

First published by Signet Eclipse, an imprint of New American Library,
a division of Penguin Group (USA) Inc.

First Printing, August 2007
10 9 8 7 6 5 4 3 2 1

Prologue

The dream awakened her just before dawn. Vanessa Abbott woke with a gasp, her heart thundering an unnatural rhythm. Her bedroom was dark except for the night-light that burned in a socket near the door.

She sat up, worried a hand through her tangle of shoulder-length dark hair and glanced at the clock on her nightstand. Almost six. She reached over and shut off the alarm that would ring in half an hour, then got out of bed.

There was no point in trying to go back to sleep; not with her heart still racing and the taste of fear in the back of her throat.

She slid out of bed and grabbed the robe on the end. She pulled it around her shoulders as she left the room, hoping the terry cloth would absorb some of the chill the dream had left behind.

She went only a short distance down the hallway before turning into another bedroom, lit by the faint illumination of a night-light.

Johnny was curled up on his side, a half smile on his face, as if his dreams were happy ones. All ten-year-olds should have happy dreams. There had been a time when she hadn't been sure her son would ever have a happy dream again.

She fought the impulse to lean over and kiss him, to feel the reassuring warmth of his forehead beneath her lips. He still had an hour to sleep and she didn't want to wake him up by indulging in her motherly need.

Instead she left his bedroom and made her way down the stairs to the kitchen. There, she turned on the small light over the stove and made a pot of coffee.

As she waited for the brew to finish, she sat at the kitchen table and stared out the window at the eastern sky transforming from the black of night to the gray of predawn.

She pulled the robe more tightly around her, telling herself her chill came from the drafts in the old three-story house rather than from the recurrence of the dream. It wasn't until she had a cup of coffee in front of her that she allowed herself to think about the visions that had awakened her.

It was always the same. In her dream she stood on a deck and Canada geese flew overhead. At first there were just a few, silently winging to the south. Then more appeared, their thick bodies and large wings blocking out the sun, turning day into night. And they were no longer silent, but honking so loudly, so discordantly, she thought she'd go mad.

It was then, when the sky was black with them, when she thought she'd go crazy with the noise, that she awakened, heart pumping with fight-or-flight adrenaline.

She wrapped her hands around the warm coffee mug and stared out the window. She'd had the dream only three other times that she could remember. The first had been when she'd been ten, the day her parents had died in a car accident.

The second time had been in college; after the dream she'd received a phone call that her grandfather, the man who'd raised her after her parents' death, had suffered a heart attack and died.

The last time she'd had the dream had been two years ago. She'd awakened just after dawn to find her husband gone from their bed, and she'd known something terrible had happened.

The something terrible had been worse than she could have imagined. It wasn't until the police officers had appeared at her door that she knew the horror the dream had portended.

They'd found Jim's car parked on the Broadway Bridge. There had been a note on the driver's seat and an eyewitness who had seen a man jump from the bridge into the cold murky waters of the Missouri River. The note had simply said, *Forgive me. I can't go on.* As if that somehow explained everything. As if that somehow made it all okay.

His body had never been found. It was as if the river had swallowed him whole. The police had told her it wasn't unusual for the river to refuse to relinquish its grasp on whatever fell into its depths.

She and Johnny had survived the devastating blow. With the loving support of Jim's family and her own strength, she'd gotten through the darkest days she thought she'd ever face.

And now she'd had the dream again. Maybe it was

because of the show tonight. Maybe the prospect of displaying Jim's work had prompted the familiar nightmare.

Still, as she watched the morning sun shyly peek over the horizon, a shiver of apprehension worked up her spine.

Chapter 1

"As you can see, there's plenty of closet space in each of the bedrooms," Vanessa said to Kate and Robert Worth.

Kate frowned, the gesture creating a slicing wrinkle between her perfectly waxed eyebrows. "The closets are nice, but I was hoping for a master bedroom that would face west. Maybe we should look at some other properties before making a final decision. Can we set up an appointment with you for tomorrow afternoon?"

"Of course," Vanessa replied, tamping down an edge of impatience. She'd been working with them for the last three weeks, showing them house after house in their price bracket. She had a feeling Robert would have been happy in any of the places she'd shown them, but Kate was another matter.

"I'll pull up some addresses this evening for you to see tomorrow," Vanessa said as she walked the couple to their car. "Why don't we say one o'clock. Would that work for both of you?"

Kate looked at her husband; then they both nodded.

Minutes later they pulled away from the house and
Vanessa got into her car and drew a deep steadying
breath.

It had not been a great day. A contract she'd thought
was a sure thing had fallen through at the last minute, and
having to deal with Robert and Kate Worth had become a
study in frustration. Kate Worth wanted a champagne
home on a beer budget. The pert, uncompromising
blonde was a Realtor's nightmare.

Vanessa turned on the heater to banish the winter chill
in the car, backed out of the driveway and headed for
home. It was after five o'clock and all too soon it would
be time for the show at Andre's Gallery.

Tonight would be bittersweet, both a celebration of
Jim's life and, at least for her, a final good-bye. When Jim
had died he'd been a promising new talent in the art
world. His oil paintings had begun to receive acclaim and
he'd had several showings.

At the time of his suicide he'd left behind a studio full
of finished works, but it had been months before Vanessa
was able to look at them, let alone sort through them to
see what was there. Since his death, art galleries had contacted her on a regular basis, eager to cash in on what Jim
had left behind.

Andre Gallagher had been the first to believe in Jim's
talent and had shown Jim's work at his upscale gallery
when nobody else would take a chance on an unknown.
When Vanessa had finally decided that it was time to let
the public see more of Jim's art, it had been Andre she'd
offered it to. He'd jumped at the opportunity, and
tonight twelve of Jim's paintings would be on display at
an invitation-only event.

And between now and then Vanessa needed to make dinner, pull up some properties to show the Worths tomorrow and make sure she and Johnny were dressed to kill for the black-tie event at eight.

As she pulled into her driveway, she stifled a yawn. "No rest for the wicked," she said to herself as she pulled in next to Scott's car.

She felt as if she'd been running on maximum speed since Jim's death. He'd left them without life insurance, without any real resources. Vanessa had gone from a part-time receptionist in a busy real estate office to a full-time agent in order to keep the house and put food on the table.

The first year had been a nightmare, as she'd struggled with grief, anger and guilt while trying to be a single parent and breadwinner.

The past six months things had gotten easier. The grief had dulled; the anger and guilt had quieted as the business of living had found laughter and joy once again.

"Hello! I'm home," she yelled as she walked into the front foyer.

She wasn't surprised when there was no reply. She knew where Johnny and Scott would be—in the third-floor attic studio.

She threw her purse on the table just inside the door and hung her coat on the hall tree, then walked up the stairs in search of her son and Scott.

This house had been her passion when she and Jim had first looked at it. It had been a diamond in the rough, a century-old eyesore at the edge of a new housing development.

Years of neglect had made it a handyman's dream, and for the first year after they'd moved in they'd scrubbed and sanded, painted and polished, to transform it into a lovely home.

It was a lot of house for just her and Johnny, and it was drafty as hell in the winter and hot in the summer, but she loved it. She felt a sense of permanence here she'd never had while growing up.

The second floor held three oversized bedrooms and two bathrooms, one in the hallway and one off the master bedroom. She had loved the large kitchen and bedrooms, which had been part of the renovation they'd done on the house. Jim had fallen in love with the attic, where he'd envisioned a place for his studio.

As she grabbed the staircase railing that led up the narrow stairs to the attic, the smell that had once been as familiar as her favorite perfume was now a sneaky assailant that assaulted her composure. The bite of turpentine battling with the distinctive odor of oil paints brought back memories of Jim. Memories both good and bad.

The stairs led directly into the studio, a large dormer room well lit not only by the ceiling lights but also by the mid-November sunshine that poured through two big skylights they'd had installed.

Both Johnny and Scott stood in front of an easel, their backs to her. Johnny held a paintbrush and as she watched he dabbed at the painting before him.

"Not too much," Scott Warren said. "You don't want to overwork it."

"Hi, guys," Vanessa said.

Both of them turned. "Hi, Mom." Johnny grinned, and as always his smile shot a wealth of heart-squeezing love through her. He was such a handsome boy. But more than that, he was a great kid.

"If this boy gets any better, he isn't going to need me anymore," Scott said.

"That's not true," Johnny replied. "I still have a lot to learn. I haven't even tried painting people yet."

"You can work for another fifteen minutes or so. Then you need to clean up," Vanessa said. "Dinner will be in about thirty minutes. Then we have to get ready to go."

Johnny turned back to his painting, obviously intending to use every second of his fifteen minutes. Scott followed Vanessa downstairs to the kitchen.

As she began taking things out of the refrigerator for the evening meal, Scott slid into a chair at the table. "Are you ready for tonight?"

Vanessa considered the question before replying. "I am," she finally said. "It's time. Besides, any money that comes out of the showing tonight is going into Johnny's college fund."

"That kid is so talented it's scary," Scott said.

Vanessa frowned as she tore apart a head of lettuce for a salad. "Sometimes it worries me, he's so much like his father."

"He's talented like his daddy, but he's also amazingly well-adjusted. He doesn't have the darkness in him that Jim did."

She flashed the handsome blond man a grateful smile as she began cutting up a green pepper. "You want to stay for dinner? It's nothing elaborate, just leftover chicken breasts and salad."

"No thanks. In fact, I need to get out of here." He got up from the table.

Vanessa smiled. "We'll see you tonight?"

"Wouldn't miss it for the world," Scott replied, and then left.

As Vanessa finished chopping vegetables to add to the salad, she thanked her stars for Scott Warren. Scott had been Jim's best friend since they had met in an art class in college.

They had been an odd couple—the pretty gay blond and the dark-haired brooding straight man—but their love of art had brought them together and mutual respect had kept them friends.

Scott had also met Eric, a defense attorney, while in college, and the two had been a couple since then. They had been frequent visitors to the house throughout the years and a huge source of support since Jim's death.

Scott worked as an art teacher at one of the local high schools, and whenever Vanessa had to work late, he stepped in as part-time babysitter and mentor to Johnny. She wasn't sure what she'd do without him.

She'd just finished zapping the leftover chicken in the microwave when Johnny joined her in the kitchen. "How was school today?" she asked as he sat at the table.

"Good, except Mr. Abery gave us a project that's due before the Thanksgiving vacation."

"What kind of a project?" She set the chicken on the table, and then joined him.

"We have to write a paper on our favorite animal or bird. He said we'd get extra credit for making pictures and doing a display on poster board." He began to fill his plate.

"And what animal or bird have you decided on?"

He frowned thoughtfully, the gesture making him look exactly like a miniature of his father. "I was thinking maybe a cardinal. I could paint a picture of one and download a birdsong from the Internet."

"Sounds like a great idea. Can you do it in the week you have left before vacation?"

"Yeah, Scott said we'd start on the cardinal tomorrow after school."

They chatted for the remainder of the quick meal, and then parted ways to get cleaned up for the night out. Vanessa took the black dress she'd decided to wear that evening from the closet. Before she closed the closet door her gaze fell on the scarlet red Dior that hung on the rack. She'd thought about wearing it. It had been Jim's favorite dress.

He'd bought it for her six years ago and had spent so much money on it that she'd been appalled. He'd insisted she wear it on each of their anniversaries and on other special occasions over the years.

She hadn't worn it since his death and doubted she would ever wear it again. She placed the black dress on the bed, and then went into the bathroom to take a fast shower.

As she stood beneath the warm spray of water a stab of loneliness gripped her. She'd never planned to be thirty-three years old and living her life alone. When she'd quit college to marry Jim, she'd expected to grow old with him.

Oh, sure, Johnny filled her life as only a ten-year-old could. But there were times when she missed the company of a grown-up male, when she longed not only for adult conversation but also for the kind of intimacy that came from sharing secrets and dreams, the kind that came from great sex.

She finished rinsing herself, shut off the water and grabbed a towel, her thoughts on the night ahead. Andre had pulled out all the stops to assure a successful evening.

He'd sent invitations to a who's who list of art critics, collectors and benefactors and to the movers and shakers in Kansas City. All of Jim's family would be there as well.

The black dress hugged her in all the right places and she pulled her shoulder-length dark hair into a fashionable bun at the nape of her neck. She put on her makeup, and then sat on the edge of the bed to put on her jewelry.

Her gaze caught on the photo of Jim she kept next to her bed. She rarely looked at it anymore, and on more than one occasion had considered packing it away. She didn't think it would bother Johnny if the photo were no longer there.

In fact, her son had surprised her in the last couple of months, mentioning to her that he wouldn't be upset if she decided she wanted to date. There were times when she thought he missed having an adult male around the house as much as she did.

With her gold earrings in place and a favorite bracelet on her wrist, she got up from the bed and went in search of Johnny. She found him standing in front of the bathroom mirror trying to fix his tie.

"Here, let me help," she said. She grabbed the ends of the black and gray tie.

"You look real pretty, Mom," Johnny said.

She finished with the tie, grabbed his chin and planted a kiss on his forehead. "And you look amazingly grown-up and handsome." He swiped at his forehead with the back of his hand. "And don't you wipe away my kiss," she said with mock sternness.

He grinned at her. "I was just rubbing it in."

As they walked down the stairs, she hoped their good mood lasted through the evening. She wanted tonight to be a celebration of life for herself and her son. They had survived a horrible tragedy and she felt that in releasing Jim's paintings, she was releasing any lingering hold his memory had on her.

He watched them as they left the house and got into their car for their big night. Tonight they were selling his paintings. First she had destroyed him and now she was cashing in on his talent.

They would pay. One by one they would all pay. All the people who had used him up and hadn't been there for him. He would destroy them all, except the boy. The boy was so much like him. He would kill them all to save the boy and his talent.

He picked the cuticles on his thumb, the pain centering him, focusing the thoughts that blew through his head with astonishing speed.

He'd thought he could handle things; thought he could let it go. But he couldn't. There were so many of them who might have made a difference but didn't, so many who might have been able to change the course of the past, but hadn't bothered.

He stared down at his thumb, where blood had welled up. Red had been his favorite color. Red, the hue of passion, the color of blood.

He was going to paint them all red.

Chapter 2

A ndre's Gallery was located in the Country Club Plaza area of Kansas City. The Plaza was known for sophisticated, upscale retail shops and residences. With breathtaking architecture and picturesque fountains, the area was a favorite for both tourists and locals.

On the outside, the gallery was an understated storefront with a small sign hanging above the door. Inside, it was a world of contrast and color, of textures and tones.

Andre's assistant, Carrie Sinclair, greeted them at the front door. "Come in," she said. She locked the door after them. "We aren't officially opening the doors until eight. Andre is in his office waiting for you."

As Vanessa and Johnny walked toward the back of the gallery where the office was located, they were surrounded by Jim's work displayed on white walls with accent lighting.

She'd expected to feel some sort of emotion when she saw the pictures here. She'd anticipated a new burst of grief, maybe a hint of residual anger, but she was surprised to realize she felt nothing except the rightness of releasing them to others.

It was at that moment she realized how completely she'd placed Jim in her past and how ready she was to go on with her future, whatever that future might be.

"Vanessa." Andre met her at his office door and took both her hands in his. "You look stunning." He squeezed her hands, then let go of them and reached out to ruffle Johnny's hair. "Good Lord, you've grown a foot since the last time I saw you."

Johnny grinned at the tall, bald-headed man. "Someday my work will be showing here."

"I'd consider it an honor." He smiled at Johnny before turning back to Vanessa. "Things have gone so smoothly it's scary. The caterers arrived and it looks like they got everything right."

He gestured outward, toward the reason they were here tonight. "What do you think of the white walls? I thought about using something else, but Jim's paintings are such an explosion of color I didn't think the background should try to compete."

"It was a good choice, Andre," she assured him. Her gaze swept the pictures and for a moment she allowed herself to think about the man who had created them.

Genius bordering insanity—that's what the critics had said about his work, and it was an apt description of the man as well. His paintings were landscapes, but with angles and lines slightly askew to give the viewer a feeling of vague discomfort. Bold colors splashed the canvas with the most dominant being Jim's favorite, red.

For a moment, myriad emotions flashed through her—

a sharp stab of grief, a whisper of guilt and finally the sadness of acceptance.

He should be here instead of in a watery grave of his choosing. She would never understand the demons that had driven him into making the choice he had made, but in the two years since his death she'd found peace and forgiveness where he was concerned.

"You okay?" Andre asked, pulling her from her thoughts.

"Fine," she assured him with a smile. She placed a hand on Johnny's shoulder. "It's nice to see his work here instead of stored in our basement, right, Johnny?"

"Yeah. When do the caterers start bringing around the stuff to eat?" he asked.

Both Andre and Vanessa laughed. "Soon," Andre replied, and looked at his watch. "It's time to open the doors and let the party begin. You want to help me on door duty?"

"Sure," Johnny replied.

As her son and Andre headed toward the front of the gallery, Carrie approached Vanessa. "Can I get you anything? Maybe a glass of champagne?"

"A club soda would be wonderful," Vanessa replied.

By the time Carrie delivered the drink to her, the doors were open and people began arriving.

By nine o'clock the gallery was packed with people. Champagne flowed freely and the noise in the place was only one decibel below that of a rock concert.

Vanessa stood in a small alcove, taking a breather from talking and smiling. As she sipped a fresh club soda, her gaze swept the room.

In one corner Jim's family was gathered. His mother

and father, three brothers and their respective wives all stood in a circle, chatting and laughing together. Johnny stood next to his uncle Brian, Jim's oldest brother.

As if he felt her gaze on him, Brian turned his head and winked at her. He was a good guy. He was the one she turned to whenever something needed to be done at the house. He was the one who had held her as she'd cried at Jim's memorial service.

When Vanessa had fallen in love with Jim, she'd also fallen for his relatives. Close-knit, at times codependent, they embodied the crazy chaos of family that had been lacking in Vanessa's life.

She recognized several of the art critics that wandered the room, along with the mayor and a couple of members of the city council. Matt McCann, Jim's agent, sat in a chair chewing an unlit cigar while he listened to a bubbly blonde with huge, nearly bare breasts.

Vanessa guessed the woman was an artist looking for representation. Matt might enjoy looking at her breasts, but it would be the woman's art talent that would decide if he represented her or not.

Scott and his partner, Eric, made an attractive couple. Scott, with his blond, pretty-boy features, was a perfect foil for Eric's sultry dark handsomeness. The two stood near a sculpture and appeared to be discussing the merits of the piece.

Thankfully the mood of the evening was upbeat, with most of the talk centered on the artwork itself and not on the tragic story of the artist.

She wasn't sure how long she'd been standing in the alcove when Andre approached her. "I've been looking all over for you," he said. "I've got somebody I'd like you to meet." He grabbed her hand and pulled her across the room, where a man stood in front of one of the paintings, his back to them.

The first thing she noticed was the broad shoulders beneath the well-fitted dark jacket. "Christian," Andre said. Instantly, the attractiveness of his broad shoulders paled as he turned around to face them.

Arresting. That's the only way to describe his chiseled features and startling smoky gray eyes. When he smiled, a whirl of butterflies took flight in her stomach. He had a great smile.

"Vanessa, this is Christian Connor, my best friend in the world and a man desperately in need of buying a home. And this is Vanessa Abbott, the only Realtor I'd trust if I were buying a house."

"Vanessa, it's nice to meet you." He reached for her hand as his gaze did a swift, almost imperceptible assessing sweep down the length of her.

"It's a pleasure to meet you, Mr. Connor," Vanessa said as he released her hand.

"Please, make it Christian," he replied.

"Oh, there's Thomas Randolf from the *Kansas City Star*. I need a word with him." Andre hurried off in the direction of a stoop-shouldered older man making copious notes on a small pad.

Vanessa had always prided herself on being able to talk to anyone at any time, but the moment Andre left her alone with Christian Connor she found herself ridiculously tongue-tied.

She cleared her throat and took a sip of her club soda as an awkward silence descended. God, the man was good-looking with his sandy-colored hair and sexy bedroom eyes.

"So, Christian, are you into art?" she finally asked.

He flashed that smile of his again and moved closer to her. "Can I share a little secret with you? I'm into drinking beer and watching football. I'm into classic rock music and working hard. I'm definitely not into art."

She found his candor charming. "So what are you doing here tonight?"

"I lost a bet. Andre and I had a bet riding on the last Chiefs and Oakland Raiders game. If the Chiefs won, Andre was going to have to spend a day working on one of my job sites. If they lost . . ." He shrugged. "So, here I am."

Although the butterflies still made lazy circles in her stomach, she felt herself begin to relax. "Then this is your first art show?"

He nodded.

"And what do you think?"

"The champagne is good, the little sandwiches are great and at the moment the company is excellent."

Was he flirting with her? It had been so long that she wasn't sure if she was reading him right or not. Still, a flush of pure feminine pleasure swept through her.

"You said if Andre had lost the bet, he'd have had to work on one of your job sites. What is it you do?" she asked.

"I own Connor Construction. We build commercial buildings, mostly strip malls. But I do need a Realtor. I'm in the market for a house. Could you help me out?"

"I'd love to." The little thrill that had swept through her a moment earlier faded away. Maybe he hadn't been flirting with her. Maybe he was just desperate for a good Realtor. She opened her purse and withdrew one of her business cards. "Just give me a call and we'll see what we can do."

He tucked the card into his pocket as he gazed at the nearest painting. "I've always admired people who had talent."

"Too much talent isn't necessarily a good thing," she replied.

Before he could respond, Johnny ran over to them and Vanessa made the introductions. "Grandma wants to talk to you," he said. "They're all getting ready to leave."

Vanessa smiled at Christian. "It was nice meeting you."

"You'll be hearing from me," he replied. He watched as she and her son hurried toward a group of people that stood near the door.

Andre had told him about her and her son and the tragedy of Jim Abbott's death. Christian's friend had spoken of Vanessa's strength following her husband's suicide. He'd raved about her parenting skills and her expertise as a Realtor. But he'd neglected to mention that Vanessa Abbott was amazingly attractive.

He watched her now, noting how the black dress clung to slender but feminine curves, how her legs were sleek and sexy beneath the knee-high skirt. He wondered how her hair would look down, and if it was shoulder-length or longer.

Her dark blue eyes had held a wariness that wasn't surprising considering her past. It must be beyond comprehension to have the man you love jump off a bridge in the middle of the night.

He turned away with a frown. Out of your league, he thought to himself. This was her world: artistic talent and pretentious people. He'd grown up in a similar world and when he'd gotten old enough, he hadn't been able to escape it fast enough.

For just a minute he thought of his father and a tiny ball of resentment pressed tight in his chest. He'd occasionally see in the society column that his father had performed at some function or another. Although Christian talked to his mother once a week, it had been years since he had spoken to his father.

He glanced back at Vanessa. It wouldn't hurt to give her a call and see if she could help him find a place to live. And maybe if he met with her to see a house, she'd have her hair down.

"We're leaving," Vanessa said to Andre.

"So early?"

"It's almost ten o'clock and Johnny has school tomorrow." She leaned up on her tiptoes to kiss Andre's cheek. "You'll call me tomorrow?"

"The minute I roll out of bed." He leaned closer to her, so only she could hear him. "The night was a huge success. Johnny should be able to go to the college of his choice after tonight."

She smiled at him gratefully. Andre knew how worried she'd been about her son's future. As hard as she worked, as many houses as she sold, there was never enough money left over after living expenses to put much away.

With a final murmur of good-bye she and Johnny left the gallery and headed for her car.

As she started the engine Johnny loudly yawned.

"You're going to be tired tomorrow. You aren't used to being up this late on a school night," she said as she adjusted the vent on the heater.

"It's okay. It was fun. Grandma was being kind of silly."

Vanessa smiled. "I think your grandma drank too many glasses of champagne."

"She said she's gonna make two apple pies at Thanksgiving so I get one of them to bring home."

"She's a good grandma."

"Uncle Garrett said maybe this weekend he'd take me to the park."

"That would be nice," she replied, although she knew her brother-in-law Garrett was terrific at making tentative plans that never panned out. He meant well, but he rarely followed through.

Vanessa pulled into the driveway as Johnny yawned again. "Directly to bed with you," she said a moment later as the two of them entered the house. "I'll be up in just a few minutes to tell you good night."

As Johnny headed up the stairs, Vanessa went into the dining room, which she used as a home office. She hadn't had a chance before they left to pull up listings of properties to show the Worths the next day.

She punched on her computer and as she waited for it to boot up, she leaned back in the chair and thought about the night.

Even if not a single painting had sold, she would have considered the night a personal success. For her, it was a final good-bye to the romantically brooding man she'd met and fallen in love with in college.

A farewell to the troubled man she had desperately

tried to understand through nine years of marriage, the man who had finally abandoned her and their son when his inner demons had shouted so loud he'd been unable to hear anything else.

She found a couple of houses and printed off the addresses, and then shut down the computer. As she climbed the stairs her thoughts turned to Christian Connor. She wondered if he'd call her.

It was a pleasant thought, almost as pleasant as standing in her son's bedroom doorway and watching him sleep. She smiled at Johnny, who had apparently fallen asleep the minute his head had hit the pillow.

Love for her son squeezed her heart, crowding out room for anything else. He'd been an easy, contented baby who was growing up to be an easy, uncomplicated young man.

After Jim's death, she'd put him in therapy for a short period of time. She'd been so afraid for him, afraid of the baggage that might fall on his young shoulders.

She knew the statistics of children who had lost a parent to suicide, knew the emotional problems that could arise. She wasn't willing to take any chances where her son's mental health was concerned. But after three months of weekly sessions the psychologist had assured her that he was fine.

Wind howled around the side of the house, rattling the window in its frame. She frowned and walked to the side of her son's bed and pulled the blanket up around him.

As she left his room and headed for her own, a chill danced through her. It had been a great night, yet there was a restless edge in her, a vague feeling of dread that had ridden her shoulders all night.

She changed into her pajamas and climbed into bed. Before turning off the lamp she picked up the photo of Jim from her nightstand. She gazed at his image for a long moment, then placed the photo in the bottom drawer of her nightstand.

It wasn't until she turned off the lamp and lay listening to the mournful autumn wind that she remembered the dream she'd had the night before.

The dream that always portended death.

"Maybe not this time," she whispered softly. "Please, not this time."

It was just minutes before midnight and there were only two people left. But Andre didn't know he had company. He thought he was alone.

The other man stood inside the back door, listening as Andre locked the front door and turned off the lights in the gallery. He tightened his grip on the granite sculpture as Andre's footsteps approached the back. Andre took one step into the office and his eyes widened.

"Surprise," the man said, and swung the granite. It made a satisfying crack as it hit Andre square in the center of his forehead. His head split like a ripe tomato and he fell to the floor without making a sound.

Paint it red.

Chapter 3

"Christ." Detective Tyler King stared at the body of Andre Gallagher sprawled on the floor in the office of the art gallery.

"My thought exactly." Jennifer Tompkins, Tyler's newest partner, stepped past the uniform at the door and into the room, carefully maneuvering around the pool of blood that surrounded what had once been Gallagher's head.

"Who called it in?" Tyler asked the young cop who stood at the door.

The officer, who looked little more than a boy, kept his gaze firmly focused away from the body. "An assistant." He flipped open a small notepad. "Name of Carrie Sinclair. She arrived for work at quarter till ten this morning and found him and immediately called 911. We've got her out back in the alley."

"Where's the medical examiner?" Jennifer asked, a trace of impatience in her voice. "And the crime scene boys? Where the hell is everyone? Taking coffee breaks longer than their vacations?" She cracked her chewing gum loudly as if to punctuate her sentence.

Tyler shot her a warning glare. God save him from rookies eager to make a name for themselves, and damn the powers that be who had given him Jennifer Tompkins to mentor. They had been partnered for eighteen days Eighteen long, agonizing days.

"Patience is one of the first things you embrace as a homicide detective," he said just under his breath.

"Patience is highly overrated," she retorted, her dark eyes holding a hint of challenge.

"Go interview Carrie Sinclair," Tyler said. It was not a request, but rather a command. It was only ten thirty in the morning and she'd already managed to push every single aggravation button he possessed.

"I'd rather stay here and see what the medical examiner has to say."

Tyler narrowed his eyes and gazed at her coldly. Less than a month with a shield and she thought she was ready to call the shots. "My crime, my call. You interview." He pointed to the door.

She held his gaze for a long moment, sighed, turned on her heels and stalked out the door. At twenty-six years old, Jennifer had the overconfidence that came from youth and inexperience, and an attitude that needed serious adjustment.

Tyler was only ten years older than her, but he'd seen enough in the last ten years to know that the very qualities that might, if tempered, make her a great cop were also the very qualities that might get her killed.

He dismissed thoughts of his newest partner and instead focused on what was important—the crime scene before him. In truth, he was grateful the ME hadn't arrived yet and he had an opportunity to stand in the silence and assess the scene before him. He knew he would have only a few minutes before the place began to fill with people.

He glanced around the neat office, looking for clues, seeking answers. The wooden shelf behind the desk held several sculpture pieces that Tyler guessed had price tags that would surpass his monthly pay.

Nothing appeared to be missing. There were no empty spaces that might suggest something had been taken. Of course, that didn't mean robbery hadn't been a factor.

The desk was neat, except for the splatters of blood and brain matter that adorned both the top and sides, and also the computer.

He returned his focus back to the man on the floor, wondering how the assistant had been able to identify him. Certainly his face was gone, shattered bones protruding from bloody flesh. It was obvious the man had been struck repeatedly by a heavy object.

He crouched down next to the body, his nose assaulted by the scent of bowel, blood and death. A streak of red decorated the front of Andre's shirt, like a lavish flourish. It wasn't blood. It was too vivid, too red. Tyler leaned closer and took a deep whiff. Paint. It smelled like oil paint.

"You communing with the devil?" The familiar deep, raspy voice came from behind him and he stood and turned to see Dr. Pip, the ME, standing in the office doorway. Pip wasn't his real name, but nobody knew him by any other.

He was a small man with a big voice and an even bigger sense of humor. Some were offended by it, some ignored it and Tyler appreciated it.

"This particular devil isn't talking much to me yet," he replied.

Pip walked over to the body, opened his black case and pulled on a pair of gloves. "Give it time. Sooner or later they always talk to you."

It was true. Tyler had an uncanny knack for crawling into the heads of the victims he mourned and the killers he sought. It probably should concern him, how easily he communed with evil, but he never gave himself much time to think about it.

He watched as Dr. Pip ran through his paces on the body, checking the stage of rigor and taking body temperature all in an effort to establish approximate time of death.

Tyler didn't have to tell him not to touch the red mark on Andre's chest. Dr. Pip carefully cut the area and bagged it, knowing it would need to be sent to the lab for analysis.

Tyler tamped down the urge to hurry the man. Pip wasn't the fastest dog out of the gate, but he was the most accurate. "Certainly cause of death appears to be head trauma. You don't have to be a rocket scientist to realize it's hard to survive when your face has been beaten into the back of your skull." He began to whistle the tune of "Rocket Man" as he continued his work on the body.

He finally closed his bag and stood. "Unless I find something surprising during autopsy, I'd say he was beaten to death and it happened sometime last night between ten and midnight."

At that moment the crime scene unit arrived and within minutes the body had been bagged and tagged and taken away so the men could begin their work of collecting potentially crucial evidence that the killer might have left behind.

Jennifer returned, her broad features squeezed into a familiar gesture of impatience and frustration. "Bad news."

"What?"

"According to Carrie Sinclair there was a fancy private art show here last night. Seventy-five people on the guest list plus the catering crew."

"Why is that bad news?"

She cracked her gum and exhaled a deep sigh. "That means we have at least eighty potential suspects."

"That's not bad news," Tyler countered. "That means we have a place to start. That's a lot more than we get most of the time."

"She told me there's a guest list in the top desk drawer."

"What artist was showing last night?"

Jennifer frowned. "I didn't think to ask." She flushed beneath his displeased glare. "Guess I'll go ask her now."

"And tell her we'll need her to come down to the station to make an official statement." Tyler watched her go.

God help him from rookies. He focused his attention back to the crime scene before him, wondering how long it might take before he was communing with this particular devil.

Chapter 4

The Wallace Realty office was located fifteen minutes from Vanessa's house. The close proximity had been one of the reasons Vanessa had gone to work there. The other reason was that in the days of Internet-based Realtors, Wallace Realty still believed in the importance of human interaction and a personal, committed relationship with clients.

A total of eight Realtors worked out of the office, although it was rare that all eight would be in at the same time. This morning they would all be there, as Dave Wallace had scheduled a staff meeting at ten.

It was just after nine thirty when Vanessa walked through the door. Alicia Richards, the receptionist, was the only other person in the office.

"How did it go last night?" Alicia asked.

Vanessa knew that nothing would make Alicia happier than Vanessa telling her that the art show had been a dismal failure. Alicia was one of those women who thrived on other people's misery. The announcement of a big winner in the lottery could make her bitchy for days.

"It was nice," Vanessa replied. She could tell that it was going to be one of those days with Alicia. An attractive blonde, her mouth was set in a slight pout and gray eye shadow rode her eyelids.

Vanessa had recognized at some point or another that she could forecast Alicia's moods by the color of shadow she wore on any given day. Blue was usually a good mood, as were green and lavender. Gray was always bad news.

Vanessa shrugged out of her coat. "I thought you were going to come."

Alicia's nostrils thinned. "Some of us have complicated lives that don't make it easy to just take off a night and spend it at the local art gallery."

Vanessa swallowed a sigh. Alicia was in rare form this morning. Whenever she was in one of her moods, her favorite target seemed to be Vanessa.

"I suppose you sold all the paintings and made tons of money," Alicia continued.

"Actually, I don't know what sold and what didn't. Andre was supposed to call me this morning, but I didn't hear from him before I left the house." She hung her coat on the rack just inside the door, then sat at the desk she shared with one of the other Realtors.

"I guess you still haven't managed to close a deal with the Worths," Alicia said, looking as smug as a poodle with a diamond collar.

"We're going out again this afternoon. It's just a matter of time before they see the right property." Vanessa turned on the computer, figuring she'd check the latest available listings before the staff meeting and update her appointment book.

Jim's family had been incredibly supportive after his death, and Vanessa had found her coworkers here at the agency equally supportive. It had been Dave Wallace who had encouraged her to get her license and leave the receptionist desk behind.

The other agents had been generous with their knowledge, teaching her little tricks of the trade that could make a difference between closing a deal or not. They had shared their wisdom and their compassion.

She cast a quick glance at Alicia, who was typing something on her computer, her sculptured nails clicking a rapid tattoo. Alicia was the only person in the business whose compassion and caring hadn't felt genuine. She said all the right words, made all the appropriate gestures, but there was no heart behind it.

However, hearing Alicia talk about her family, the men she dated and the things she did, Vanessa suspected that it wasn't a beating heart that kept Alicia alive, but rather a miserable unhappiness and a competitive drive.

With her blond curls and blue eyes, she was a pretty woman, but her attractiveness was tempered by the hard gleam in her eyes and the hint of a sneer that threatened to take over her features at any moment.

Within minutes the other agents began to arrive and the office filled with easy laughter and the camaraderie of people who shared a common interest.

The staff meeting took place in a large room in the back of the building and lasted almost an hour. Dave Wallace, the owner, spoke with excitement about the booming real estate market and encouraged each of them to set new personal goals for sales.

His broad face reddened as he talked passionately

about how many people were choosing to make their homes in the Kansas City area and the fact that there was no reason why each and every one of the Realtors couldn't see incomes they'd only dreamed about.

Vanessa knew she'd never get wealthy doing this work. She wasn't driven enough, set too many limitations for herself. She tried not to show in the evenings and worked on Saturday or Sunday only if it was absolutely necessary. She preferred to spend her evenings and weekends with Johnny.

As long as she generated enough sales to pay for the living expenses and have a little extra to tuck into savings or for a movie or dinner out, she was satisfied.

"He should have been a motivational speaker instead of a Realtor," Buzz Braxton whispered to her. "He could motivate a dog to fly."

Vanessa grinned, and then directed her gaze back to Dave. Buzz was a nice guy. His wife had recently left him, and Vanessa had a feeling he was working up his nerve to ask her out. As nice as he was, Vanessa wasn't interested.

There were no sparks, no magic, with Buzz. She wanted magic. If she decided to get into another relationship, she needed magic.

She'd had it once, in those early days of her relationship with Jim. The first moment she'd laid eyes on him her heart had quickened and butterflies had danced in the pit of her stomach. She'd known in that first glance that he was the man she wanted to marry, the man she wanted to spend the rest of her life with.

Unfortunately, that magic had lasted only months into the marriage. By the time she was pregnant, she began to see the emotional cracks in the man she loved, cracks that became wide fissures that swallowed up whatever magic had once existed.

The staff meeting broke up, but everyone lingered, helping themselves to the doughnuts and coffee Dave had provided. "Sorry I didn't make it last night," Helen Burkshire said to Vanessa; then she bit into a crusty cruller that dropped crumbs all over her black sweater. "How did it go?"

"It was nice." Vanessa picked up a glazed from the tray and leaned closer to her friend. "Andre pulled out all the stops. Things went well, much to Alicia's dismay."

Helen brushed the crumbs from the front of her. "Alicia is a bitch. She's just working here until a handsome millionaire walks through the door and sweeps her off her feet."

Vanessa smiled. "That might be hard to do, considering the fact that most of the time Alicia's feet are in her mouth."

Helen laughed. "How's that handsome boy of yours? Did he handle things okay last night?"

"He's great and he seemed to be fine with the show." Vanessa bit into her doughnut and chewed thoughtfully for a moment. "I worry about him sometimes. He seems so well-adjusted that I'm afraid there might be things I'm missing."

Helen lightly touched Vanessa's arm. "Stop it. Stop it right now. Don't look for trouble. The bad times are behind you now."

"You're right," Vanessa replied, and tried to ignore the tiny sense of inexplicable dread that had whispered through her ever since she'd had that familiar, haunting dream.

She finished her doughnut and chatted with Helen and several of her fellow agents for a few minutes longer before heading back into the main room.

She stopped short in the doorway as she saw the man talking to Alicia. The night before, he'd been handsome as sin in his dark suit. Now clad in a pair of worn jeans and a knit shirt that stretched across his broad chest, he made her heart skip a beat.

Christian Connor. He looked up as she took another step forward and the smile that lit his features momentarily stole her breath.

Alicia turned her head to see Vanessa, and her flirtatious smile fell from her face. "Vanessa, this gentleman is here to see you," she said.

"Mr. Connor," she said as she approached where he stood.

"I thought we'd agreed last night that it was Christian and Vanessa," he replied, a slight chiding tone in his voice. "I was in the area and thought I'd stop by to kind of get the ball rolling."

"Yes, of course." She glanced over to her desk, relieved that Mike Scalon, the agent she shared the space with, was nowhere to be seen. She gestured him toward the desk. "Why don't we have a seat and chat a bit so I can pull up some properties that might interest you."

She was ridiculously self-conscious as he followed her to the desk. A million thoughts flew through her brain. She was glad she'd decided to wear the pencil-thin blue slacks that complemented her long legs.

She was grateful that she'd coupled the slacks with her

favorite blouse, a shimmery blue gray that brought out the blue of her eyes. Then she quickly chided herself for focusing on things that didn't matter.

He was here to find a house. That was her job. It didn't matter what she wore. All he cared about was her expertise in fitting the right house with the right person.

She slid into the chair behind the desk as he sat in the chair next to her. She was immediately aware of the scent of him, a heady combination of warm sunshine, crisp wintry air and spicy cologne.

"I have a questionnaire that I have potential clients fill out," she explained as she opened her top desk drawer to withdraw the questionnaire.

"Does it ask me about my deepest, darkest fantasies?" One of his eyebrows quirked upward as a teasing smile curled his lips. God, the man had great lips.

Once again a slight flutter went off in the pit of her stomach. How long had it been since an attractive male teased with her? She couldn't remember the last time.

"It does," she said, responding with a light teasing tone of her own. "It asks those burning, need-to-know questions like how many bathrooms you prefer, if you're interested in a ranch or a two-story and what kind of a lot you'd like the house to be on."

"Wow, really digging deep into my psyche." He took the questionnaire from her and began to fill it out. While he did that, she pretended to be busy at the computer. But her gaze kept going from the screen to him.

Christian Connor had none of the physical qualities that had initially drawn her to Jim so many years ago. Jim had been all shadows, brooding intensity and dark secrets.

Christian had an openness to his features, a sparkle in his eyes and a warmth to his smile that was infinitely appealing to a woman who felt as if she'd walked in the shadows for too long.

Out of the corner of her eye she saw Alicia stand, smooth the black skirt that barely covered her shapely butt and approach where she and Christian sat.

"Would you like a cup of coffee, Mr. Connor?" Alicia asked. "We have some fresh brew in the back. I'd be happy to pour you a cup." By the look in her eyes she would have been happy to do more than that for the tall blond.

"No thanks, I'm fine." He barely glanced up from the piece of paper. Alicia's lips thinned in displeasure as she stalked toward the back room with her coffee cup in hand.

Christian finished filling out the questionnaire and handed it back to Vanessa. "What happens now?"

Vanessa scanned the answers he'd written, then looked back at him. "Now I'll do my best to match up your wants and needs with the perfect house. When would you be available to go out and take a look at some places?"

"Now, if you're available."

"All right, then let's take a ride and see what we can find." She shut down her computer, her mind already filling with several potential properties. One of the questions he'd answered on the form was about price range. If she could make a sale to him in the price range he'd indicated, it would be one of the largest commissions she'd earned since getting her license.

She grabbed her purse and shrugged on her coat. By that time Alicia was back at her desk. "I'm taking Mr.

Connor to see the Waddell and the Simmons properties," she told Alicia. She turned to Christian. "Ready?"

It was a safety plan that Dave had implemented for the women Realtors, letting Alicia know where they were taking clients. When Vanessa arrived at each of the locations and before she left she would call Alicia again.

It wasn't the only safety measure they took. Each Realtor was armed not only with a cell phone but with pepper spray. In the year that Vanessa had been working as an agent, she'd never felt uncomfortable or unsafe while working.

Despite the roominess of her minivan, Christian Connor seemed to fill the interior as he got in on the passenger side. Vanessa's insides clenched in an altogether not unpleasant way.

"So tell me, how do you know Andre?" she asked once she'd backed out of the parking space and was headed toward the first home.

"I met Andre about five years ago in Chicago. I was there working on a shopping mall and he was there buying art. We met in the lobby of the hotel where we both were staying, and struck up a conversation. We had a couple of drinks, and then decided to play golf together the next day. By the end of the golf game we'd become good buddies."

"Andre is terrific," she agreed.

"He's great. When I told him I was thinking of relocating from my home base in Denver to Kansas City, he opened his home to me, showed me around town and did everything in his power to make the transition as smooth as possible."

"How long have you been here in Kansas City?" She'd

thought that after the initial shock of seeing him standing at the front desk vanished, some of her nervous tension would ebb, but for some reason it hadn't. She was acutely conscious of herself and even more conscious of him.

"I've been here three years and it was the best move I ever made, both personally and professionally."

"Is there a Mrs. Christian Connor in the picture?" she asked, quickly adding, "I was just wondering if a special woman in your life will be helping you make the house-buying decision."

"No wife, no special woman, although I certainly wouldn't mind you giving me a woman's perspective on things. Eventually I'm hoping to find that special woman to share my life with." She felt his gaze on her. "What about you? Any special man in your life?"

"Definitely. You met him last night. My son, Johnny."

"Right, he's a good-looking kid."

"Best of all, he's a great kid."

"It must have been tough on him, losing his dad the way he did. Must have been tough on both of you."

"It was, but we're doing just fine." As always, she found talking about Jim's death difficult. There were still pieces of that tragedy she'd never shared with anyone, feelings she didn't even want to explore herself.

"Here we are," she said as she pulled into the driveway of a large two-story stone home. It was in a neighborhood of upper-bracket houses with manicured lawns and had a feeling of permanence despite the fact that it was in a relatively new development.

She got out of the car, somewhat relieved for the bit of distance from him. She walked over to the lockbox mounted next to the garage door and retrieved the house key, aware of his gaze following her movements.

"There's an association fee of five hundred dollars yearly," she said as they walked toward the front door. "That takes care of snow removal and landscaping at the entrances of the development."

"Sounds reasonable," he said.

She opened the door and they stepped inside, their footsteps echoing in the large tiled entry hall. It didn't take them long to go from room to room. Unlike most prospective buyers, Christian was obviously more interested in the quality of the construction and materials used than in how big or airy the bedrooms were.

As they walked through the house Vanessa fell into her salesman mode, pointing out the special features of the house. The thrum of nerves that had assailed her from the moment she'd seen him standing in the real estate office quieted as she focused on what she did best: selling property.

The nervous tension didn't reappear until she found herself with him in the large walk-in closet off the master bedroom. He blocked the entrance and for a moment her heartbeat resounded in her ears, crashing with the beat of flight-or-fight.

Logically she knew this man posed no physical danger to her. He was a close friend of Andre's and Andre didn't give his friendship lightly. But the danger she felt came from the fact that she found him so attractive, she responded to his nearness in a way that was half-frightening, half-exhilarating.

"As you can see, there's plenty of built-in shelves.

There's a place for shoes, a pants rack and the overhead shelves that could be used for almost anything."

She smiled and from the smile, from the slight tremor of her tone, Christian could tell she was nervous. Her hair was loose today, cascading over her shoulders in rich dark waves that beckoned his fingers to touch it.

She'd been beautiful the night before, but today she nearly took his breath away. The blue tailored blouse emphasized the thrust of her full breasts and matched the hue of her dark-lashed eyes.

It had been a long time since Christian had enjoyed a relationship with any woman. Too damn long. Work had been his lover, his taskmaster, since he'd moved his business from Denver to Kansas City. There had been no time to pursue any personal relationships.

The business was running smoothly, more successful than he'd ever dreamed, and he realized he was hungry for female companionship and more.

Aware he'd been staring at her, he tore his gaze away and focused on the shelves. "Great closet," he agreed, and stepped out. "Great house, but I have to confess it isn't what I'm looking for."

"Then tell me what you like and what you don't like about this one and I'll see what I can do to show you a property more to your taste."

They moved out of the master bedroom and headed toward the front door. She walked in front of him and he tried not to look at the sway of her hips, the rounded cheeks of her ass. She had a great ass.

She reached the front door and turned around to face him. She must have realized what he'd been looking at because her cheeks turned a becoming pink.

"I was just thinking maybe we could discuss the particulars over dinner this evening." The invitation came from him without warning, but the moment it left his mouth he realized he wanted to have dinner with her.

Her eyes widened slightly. He couldn't tell if it was with pleasure or disdain. "I'm sorry, but I'm not available for dinner this evening. I'd have to make arrangements for somebody to be with Johnny."

Her son. He'd forgotten about her son. He wasn't interested in children—having them or raising them. The fact that she had a kid should have been enough to make him rethink his desire to have anything to do with her.

"What about lunch?" he countered. It's just a meal, he told himself, certainly not the basis for a long-term relationship of any kind.

She looked at her wristwatch, then back at him, a slight wariness in her eyes. "It would have to be a quick lunch. I have an appointment with other clients at one o'clock."

"We can make it fast," he agreed.

"You have family here in town?" he asked minutes later when they were back in her car and headed toward a restaurant not far from her office.

"Just me and Johnny. My parents died when I was young. I was raised by my paternal grandfather and he passed away when I was in college," she said. "Jim's family is all here in town and they're terrific."

"No siblings?" Her scent filled the interior of the car, an exotic, spicy scent. He'd love to find the exact locations where she'd dabbed or sprayed it on. Perhaps in the hollow of her throat, behind an ear? Or maybe between her breasts or on her inner thigh.

"No, just me. What about you?"

"I'm an only child, too. My parents are in Denver."

She cast him a quick glance, then focused back out the front window. "Must have been hard to leave family behind and move away."

"Not really. Denver isn't that far away for visits home and besides, my parents lead very busy lives." In the three years he'd been living in Kansas City he hadn't made a single trip back home, nor had his parents come to visit. Once a week he made the obligatory call to his mother, asked about her and his father, then put them out of his mind until it was time to make the next call.

She pulled into the restaurant parking lot and together they got out of the car and headed for the entrance. "I insist that I pay for lunch," she said. "I consider this a business lunch."

"I'm not used to a woman buying my lunch," he replied. "And I'm not sure I like the idea of being nothing more than a business expense." She frowned, as if worried she'd offended him. "Vanessa, I was teasing," he said softly.

The frown fell away and she smiled, a real genuine gesture that lit her eyes and warmed her features. The warmth of that smile formed a ball of heat in the pit of his stomach.

"It's been a long time since I've been teased," she said as they entered the Applebee's.

She was a woman who should be teased often to bring that light into her eyes, Christian thought as they were led to a table. There was something sad about her, a whisper of shadows in her eyes. She'd had parents who had died when she'd been young and a husband who had committed suicide. Life hadn't been particularly kind to Vanessa Abbott.

It wasn't until the waitress had departed with their orders that Vanessa pulled out a small notepad and a pen. "Now, tell me what you liked and didn't like about the property so I can find the perfect place for you to call home."

Home. He'd never felt like he'd had one. Certainly the mansion where he'd grown up wasn't a home. It had simply been a place to survive until he was old enough to get out.

"I'd like some land with the house, maybe five acres or so with lots of trees. I'd prefer a master bedroom on the main level and guest bedrooms upstairs."

She bent her head to take notes, her hair falling forward, and once again he fought the impulse to reach out and touch a strand.

He sat back in his chair, wondering when in the hell it had happened that he'd become starved for soft and pretty. That he yearned for sweet-smelling and sexy.

"What else?" She looked up at him, pen poised over the paper.

"What do you do when you aren't selling real estate?"

She set the pen down and leaned back in her chair. "I pretty much juggle my time between my career and my son."

The conversation halted as the waitress arrived with their orders. As they ate they fell into an easy conversation. They talked about the Kansas City area, more about what he'd like in a house and about their respective plans for Thanksgiving.

"We always spend the day with Jim's family," she said

as they finished up their meals. "It's total chaos with all the family together, but chaos in a nice way."

"Family is important to you," he observed.

"Isn't it to everybody?" she countered, then glanced at her watch and looked back at him. "I'm sorry, but I've got to get back to the office."

He picked up the check the waitress had left behind. "I insist that I take care of this. This was more pleasure than business as far as I'm concerned."

He was rewarded with another of her blushes and was grateful she didn't attempt to argue with him. "Thank you," she said graciously.

"I'll do a little research this evening to see what's available on the market that might be more to your taste," she said once they were back in her car.

"When we get to your office I'll give you my home and cell phone numbers so you can get in touch with me," he replied.

"You might want to go ahead and speak with your banker or wherever you intend to get your mortgage. They can prequalify you and save some time when you do find something."

Christian nodded. He was disappointed by the brief lunch with her. Although the conversation had been pleasant and she was incredibly easy to look at, he felt like he didn't really know any more about her now than he had before.

And he wanted to know her. It had been difficult to put her out of his head after the art show the night before. Something about her drew him and it was something he wanted to pursue.

She should be the last woman he wanted to get involved with anyway. She had two major strikes against her. If last night was any indication, she was comfortable in a lifestyle that had nearly destroyed him.

The second strike against her was the fact that she had a son, a boy who had no father in his life. Christian couldn't, *wouldn't*, parent any child. He'd learned nothing at his own father's knee to teach him how to be a good parent.

It would be best for him if he'd just let her find him a house, and then be on his way. As they arrived at the real estate office, Christian wondered why he never did what was best for him.

Chapter 5

Lunch had been nice, but Vanessa had been tense throughout the meal, aware of her attraction to Christian Connor and equally aware of his attraction to her.

While she was finally at a place where she felt ready to move on with her life, she was afraid to trust in any man, in the potential for any real happiness, too soon.

It was almost a relief when they arrived back at the office. "I'll just come in and give you those phone numbers," he said as they got out of her car.

"I feel confident I'm going to be able to find you exactly what you want," she replied, then cautioned, "although it might take a little bit of time."

He smiled. "I've been in the apartment for the last two and a half years. A little more time there won't hurt me."

They entered the office and Vanessa stopped short at the sight of a tall, dark-haired man and a big-boned, hard-eyed blond woman who sat in the waiting area. They both stood as Vanessa and Christian entered.

Vanessa's stomach twisted as she realized they'd been

waiting for her. The very first time she'd met the dark-haired man was in the early-morning hours when he'd come to tell her about finding Jim's car on the bridge. The last time she'd seen him was when he'd come to her house to let her know they were officially closing the case on Jim's suicide. Detective Tyler King.

"Detective King," she said as a million questions tumbled around in her head. What was he doing here? What could he want? After all these years had they finally found Jim's body?

"Mrs. Abbott." He held out a hand to her. The handshake was firm and brisk; then he gestured to the woman standing next to him. "This is my partner, Detective Tompkins."

The woman glared at her, as if she were personally responsible for every crime that had been committed in the general vicinity.

"We need to talk to you. We were wondering if you could come with us to the station," Detective King said.

A flare of panic torched through her. "Is this about my son? Has something happened to Johnny?"

"No, nothing like that," Detective King quickly assured her.

"Have you found Jim's body?" He shook his head. "Then what's going on? What's this about?" She was vaguely conscious of Christian standing just behind her, of gossipy Alicia seated at her desk wearing the hungry gaze of an animal sniffing the fresh scent of meat.

"It's about the art show last night. We need to get some information from you," King replied.

"What about it? Please, tell me. What's happened?" She looked first at King then at his partner.

"Sometime last night somebody bludgeoned Andre Gallagher's head. He's dead," Detective Tompkins said.

Vanessa scarcely registered the harsh glare Detective King shot his partner as shock rocked through her. She swayed slightly, surprised when Christian's hands grabbed her shoulders from behind to steady her.

"I'm Christian Connor," he said. "I'm not only Andre's friend, but I was also there last night."

"Then we'll need you to come down to the station as well," Detective King replied. "We'd be more than happy to transport you to the station, and then return you here when we're finished."

Christian still held on to Vanessa's shoulders and she was grateful for the support as a cold, unrelenting wind blew through her.

The dream.

Always the portent of death.

Andre was dead, murdered.

"We'll go in my car." Christian's fingers squeezed lightly on her shoulders. "I'll drive, Vanessa. Then I'll bring you back here. Is that all right?"

She nodded her assent, knowing she was too shaken up to drive. "Call the Worths and cancel my appointment," she said to Alicia, and then allowed Christian to lead her out the door and toward his car.

"It must have been a robbery," Christian said as they followed behind Detective King's car. "I can't imagine anyone who would want to hurt Andre."

She heard the barely contained emotion in his voice and realized that as stunned as she'd been to hear about Andre's murder, Christian had just lost a dear friend.

Her heart clenched as sorrow engulfed her. "I'm sorry for you, for your loss," she said.

His hands tightened on the steering wheel, his knuckles turning white. "He was a good man, a great friend."

"You think they'll be interviewing everyone who was at the show last night?"

"I'm sure they will."

Vanessa stared out the window and wished she didn't have such a vivid imagination, wished Detective Tompkins hadn't told them that Andre's head had been bashed in. All she could think about was that beautiful face of his destroyed, his shining spirit smashed out.

"I can't imagine anyone who attended last night being capable of something like this," she said, her voice a little steadier than it had been before.

The shock was wearing off and grief had not yet grabbed her, leaving her in a strange kind of emotional limbo. "Thank you for driving me," she said. "I'm not sure I could have driven myself."

He flashed her a tight smile. "It appears that for the moment we're in this together. Hopefully it will only take a few minutes for them to get our statements and let us go."

She clasped her hands together in her lap, dreading the moment she would have to walk through the police station doors. She'd hoped she'd never see the inside of the police station again.

The week following Jim's jump off the bridge, she'd been called down there several times to talk with Detective King about her life, her husband and the state of her marriage.

She'd found the detective to be probing but compassionate. He was sharp and she knew if anyone could find out what had happened to Andre, it would be Detective Tyler King.

Christian pulled into a parking space in front of the station. He cut the engine, then turned and looked at her. "Are you okay?"

"I'm fine." She stared at him for a long moment. He was little more than a stranger to her, and yet she was comforted by the fact that he would be beside her as they went inside, comforted that he would once again be at her side as they left the police station.

"Ready?" he asked.

She nodded and together they got out of the car and headed for the building where the detectives would be waiting to speak to them.

Vanessa was grateful that it was Detective King who led her to an interview room. Although the circumstances that had brought him into her life two years before had been devastating, she knew he would make this process as painless as possible.

She had no information to give him and knew that she was only one of many whom he would talk with in order to find out who had committed the heinous crime.

The interview room he led her to smelled just like she remembered, bringing back memories of those days immediately following Jim's suicide. Stale coffee, a lingering scent of fast food and, beneath all that, the scent of sweat and fear. It permeated the very walls that surrounded them.

She sat in one of the chairs at the long conference table and tried not to emotionally slide back into the place she'd been when she'd last been here.

Detective King sat in the chair opposite her, his eyes as dark and fathomless as she remembered. "I'm sorry to bring you down here like this, but we need to get some answers as quickly as we can."

"I understand, although I'm afraid I don't know anything that's going to be any help." She clasped her hands tightly in her lap.

"Do you mind if I record your statement?"

"No, that's fine."

He pulled out a small handheld tape recorder and set it in the center of the table. He flipped the button, indicated the time and date, then began his questions. "I understand the art show last night featured paintings by your late husband. How did that come about?"

"Since Jim's death I've had a number of gallery owners contact me about the possibility of showing his remaining work, but I always knew when I was ready, it would be Andre who would show it."

"And why is that?"

"Andre was the first person who really believed in Jim's talent." Despite the fact that she had absolutely nothing to be nervous about, nerves jangled inside her, convulsing in her stomach with cramps.

"What time did you leave the show last night?"

"It was just before ten. Johnny, my son, had school this morning, so I wanted to get him home and into bed." There were so many questions she wanted to ask, such as what they knew, whom they suspected. "Was it a robbery?" she asked.

She wouldn't have thought it possible for his eyes to grow darker, but they did. "I can't discuss the particulars with you. Did you go straight home when you left?" She nodded and he continued. "Did you and Andre have any disagreements? Problems with the way the paintings were displayed or the split on the profits from the sales?"

"No, and you can't really believe that I had anything to do with Andre's death." There was no self-righteous indignation in her voice, only a soft chiding tone.

"We're questioning everyone who was at the show last night," he replied. He leaned back in his chair, lines of stress etched deep across his forehead. "You know anyone who was giving Andre problems?"

She shook her head. "My relationship with Andre was pretty much a working one. We were more acquaintances than friends. If he were having problems with anyone, he probably wouldn't have shared that information with me."

"The show went well?"

Unexpected tears burned hot in her eyes. "The last thing Andre said to me before I left was that the night had been a huge success."

He frowned and tapped the end of a pencil against the tabletop, then leaned over and shut off the tape recorder. "I think that's all I need at this point. I'm sorry we had to meet again under these circumstances."

She nodded, a thick lump of emotion in the back of her throat. "Andre was a nice man. Just please find the person responsible."

They got up from the table and he walked with her back to the reception area. "You can wait here for your friend. I'm sure we'll be finished with him in just a few minutes."

She sat in one of the bright yellow plastic chairs in the reception area to wait for Christian. The dream. That damned dream. She'd never had it without death intimately touching her life. Death's touch had been less intimate this time, but no less devastating.

Although she knew it was ridiculous, she felt responsible for Andre's death, as if by having the dream she'd signed his death warrant. The ball of emotion in the back of her throat grew bigger and she swallowed hard once . . . twice . . . to force it away.

She waited only about fifteen minutes; then Christian appeared, looking pale and stressed. He didn't speak until they were out of the police station and in his car.

"Detective Tompkins is definitely a cop with an attitude," he said as he started his car. "She had me ready to confess to anything just to shut her up."

"Did she tell you anything about what they think might have happened?" Vanessa asked.

He shook his head and shot her a wry grin. "I have a feeling that woman wouldn't have given me the emergency number if I'd been dying on the floor."

Vanessa settled back in the seat. "This all feels so surreal."

"Yeah, it definitely hasn't hit me yet that he's gone."

An edge of pain radiated in his voice, a pain that called to her, that made her remember how badly she'd longed for human touch in the days and weeks after Jim's death.

She reached over and wrapped her fingers around his forearm, wanting to comfort but knowing nothing she did could take away his loss of a valuable friend. "I'm so sorry, Christian. I know this has to be hard on you." His skin was warm beneath her fingers, as if fevered.

Although he flashed her a smile, his fingers tightened on the steering wheel and she felt the tautness of his arm muscle. "I'll be fine. I just want whoever is responsible for this behind bars."

She pulled her hand away, finding the feel of his warm skin far too pleasurable. "I know Detective King. He was in charge of Jim's case. He's a good man. A good detective. If anyone can find out who's responsible, he can. Did Andre mention to you that he was having trouble with anyone?" she asked.

"No, never. Andre was the most laid-back man I ever knew. In the years I knew him I never heard him having a problem with anyone." He sighed in obvious frustration and they both fell silent for the remainder of the drive.

When they reached the real estate office, he pulled in next to her car and turned to look at her. "This was not exactly the way I wanted to end a first date."

She eyed him with surprise. "Is that what this was? A first date?"

"Anyone could sell me a house, but it's not anyone I want to take out to lunch."

The timing was awful for the pure pleasure that seeped through her. Andre was dead, the police had just questioned her about his murder and yet a sweet heat of delight filled her as she saw the smolder of his smoke-colored eyes.

"I didn't realize this was a date. If I'd known, I would have put on fresh lipstick."

The smolder of his eyes seemed to deepen. "Your lips look just fine to me." For a long moment their gazes remained locked and it was she who broke the contact, afraid that if she held it a minute longer, she would be unable to breathe.

"I've got to go." She felt as if she were in overdrive, as

if too many emotions battled one another for dominance in her head.

"You'll call me when you have some more properties lined up?"

"Of course." She opened the car door and got out. "When we go looking at other properties, shall I consider it a second date?"

He smiled and it was as if the sun came out from the clouds and some of the pall of gray that had hovered over her burned away momentarily. "I'll let you know."

She stood next to her car and watched as he pulled out of the parking lot. The minute he disappeared from her sight the gray pall surrounded her once again.

She eyed the office, but didn't have the stamina to face Alicia and her endless tactless questions. Instead she got into her car and headed home, needing peace and quiet, needing to settle the nerves that once again jangled inside her.

Johnny wouldn't be home from school for another hour and a half and she could use the quiet time to process the highs and lows the day had brought.

Murdered. Andre had been murdered. Her heart squeezed painfully as she thought of the man who had been both gracious and kind, a man who had seen the potential in Jim and had brought him a level of success few artists ever saw.

After Jim's death Andre had continued to be supportive, calling occasionally to check in with her, letting her know he was available to talk to her whenever she felt ready to let go of the last of Jim's work.

Certainly she'd recognized that Andre's interest wasn't strictly altruistic, that he was a businessman above all else. But he'd never pressured her, never encouraged her to do anything she wasn't emotionally ready to do. And now he was gone.

She returned home and went directly into the kitchen. The one thing she'd discovered that settled her mind, soothed her soul whenever she was upset or unsettled was baking.

Apples, cinnamon, flour and butter were lined up on the countertop. Strudel, she'd make an apple strudel for dessert. As she peeled the apples the horror of the day slowly ebbed. She loved to bake, but rarely had the time. In the weeks after Jim's death she'd filled the house with cakes and pies, finding a small modicum of solace in the act of cobbling recipes to make culinary magic.

It wasn't until she had the strudel in the oven that she allowed herself to once again think of Christian Connor. She sank down at the table with a cup of hot tea and thought about the look that had been in his smoke gray eyes. He hadn't looked at her like a client, but rather like a man interested in a woman.

The kitchen began to smell with the scrumptious scents of baking apples and cinnamon. She stirred a spoonful of sugar into her tea and thought about the man who had raised her.

Grandpa John had been a wonderful man with a multitude of talents. He'd played the piano by ear and most mornings she woke up to the soft sounds of "Autumn Leaves" or the house-hopping "When the Saints Go Marching In."

He tinkered on the piano, grew lush, gorgeous plants and flowers in his garden and could have opened his own bakery. Rarely had there been a day that Vanessa hadn't come home from school to the scent of a velvet cake or a fresh peach pie baking in the oven.

Her parents had given her life, but it had been Grandpa John who had taught her about the lust for life. When he'd passed she'd feared he'd taken all the music, all the beautiful flowers and all the sweetness of life with him.

She'd still been in that place of grief when she'd met Jim. Perhaps it had been the darkness of her grief that had drawn her to the darkness of his soul. But time had healed her grief, and Johnny's birth had brought her a kind of happiness she'd never known before.

As she finished her tea, her thoughts once again went to Andre. Even though she knew his death had nothing to do with her, she couldn't forget the dream, the dream that always brought death close to her.

By the time the strudel was finished baking she'd whipped up a dozen banana-nut muffins as well. They were still in the oven when Johnny came home from school.

He came into the kitchen, a worried frown wrinkling his nose. "What's wrong?" he asked before saying hello.

"What makes you think anything is wrong?" she asked in surprise.

He flopped his backpack on the top of the table; then he sat and pointed at the strudel cooling on the counter-top. "The house smells just like it did when Dad died. It smells like something bad happened."

Vanessa stared at her son in stunned surprise. How awful that he related the smells of baking to terrible things. She made a silent vow to bake more often, on happy days when she had no bad news to impart to him.

But today she did have bad news. As they sat at the

kitchen table she told him about Andre. Johnny accepted the news about Andre's murder stoically. Then, with the resilience of youth, he changed the topic to what had happened in school that day and how excited he was to start painting the cardinal for his school project.

They ate dinner and passed the evening with Johnny writing the report that would accompany his painting, while Vanessa worked on her laptop, pulling up properties she thought might be appropriate to show Christian.

It was nine o'clock when she tucked Johnny into bed and walked wearily into her own bedroom. The day felt as if it had lasted a month and she couldn't remember the last time she'd been so ready for bed.

She went directly into her bathroom and stripped off her clothes. Pulling on her comfortable flannel pajamas, she recognized her exhaustion was not only physical but mental.

The last thing she wanted to do was think anymore. She'd thought the events of the day to death. She left the bathroom, her bed beckoning with the promise of sweet oblivion.

She crawled beneath the sheets and reached over to turn out the bedside lamp. Her hand froze in midair as Jim stared at her from the framed photo on the nightstand.

Hadn't she placed the picture in the drawer the night before? So how had it gotten back on the nightstand? Johnny hadn't been in her room since the night before and in any case she doubted her son would have noticed the missing picture, nor would he have returned it to this place of honor.

There was a box of tissues in the drawer; surely she

must have reached for a tissue in the night while asleep and set the photo back on the top of the nightstand. That was the way it had to have happened, for nothing else made sense.

Her hand trembled slightly as she placed the photo back in the drawer, then shut off her light and lay in bed, watching the play of moonlight drifting in through the window.

In the two years since Jim's death, she'd never suffered a moment of fear in this big old house. She recognized each and every noise, had always felt safe and secure here.

But even though she knew there had to be a logical explanation for the reappearance of Jim's picture on the nightstand, she couldn't help the uneasy flutter of her heart, the chill that stole up her spine, forcing her to pull the covers up more tightly around her.

Chapter 6

"Vanessa, how about another slice of pumpkin pie?" Annette Abbott worked the serving knife like a surgeon wielding a scalpel. "That last piece you had was so tiny, and I know it's your favorite."

It wasn't her favorite, but somehow Jim's mother had gotten it into her head that it was. "Honestly, I couldn't eat another bite," she replied.

"Ma, if you're done fawning over Vanessa, I'd take another piece of that pie," Jim's brother Steve said.

Annette cuffed him affectionately on the side of his head. "You don't need another piece, and I don't fawn over anyone."

This statement started a good-natured argument among the three brothers. Vanessa sat back in her chair at the long wooden kitchen table and soaked in the feeling of being part of something bigger than herself.

When she'd married Jim, she'd gotten a package deal: three boisterous brothers-in-law, two with wives, and Annette and Dan Abbott, the beleaguered, loving parents.

There was no question of who wore the pants in the

Abbott family, and it wasn't quiet Dan. Jim had once told Vanessa that he loved his mother to distraction, but had never gotten over his fear of her wrath.

In the years of Vanessa's marriage, she'd recognized that Annette was manipulative and intrusive, but nobody could ever question her devotion and at times completely blind love for her sons.

The Abbotts were a handsome family, all of them dark-haired and dark-eyed. Brian was the eldest at forty-one. He was a tall, stocky man always fighting an extra twenty pounds and devoted to his wife and two little girls. Brian worked as a graphic design artist.

Steve was thirty-nine, quick to temper and equally quick to cool down. He was married and had a son who was two. He owned a shop called Mosaic Magic that sold stained-glass windows and mosaic items that he created.

Then there was Garrett, who was thirty-seven, single and the only member of the family who didn't seem to have an artistic bone in his body. He worked as a math teacher at one of the local high schools and on the weekends dated an endless bevy of women in his effort to find Ms. Right.

Jim had been the baby of the family, but Garrett had many of the characteristics of a spoiled youngest child.

"Personally, I think we should all have an extra piece of pie," Brian said. "I think we can agree that it's been a tough week."

"And pie heals all wounds?" His wife, Dana, raised an eyebrow in amusement.

"Something like that," he replied with a grin.

Vanessa knew the difficulty of the week he'd referred to was that all of them had been called down to the police station to give statements, and then on Tuesday they had all attended Andre's funeral.

Christian had been there, supporting Andre's mother, who wore the look of a shell-shocked soldier in the midst of a war she didn't understand. Andre's sister stood next to them, weeping uncontrollably throughout the solemn ceremony.

When the ceremony was over Christian made his way to where Vanessa and Johnny stood. He took her hands in his, asked how she was doing and made her heart turn somersaults in her chest.

They'd set up for him to meet her first thing Monday for a morning of house hunting. As she listened to the conversation flowing around her she wondered where Christian was spending the Thanksgiving holiday. She hoped he'd flown home for the holiday and was enjoying a feast with his loved ones.

"Who was that hunk I saw you talking to after the funeral?" Bethany, Steve's wife, asked, as if she'd crawled into Vanessa's head and knew she'd been thinking of the handsome blond.

"He's a client," Vanessa replied. "I'm working with him to find a house."

"For him to be just a client, your eyes sure are sparkling," Bethany said with a smile.

A blush warmed Vanessa's cheeks. "He's a nice man."

"I'd love to find a nice woman," Garrett said with a deep sigh. Garrett had a penchant for dating women who needed rescuing. He rescued; then they found true love with another man. Unfortunately Garrett also had a fondness for drinking too much. His boozing, coupled with a lack of responsibility that had him still living at home with his parents, didn't make him terrific potential-husband material.

It wasn't until the men had retired to the family room to watch a football game and the women worked in the kitchen to wash the dishes that Annette questioned her further about Christian.

"This client of yours, this nice man, he's somebody maybe special?" One of her dark eyebrows arched upward with interest as she squirted orange-scented dish soap into a sink full of water.

"Oh, I don't know. I only met him the night of the art show." Vanessa grabbed a dish towel, uncomfortable with the turn of the conversation.

She and Annette had never talked about Vanessa's life after Jim. Vanessa had always felt like Annette wanted her to be nothing more than her grieving daughter-in-law for the rest of her life.

Annette dunked a pot into the soapy water. "Dana and Bethany, why don't you two go into the dining room and take the tablecloth and linens to the laundry room."

Vanessa tensed as her two sisters-in-law scooted out of the room as if the hounds of hell were nipping at their heels. For a few minutes Annette used a scrub brush to scour out the pot. It wasn't until she rinsed it and handed it to Vanessa to dry that she finally spoke.

"It's good to have uncles. Steve, Brian and Garrett have tried to be good uncles to Johnny."

"The best," Vanessa agreed.

"But Brian and Steve have their own kids, their own lives, and Garrett is too busy trying to find a life to have any real time for his nephew." She plunged another pot into the soapy water. "But as nice as it is for a boy to have uncles, he needs a father more." Her dark brown gaze held Vanessa's. "And a woman needs a man."

Vanessa looked at her in surprise. "Annette, he's just a client," she protested.

"But I want you to know that if he, or if anyone, becomes special in your life, it's okay with me. It's okay with us." She pulled her hands from the water and dried them. Then she laid warm, plump fingers on Vanessa's cheek.

"I know how much you loved my son, but he's been gone a long time now. Life goes on and your life needs to go on." She removed her fingers from Vanessa's face and once again plunged them back into the water. "You're a strong woman, Vanessa. Despite all the hardships you've faced over the last two years you've never asked for help."

"You have no idea in how many ways you've helped me and more importantly helped Johnny over the last two years," Vanessa replied.

"I know that when you build a life for yourself, if and when you find a special man, we'll still have a place in that life. You know how important you and Johnny are to us."

Warmth filled Vanessa's heart for this woman, for this family, who had embraced her the moment of her marriage and who she knew would continue to embrace her until she died. She also felt a bit of relief, as if she'd been released from what might have become a prison of love. Annette was letting her free at a time when Vanessa had begun to seek freedom.

"Anyway," Annette continued, "whether this client is somebody special or not, I think you should take a page from Garrett and get out there and start dating. I'll sit with Johnny any time you need me. You need to go out, have some fun; flirt a little and remember that you're too young to be a widow the rest of your life." She turned toward the doorway leading out of the kitchen. "Bethany and Dana, you're probably hovering right outside the door. You both can come back in and help with the last of these pots."

The rest of the afternoon passed pleasantly. The women sat at the table and drank coffee, the kids played in the playroom, which had once been Jim's bedroom, and the men groaned and shouted from the living room as the football game continued.

"How are things at the shop?" Vanessa asked Bethany.

"Too busy," Bethany replied. "It seems like Steve and I hardly see each other anymore. He's always at the shop or meeting wholesalers or developers."

"Developers?" Dana frowned. "Why is he meeting with developers?"

"We're opening another store down south. Steve feels confident that business is good enough to sustain two locations."

"But that's wonderful," Vanessa said, pleased with their success. Bethany and Steve had always been her favorites. "I can see it now, Mosaic Magic chain stores all across the nation."

Bethany laughed. "Bite your tongue. I don't see enough of my husband now."

"Maybe things will settle down once the new store is up and running," Annette said. "You know, success sometimes takes sacrifices. Five years from now when you're living the good life, you won't mind that for a little while you didn't see enough of your husband."

"I suppose you're right," Bethany agreed. "It's just that lately Steve's ambition seems to fill every waking moment. It's been that way for a while."

Annette nodded. "Since Jim died. None of them have totally adjusted to Jim's death." She took a sip of her coffee, her dark gaze filled with sadness. "All the boys showed an unusual amount of talent when it came to drawing and such when they were little, but it was Jim who stole our breath away with his talent."

Vanessa had heard this story before, about Jim's exceptional talent brought to Annette and Dan's attention by an art teacher when Jim had been in third grade. They had immediately enrolled him in classes to encourage and develop his talent.

"Jim was everyone's hope for the Abbott name meaning something in the art world," Annette said.

"And now Johnny can carry the torch," Dana said. "Did Brian tell you about the contest?" she asked Vanessa.

"What contest?"

"There's a young-artist contest being sponsored by one of the community colleges. Brian was going to encourage Johnny to enter one of his paintings."

"I see my wife is one step ahead of me," Brian said as he came into the kitchen and went to the refrigerator. He leaned down and grabbed a cold beer, then straightened and looked at Vanessa. "I was going to get the official paperwork before I mentioned it to you."

"I don't know." Vanessa frowned. "Sometimes I worry

because he doesn't seem to want to do anything else but paint."

"Just like his father," Annette said with a nod. "Jim never wanted to play ball or anything else. All he wanted to do was draw and paint."

"If it's what he loves to do, then you shouldn't worry," Dana said, and lightly touched Vanessa's hand.

"You're right. He's happy and healthy and today is a day not to worry but to count my blessings," she replied.

It was almost seven when she and Johnny finally left the Abbotts' to go home. Johnny carried on his lap the apple pie his grandma had made for him and as they drove the short distance to their house he chattered about his cousins, the food and what a great day it had been.

Later that night as Vanessa stood in Johnny's doorway after tucking him in, she thought once again of her blessings. Yes, they'd all suffered a terrible tragedy, but her life was filled with things to be thankful for, like Jim's family, her friends and Johnny.

She pulled her robe more closely around her as the wind howled around the house, rattling tree branches against the windowpanes. She smiled to herself and turned to go into her bedroom.

Electric blankets. She was definitely thankful for whomever had invented electric blankets, at least until the time she might have a man to wrap his arms around her and keep her warm through the cold wintry nights.

Matt McCann hated Thanksgiving. In truth he hated most holidays, but he personally thought Thanksgiving was one of the lamest. If anyone had anything to be thankful for, it was his two ex-wives, who'd sucked him dry when each had left him.

He should have been a divorce lawyer. His marriages had made two attorneys hefty paydays. Friggin' shysters had made out almost as well as the two bimbos he'd made the mistake of marrying.

While everyone else in the United States had spent the day feasting on turkey and stuffing with loved ones, Matt had spent the day with the person he loved most . . . himself. He'd eaten take-out Chinese and drunk half a bottle of Scotch for dinner.

He now got up from his desk and went into the kitchen, where he poured himself another healthy shot of Scotch, lit a cigar and perched his fat ass on one of the barstools.

A holiday was nothing more than a waste of working hours. He hadn't been able to accomplish anything today with all the art galleries closed. Hell, it would probably be Monday before anyone was in to conduct official business.

He leaned back on the stool and sucked in a deep lungful of the Cohiba Double Corona cigar. He'd smoke half of it, and then stub it out. At almost fifteen hundred dollars for twenty-five of the suckers, he rarely finished one in a single pop.

As he smoked his stogie and sipped his Scotch, he looked around the pristine, state-of-the-art kitchen that was a rarely used part of the half-a-million-dollar place he called home.

On one wall was an abstract painting he'd done when he was in his early twenties and believed he was destined to set the art world on fire. His mother, God rest her soul, had relentlessly encouraged him to be a stockbroker, certain that he didn't have the talent to be able to support himself in the art industry.

She'd been half-right. Matt hadn't had the talent to be an artist, but he'd been smart enough to realize he could represent artists and make tons of money from them. He had a knack for recognizing real talent, and had made enough contacts with art galleries over the years that he'd become successful beyond his wildest dreams.

He finished his Scotch, stubbed out the cigar and left the stool, deciding that he might as well call it a night. Even though it wasn't even ten o'clock, he'd drunk more than usual this evening and suspected a hellacious hangover was in his very near future.

He'd just headed down the hallway toward the master bedroom when the doorbell rang. Damn. He hoped like hell nobody had got to wondering what good old lonely Matt was doing and had decided to come for a little Thanksgiving visit. God help him from well-meaning friends.

"This better be good," he said as he yanked the door open. The baseball bat hit him in the face, shattering cheekbones and breaking his nose.

He careened backward, blinded by blood and senseless from the pain. Oh God. The pain. He never saw who'd swung the bat, never had a chance to ask why as he was struck again and again until the pain was gone and he knew nothing more.

The killer shuddered as he hit Matt one last time. Oh God! A rush like he'd never known shot through him. He gasped for breath, the noise breaking the otherwise silent house.

He tossed the bat aside and for a moment simply stood and allowed the rush of the kill to fill him. It felt so good, so right.

He'd expected the feeling of self-righteousness and had anticipated the sweet vengeance, but he hadn't expected the excitement. He shuddered again, then drew a couple of deep steadying breaths through his nose.

It had been so easy, so incredibly easy. The first time with Andre he'd worried that he couldn't do it, that something might go wrong or he'd lose his nerve. But it had gone so smoothly and afterward he'd felt more alive than he had in years.

He'd dreamed of this revenge for two long years. He'd made lists in his mind of the people who had taken advantage, used everything there was to give. Although the killing fantasies had become stronger and stronger with each passing day, he'd never really thought he'd follow through on them in reality. Until the night of the art show. It was that night that something snapped and he knew it was time to make his fantasies a reality.

The cops didn't have a clue. The investigation had gone nowhere and with each day that had passed he'd felt safer, stronger.

The fact that the bastard Matt lived alone in a house set on a three-acre lot had made this easy. Even if he'd screamed, there wasn't much chance that anyone would have heard him. But he'd never had a chance to scream. The stupid bastard had opened the door to death.

A giggle escaped the killer, a giggle that quickly changed to full-blown laughter. He laughed until tears blurred his vision, until his stomach ached.

Andre had paid. Matt had paid. But there were others who needed to taste his brand of revenge.

She would be last. Vanessa would pay, but he imagined a particular kind of torment for her before she met her untimely end.

She would know what it was like to feel as if the entire world had turned against her. She would learn what it was like to be alone, to be afraid and have no place to turn.

A new shudder slowly worked up his spine as he thought of the woman he blamed more than anyone else in the world. Vanessa. He wanted to see her cry. He wanted her to feel a special kind of agony. A bat to the head would be too easy for her, too quick.

He closed his eyes and for a moment saw a vision of her in his head, her blue eyes filled with tears and terror. Ah yes, that was the future he'd deliver to her. Tears and terror. She deserved no less.

Opening his eyes, he stared down at Matt McCann's lifeless body. The man had been a pig, sucking artists dry while lining his own pockets.

There was still work to be done. From his pocket he pulled out a plastic bag that held a tube of paint and a paintbrush. He uncapped the tube, squeezed some of the crimson paint on the brush and swept it down the front of Matt's shirt.

He repeated the process several times until a long slash of the paint mingled with the blood spatter. When he was finished he recapped the paint and returned both the tube and the brush to the plastic bag. He stood and smiled.

Paint it red.

Chapter 7

Nervous tension twisted and turned in Vanessa's stomach as she drove to work Monday morning. She told herself it was ridiculous to be nervous, that today would be just another day at work. Still, she'd taken extra care with her appearance because her first client of the day was Christian.

She felt like a teenager, half-giddy with anticipation. It had taken her an extra thirty minutes to get ready. She'd put on three outfits before settling on a pair of black slacks and a teal-colored V-neck sweater. Black and teal beaded earrings and a matching bracelet completed the casual business look.

She had several properties to show him and had blocked out half the day for him. That afternoon she was once again meeting the Worths, hoping they would make a final decision on a house.

The holiday weekend had flown by. She and Johnny had spent a quiet Friday and gone to the movies on Saturday when Garrett hadn't called to follow through on the day in the park with Johnny.

Then on Sunday she and Johnny had put up their Christmas tree. Although it was a bit early for the tree, Vanessa loved Christmas and went a little crazy with decorating the house.

A few spits of snowflakes dotted her windshield as she pulled into the realty office and parked. The weather forecast was for blustery cold with a chance of snow flurries. She loved Christmas, but she hated winter.

"Good morning," she greeted Alicia as she walked through the front door.

"Back at you," Alicia replied. Today blue shadow rode her eyelids, always a good sign. "How was your holiday?"

"It was okay." Vanessa shrugged out of her coat and hung it on the rack just inside the front door. "Johnny and I spent the day with Jim's family. What about you?"

Alicia's mouth curved up in a satisfied smile. "I met a guy. We met Wednesday night and spent the entire long weekend together. It was amazing. He's amazing."

Vanessa sat in her chair. "What's his name?"

"Guy Merrick." She leaned forward, her eyes glittering. "He's a total hunk. We met at Seventy-seven—you know, that club off Main Street. Anyway, he works for a cable company and is divorced. No kids, so if things go well, I won't have to play the role of stepmom."

In the two years since Alicia's divorce, Vanessa had seen her infatuated with dozens of men. She dived into a man and the relationship was hot and heavy for a month or two; then suddenly the man disappeared and Alicia was left devastated.

Vanessa wanted to tell Alicia to go slow, to build

something meaningful, but she knew Alicia wouldn't take her advice in the way Vanessa intended it.

"Sounds great," she said. There was nothing she could do but enjoy the honeymoon of Alicia's happiness. All too soon it would probably be over and the woman would be more bitter and hateful than ever.

At that moment Christian came through the door, bringing with him the crisp scent of the cold weather and warm male. The smile he gave her nearly took her breath away and once again she felt like a silly teenager, giddy with pleasure because the captain of the football team had smiled at her.

She stood and returned his smile, her heart thudding with a quickened pace. "Hi."

"Hi, yourself." He gave a curt nod in Alicia's direction, but his gaze remained intently focused on Vanessa. "You ready to do this?"

God, if he kept looking at her like that, she'd be ready to do anything. The man looked positively lethal in a black leather jacket, a pair of jeans and a gray sweater that perfectly matched his eyes.

"All set," she said briskly. She'd just been mentally chiding Alicia for moving too fast and now had the impulse to make the same kind of mistake with a man she barely knew. She needed to get a grip.

She grabbed her keys and handed Alicia a list of the properties she intended to show Christian. "I'll check in from each location," she said.

"I'll be here," Alicia replied.

Together Vanessa and Christian left the office and got into her car. "How was your holiday?" he asked once they were settled in.

"It was nice. What about yours? Did you fly back to Denver to be with your family?"

"No. I stayed here in town. It was a working weekend for me, as I had some blueprints to study of a new project. My Thanksgiving feast was a turkey-and-dressing Hungry-Man TV dinner."

"That's awful," she exclaimed.

He grinned. "Actually, it was pretty good. I'm a connoisseur of anything that cooks in a microwave."

"Nobody should spend Thanksgiving alone," she replied.

Those broad shoulders of his shrugged. "I'm used to spending most of my holidays alone. My parents travel quite a bit, and in any case, they've never observed many of the traditional holidays. So, what have you got to show me this morning?"

It was an obvious move to change the topic of conversation and made her wonder about his relationship with his parents. "I've got four houses lined up to show you, all of them in the Northland area and all of them on some acreage."

"Sounds good," he said. "And will you have time to get some lunch afterward?"

Her heart did a crazy flutter dance. "I might be able to work you into my busy schedule," she said lightly.

"If we have lunch, it will be our second date. Do you kiss on the second date?"

Oh, this man was a temptation in a life that had held very few temptations. She laughed a shaky little laugh. "It depends," she replied.

"On what?"

She shot him a quick glance and then looked back at

the road. "Depends on how much I enjoy the second date. Depends on if I'm really interested in the man."

"I can tell you for a fact that the man is interested in you." His smooth deep voice evoked a warmth in her that rivaled the hot air blowing from the heater vents. "Am I moving too fast?"

"To be honest? I don't know. I don't know what the norm is when it comes to dating or whatever."

"You haven't dated at all since your husband's death?"

She shook her head. "I haven't felt ready until lately. After Jim's death there were so many things to take care of. Getting a job, paying the bills—before he died I had worked only part-time. But then it was up to me to figure out a way for us to keep the house and eat." She broke off, aware that she was telling him far more than he'd asked. "What about you? Any ex-wives in your past?"

"Not a one. Got close once, but we both realized we had different belief systems, different values, and a marriage between us probably wouldn't have lasted."

"At least you were smart enough to recognize that before taking the vows." She pulled into the long driveway that led to the first house on her list. She grabbed her cell phone from her purse. "I just need to make a quick call to the office to let them know we're here." She made the call, then returned the phone to her purse.

"Is that usual? Making calls whenever you get to a house?" he asked as they walked from the driveway to the house.

"Dave Wallace, my boss, calls it the buddy system. From what I understand it was implemented about four years ago after a woman Realtor was attacked while showing a house. She didn't work for our company, but her client beat her up and stole her purse and left her unconscious. Her husband called the police when she didn't come home, but nobody had any idea where she was."

She opened the lockbox and withdrew the key to the house. "She survived the attack, but it was after that that Dave insisted his female employees call to check in whenever they're out in the field. Alicia keeps a log of where we are and with whom." She turned to unlock the door, acutely conscious of Christian standing just behind her.

"Have you ever felt unsafe when showing a house?"

Only at this moment, she thought, with you standing so close and warming me with your body heat. "Never," she said aloud as she pushed open the door and stepped inside.

As they walked through the house, Vanessa found herself watching him, studying his features with feminine interest. What was it about him that made her feel so edgy? Whenever he was near, she felt as if there weren't enough air to fill her lungs, enough oxygen to feed her brain.

Certainly he was easy on the eyes, but she'd been around dozens of handsome men since Jim's death. Still, none of them had affected her on such a visceral level.

His sandy-colored hair was shot through with strands of white, as if some of it had been bleached from hours in the sun. His lean, angular face was tanned, making his long-lashed gunmetal eyes incredibly sexy.

She watched as he ran his fingers down the length of a wooden banister. She'd noticed his hands in the car, neatly clipped nails on blunt fingers. Not an artist's hands but the hands of a laborer.

As he caressed the rich mahogany she could almost

imagine the feel of his big hands on her skin, sliding down her shoulders, across the length of her back. She fought back a shiver that had nothing to do with fear and everything to do with desire. And wondered, why now, why with this particular man had her sleeping hormones decided to awaken with a roar?

It was crazy, to want a man she hardly knew, to wonder what his arms might feel like surrounding her. She had to take care, couldn't be impulsive when it came to her love life. Not because she worried about her own heart, but because she worried about Johnny's.

"It's nice," Christian said when they'd been through the entire house. "But it's not right."

"What's wrong with it?" she asked curiously.

"I'm not sure." He smiled apologetically. "I don't know what's wrong. I only know it isn't right. I'll know right when I see it."

"Then let's go take a look at the next one on my list."

Within minutes they were back in the car. The snow flurries that had dotted the windshield earlier had disappeared and the sun peeked out from beneath fast-moving, low-hanging gray clouds.

"Do you like what you do?" he asked. "Being a Realtor?"

She considered the question before answering. "I don't know. I don't think about it much. When Jim died I had to make a decision fast about what I was going to do. I was already working at the Realtors' as a receptionist, and Dave encouraged me to get my license and work for him."

"But that doesn't answer my question." His deep, smooth voice held a teasing tone.

She flashed him a quick smile. "I guess I didn't." She frowned thoughtfully. "There are a lot of things I like about this job. I've met lots of interesting people. I love sharing in the happiness of bringing people together in a perfect house."

"And what don't you like about it?"

She cast him a sideways glance. "Are we playing twenty questions?"

"How can I get to know you better if I don't ask questions?" he countered.

She laughed. "Okay, I'll answer your questions, but keep in mind, turnabout is fair play." She drew a breath, savoring the scent of him. "What I don't like about this job is that so much of the work takes place on the weekends or in the evenings. I don't like that unless I hustle and make sales, there's no paycheck at the end of the month. So far I've been lucky. The real estate business is booming. Now, your turn."

He leaned forward and smiled. "Ask me anything. I'm an open book."

"Do you like what you do?"

"I love it. I love every aspect of it. There's nothing I like better than the weight of a hard hat on my head and a hammer in my hand." There was passion in his voice as he leaned forward slightly and continued. "I love the fact that I take a simple set of blueprints and transform them into something real, something useful."

He leaned back in the seat and released a small burst of laughter. "I didn't mean to get carried away."

"Don't apologize," she replied. "It's nice when you can do something you love."

He nodded. "I love my work, but it's not all of who I

am. I also love popcorn and watching movies. I like going to football games, eating nachos and hot dogs and cheering with the crowd." He flashed her one of his charming grins. "In other words, I love my work, but I love my play also."

By that time they'd reached the next property on her list. The morning passed quickly. She showed him four houses and when they were not talking about the properties, they small-talked in the way people did when they were getting to know one another.

He was incredibly easy to talk to, and asked questions that required answers that would let him know what kind of person she was and what was important in her life.

By the time they went to lunch her nerves had settled. There was still a simmering tension between them, but instead of fighting it, she found herself enjoying it.

He insisted they go to one of his favorite restaurants, Café Italia, on the corner of North Oak and Barry Road. It wasn't far from the office and they passed one of his construction sites on the way.

"You must be a very good boss," she said once they were seated at a secluded table inside the restaurant.

"Why do you say that?" One of his eyebrows quirked upward.

"You must feel you have things under control to be able to take off so much time to house hunt and lunch out." She pulled the red napkin from the table and placed it on her lap.

"I'm a great boss—smart enough to have competent people I trust working for me. I'll check in later this afternoon on the site and make sure things are running smoothly."

The waitress appeared at their table, halting any further conversation as they placed their orders. All morning Christian had found himself enchanted with Vanessa.

He'd asked question after question, seeking a reason to back away, seeking something that would turn him off, but it hadn't happened. If anything, every little piece of information he learned only increased his interest in her, an interest that was growing from just strictly physical desire.

He waited until the waitress had placed a loaf of freshly baked bread on the table and had made them each a plate of Italian butter. Then he asked Vanessa how she'd met her husband.

"We met in college. I was a junior and Jim was a senior." She reached for a slice of bread, broke it in two and dipped a piece of it into the olive oil.

"Was it love at first sight?"

She smiled. "I'm not sure I really believe in love at first sight, but it was definitely a strong attraction. He asked me out for a drink one night and we ended up sharing a bottle of wine and talking into the wee hours of the morning."

She paused to take a bite of her bread, then continued. "After that first night, things between us moved very quickly. Within six months I'd dropped out of school and we were married."

"It was a good marriage?"

She broke eye contact with him and instead looked at some unidentifiable place over his shoulder. "It was a normal marriage, with ups and downs," she said after a long pause.

Her answer pleased him. Christian had dated a widow

once before and the experience had been frustrating. In death the woman's husband had risen to saint status. It had taken Christian three months to realize no mortal man could ever live up to what the dead man had become in the widow's mind.

"You mentioned the other day that a grandfather had raised you. Tell me about him."

Her eyes sparked with warmth and a new smile curved her lips, a smile that held happy memories and love, a smile he wanted directed at him because he evoked that emotion in her.

"Grandpa John. He was a wonderful man. We lived in a little cottage and most of the yard was a combination flower and vegetable garden. He had a magic with growing things, loved to bake and played the piano by ear. But best of all, he loved me unconditionally and taught me about the real value of life."

"You were lucky to have somebody like that in your life."

"You didn't?"

His childhood had hardly been idyllic, nor was it something he was prepared to talk about with her at this moment. "Not quite," he replied lightly. "But that's another story for another time."

He was saved by the appearance of the waitress bringing their orders. The conversation while they ate remained light. She talked about her son, who was obviously the shining star in her life, and they good-naturedly argued politics and steered clear of religion.

All too soon she glanced at her watch and he knew it was time for her to get back to the office. "Have dinner with me, Vanessa," he said as they left the restaurant and walked back to her car. "You pick the night. Let me take you out someplace nice."

"And maybe do a little dancing after dinner?" She smiled, her blue eyes holding a touch of wistfulness. "I used to love to dance, but it's been years."

"Then I'll make sure we do some dancing. Come on, what do you say?"

"Okay. Friday night. I'll make arrangements for Johnny to stay with his grandparents."

The flush of pleasure he felt surprised him. He couldn't remember the last time he'd looked forward to a date with this much anticipation.

When they got back to her office, she walked him to his car. "I'm sorry we didn't connect on any of the places today," she said.

"There will be other houses. I have confidence that you'll find me the right place." Despite the scent of winter that lingered in the air he could smell her perfume, that spicy scent that tightened his muscles and made him think of rumpled sheets and naked flesh.

"Now I have a much more serious question," he said, and took a step toward her, knowing he was invading her personal space.

She didn't take a step backward, which emboldened him. The tip of her tongue danced out to wet her upper lip and the cold air that surrounded them seemed to warm by twenty degrees. "What's your question?"

"How much did you enjoy lunch?" He could tell from the shine in her eyes that she knew where he was going.

"The food was delicious." Her cheeks were pink and he suspected it wasn't just the cold bringing them color.

He took another step closer to her and fought the impulse to raise his arms and wrap them around her. "And how was the company?"

"The company was wonderful." She knew he was going to kiss her; he could see it in her eyes.

"Wonderful enough for a kiss on the second date?"

Her lips curved upward and she gave a quick nod of her head. It was all he needed. Still keeping his arms at his sides, he took her mouth in what he'd intended to be a soft, quick, casual kiss.

But the moment he tasted the warm softness of her lips, the kiss became anything but quick and casual. Fire licked in his veins as she opened her mouth to him, allowing him access to deepen the kiss.

It was only when he felt himself becoming fully aroused and remembered that they were in the parking lot of her place of business that he broke the kiss and stepped back.

Her eyes were glazed, as if she'd been momentarily drugged, and he wanted nothing more than to kiss her again, this time with their bodies so close he could feel her heartbeat. But he didn't.

He took another step back from her and smiled. "That was the best second-date kiss I've ever had."

She laughed. "It was the only second-date kiss I've ever had."

He pulled his car keys from his pocket. "I'll get out of here. I know you have a one o'clock appointment and I need to get back to work. I'll call you in the next day or two to finalize plans for Friday night."

He got into the car and rolled down the window. "Vanessa, I have a feeling our house hunting together is going to take a long time. It might take months of looking and lunching."

She smiled. "Somehow I suspected that."

"I'll call you." He rolled up the window and started the car. As he drove out of the parking lot, he saw in his rearview mirror that she stood in place and watched him leave.

He had no idea how far he intended to go with her, how willing he was for a long-term relationship. Although he was at a place in his life where he'd like to have a woman by his side, sharing his life, he wasn't convinced Vanessa was that woman.

She had two strikes against her as far as he was concerned. The first was that she hadn't dated since her husband's death. The last thing Christian wanted to be was some kind of transition man in her life.

The second strike she had against her was Johnny. It wasn't that Christian didn't like kids. It was simply that he had no illusions about his ability to parent a child. Vanessa's son had already suffered a terrible tragedy in his life. He didn't deserve the second tragedy of having a stepfather who didn't know how to be a good parent.

Still, despite these two drawbacks, he wasn't ready to walk away from her now. She touched something deep inside him. Aside from the intense physical attraction he felt for her, there was something about her that tugged at his compassion, that made him want to make her smile.

She was a woman who deserved to be happy, to be loved. Whether he was the man to give her that was still up in the air.

As he drove toward the job site he shoved thoughts of Vanessa away and instead focused on work. They had another two weeks to finish up the latest strip mall. In the years that Christian had been doing this kind of work he'd never brought in a project over budget or late.

He had the one mall to complete, another framed in and contracts to break ground on two more in the early spring. Unfortunately, he was always at the mercy of the weather. This year the forecast was for a mild winter, which would definitely make things easier on all the area builders.

For the past three months he'd been looking for a piece of land to put his pet project, an upscale strip mall that he would own and operate. It was merely a set of blueprints and a dream at the moment, but he was finally in a position to go after his dream.

As he drove onto the property, where the latest project was up and most of the work was inside, he saw Jason Weir, his supervisor, standing in front puffing on a cigarette.

"Shit," he muttered, knowing that if Jason was smoking, there were problems.

He got out of his car and approached the big, burly man he trusted like a brother. Jason's grizzled gray brows met in a frown across the bridge of his oversized nose.

"I hate that look on your face," Christian said.

Jason took a last drag off his cigarette and flicked the butt aside. "Kevin didn't show up for work this morning and I had to send Ted home after lunch."

"Six-pack lunch?" Christian asked.

"Maybe, but I think it was more than beer. I think he's doing drugs." Jason sighed. "He misses more days than he's here, and even when he is here I can't get a day's worth of work out of him."

Christian frowned. "I was hoping he'd shape up, but I guess it's not happening. When he gets here in the morning, send him to the trailer and I'll give him his walking papers."

Together the two men headed for the small trailer next to the building to discuss what Christian had missed that morning and what needed to be accomplished before the workday was finished.

He drove by slowly, watching the tall blond and the big, gray-haired man disappear into a small trailer. He pulled over to the curb a block away and parked, needing to get hold of the rage that ripped through him, the rage that had been building and building with each day that passed.

He'd seen them. Vanessa and the tall blond man. He'd seen them kissing in the parking lot of the real estate office. Like two horny teenagers unable to wait for the cover of dark. Like two animals eager to rut without caring who watched.

He'd learn everything there was to know about the bastard. Vanessa thought she could just pick up the pieces of her life and go on. She believed she could put her past behind her and find happiness. Like he'd never existed. Like he'd never mattered.

He raised his thumb to his mouth and bit the nail, wincing as he razed the quick. But the pain felt good. It centered him. He drew several deep, cleansing breaths, started his car and pulled away from the curb, his thoughts firing first one direction, and then another.

Maybe he'd do nothing for a while. Maybe he'd just stay back in the shadows and see what happened between

Vanessa and her new man. Let them build something meaningful, let that bitch think that happiness was in the palm of her hand. Then he'd slap it out and make her pay. Just like he was going to make them all pay.

Chapter 8

The flowers were delivered on Wednesday evening. Vanessa and Scott were seated at the kitchen table drinking coffee and filling out the entry forms for the art contest Johnny's uncle Brian had mentioned on Thanksgiving Day.

The doorbell rang and when Vanessa answered, a floral-delivery truck and a huge bouquet of long yellow roses in a lovely pink vase greeted her. She took the bouquet from the smiling delivery woman and leaned for a long moment against the wall in the entry hall, an intense sense of déjà vu sweeping through her.

The pink vase and ribbon perfectly matched the pale pink edges of the delicate yellow blooms. Peace roses. How many times in her marriage had she received a bouquet just like this one? Too many to remember.

Jim.

His name screamed through her head. Jim had always sent her these roses when they'd had a fight. For a crazy moment she wanted to drop the vase to the floor. Her skin crawled. It was as if the flowers had been directly delivered from a man in a watery grave.

Although her impulse was to drop the vase, she clung tight. "Jim's dead," she whispered. "He didn't send the roses. He couldn't send the roses." She drew a deep breath to steady herself and slowly walked back toward the kitchen.

With each step she took, the initial horror faded as rational thought returned. Christian. He must have sent the bouquet. He couldn't have known what these particular roses meant to her personally. He probably had just seen pretty yellow roses and sent them to her.

"Whoa!" Scott's eyes widened as she entered the kitchen. "Where did those come from?"

"I'm not sure, but I could make an educated guess." She set the vase on the table and searched for a card. "There's no card," she murmured more to herself than to Scott.

"Hmm, and the plot thickens. Looks like somebody has a secret admirer."

She returned to her chair across from him and forced a smile. "It's not exactly a secret admirer. I have a date Friday night and he must have sent them."

One of Scott's blond eyebrows rose. "A date? Do tell. What's his name, what does he do? Where did you meet him? Have you run a background check?"

She laughed. "His name is Christian Connor and I met him the night of the art show. He was a close friend of Andre's."

"The tall blond with the broad shoulders and killer eyes?"

She nodded. "He's in the market for a house and I've

taken him out to look at properties a couple of times and one thing led to another and we're going out Friday night."

"Good for you. It's about time. And I'm only just a little bit jealous that you caught such a hunk."

She laughed once again. "If Eric heard you talking like that, he'd pin your ears back."

"Eric knows all of my faults and loves me anyway." Scott got up from the table and poured himself a second cup of coffee. "Oh, I meant to tell you. Guess who I ran into the other day? Gary Bernard."

"Gary?" She leaned back in her chair with surprise. "Is he just back for a visit?"

"Nope. He's moved back. He's living in the Willow Hills Apartments and looking for work in one of the galleries in town."

"When he left here for Arizona after Jim's death he swore he'd never return," she mused. Gary had been another artist friend of Jim's. After Jim had died, Gary had moved to Arizona to get in touch with his Southwestern roots and sell his Native American artwork.

"He told me he'd had enough of red rocks and dust." Scott tapped the entry forms on the top of the table. "We need to finish filling these out. I need to turn them in tomorrow."

Vanessa stared at the forms, wondering why she was dragging her feet. Certainly Johnny was excited about the contest. He'd already begun working on a painting to enter. She picked up the pen and twirled it in her fingers.

"What's wrong?" Scott's voice was soft. He reached out and covered her hand with his. "What are you thinking, sweet Vanessa?"

She looked into his warm blue eyes. He knew her so well and he was such a dear friend. "I don't know. I worry sometimes."

"You worry too much," he chided. "Is this about Matt McCann?"

She pulled her hand from his, dropped the pen on the table and leaned back in her chair. The day before, she'd heard the shocking news about Matt McCann's murder.

"Vanessa, we both know Matt was a terrific agent, but he was also a slimeball."

"It's just weird, first Andre, then Matt. Both of them worked in the art world."

"And nobody knows what nefarious activities Matt might have been involved in that had nothing to do with art. I know he was quite a gambler and he loved the ladies. The man was a pig and I imagine he pissed off the wrong person."

He leaned forward. "Johnny has a God-given talent and it would be tragic if you didn't allow him to pursue what he obviously loves doing." He picked up the pen and held it out to her. "It's a contest for kids, Vanessa. Don't make it bigger than what it is."

She took the pen from him. "You're right." It took her only minutes to finish filling out the forms. She'd just finished up when Johnny came into the kitchen.

"Cool flowers. Where did they come from?" he asked.

"Your mother's new beau," Scott replied.

Johnny looked at her. "The guy you're going out with Friday night?"

"There's no card, but I'm pretty sure that's who sent them," she replied.

"What are you going to do Friday night?" Scott asked Johnny. "Are you going out on a date, too?"

Johnny grinned and punched him in the shoulder. "I'm spending the night at Grandma's. We're going to play poker and eat popcorn."

"If you're playing poker with Grandma, you'd better watch her like a hawk," Vanessa said. "She cheats."

Johnny giggled and scooted into the chair next to Scott's. "How come you're still hanging around?"

"Eric is working late and I hate going home to a silent house," Scott replied. "Besides, I like hanging around here and tormenting your mother."

Johnny laughed again and his eyes brightened as he saw the forms on the table. "Did you sign them, Mom?" he asked eagerly.

"I did."

"Cool. First prize is a five-thousand-dollar savings bond. I could put it in my college fund." He cast a sly glance at Vanessa. "Or I could buy lots of new paints and canvases."

"You have enough paint and canvases now to last for another five years or so," Vanessa replied.

For the next few minutes they chatted, talking about school and Christmas wish lists and the contest. At eight thirty she sent Johnny upstairs to get ready for bed.

"I guess I'd better head home," Scott said, also getting up from the table.

She walked with him to the front door, his slender arm slung around her shoulder. "You know, not everyone who has artistic tendencies is dysfunctional," he said.

"Van Gogh cut off his ear," she said dryly.

"Doesn't count," he replied. "Van Gogh had epilepsy

and cut off his ear during a seizure. Look at me. I'm an artist and I'm well-adjusted." He dropped his arm from her shoulder and grinned wryly. "Okay, I'm gay, but that's not dysfunction. That's just a fact of my life."

"You're good for me, Scott," she said with a laugh. She leaned forward and kissed him on the cheek. "If you were straight, I'd marry you."

He smiled at her fondly. "If I was straight, I'd let you. But if that happened, Eric would be heartbroken and your new beau would have wasted all that money on roses."

She opened the hall closet and pulled out Scott's coat. "Get out of here," she said. "I've still got an hour's worth of computer work to do before I can go to bed."

Scott pulled on his coat, leaned over and kissed her on the forehead. Then with a wave he went out the door. She watched until he was in his car; then she closed and locked the door and went upstairs to check on her son.

Johnny was in bed, but not asleep. She sat on the edge of his bed and breathed in the scent of minty soap and bubble-gum-flavored toothpaste. "Do I need to check behind your ears and knees and elbows to make sure you washed good?"

He grinned. "You haven't done that since I was about five."

"When you were five I had a terrible time getting you to take a bath. You had decided that baths were a waste of time and preferred to stay dirty."

"I was a weird kid."

She leaned forward and swiped a strand of his dark hair away from his forehead. "You were a normal kid."

He yawned and turned on his side to face her. "If I win that contest, we don't have to put the money in my college fund. You could use it to buy something you want or whatever."

Her heart squeezed tight as love nearly overwhelmed her. "What on earth would I do with all that money?"

"I dunno. You could get your nails done or buy yourself something special. Grandma says you work too hard and never do anything for yourself." He yawned again. "Grandma says someday I'll be a rich, famous artist and then nobody will have to worry again."

Vanessa stroked the softness of his cheek. "Johnny, you don't have to worry about being a famous anything. You just be a good boy—that's all I expect from you. It's not your job to take care of anyone but yourself, okay?"

He nodded and his eyes drifted to half-mast. She leaned over and kissed his forehead. His hand crept up to swipe at the place where she'd kissed.

"You better not be wiping that off," she said with mock sternness.

A corner of his mouth curved up in a grin. "I'm rubbing it in," he said, his voice slurred with sleep.

Vanessa left his bedroom and went back downstairs to the kitchen, where the roses greeted her on the table. As she washed out the coffeepot and put the cups and saucers in the dishwasher, she kept her gaze averted from them.

It was ridiculous to feel such unease whenever she looked at them. Christian couldn't have known what memories those particular roses would evoke in her.

She wanted to throw them away. She didn't want to wake up in the morning, stumble into the kitchen to make coffee and see them sitting there. But it seemed sinful to throw away such beauty.

She needed to focus on the man rather than the roses. Certainly the kiss they had shared had lingered in her head. In fact, she'd hardly been able to think of anything else through the week.

The kiss had shocked her. She'd expected something light and uncomplicated, but the moment his mouth had claimed hers it had been anything but uncomplicated. She'd wanted to melt against him. She'd wanted that kiss to last forever. Her intense longing had stunned her.

She left the kitchen and went into the dining room, where her computer awaited her. She didn't have just the Worths and Christian on her client list, but also two new young couples who were looking to buy their first home.

This kind of client was her favorite. She loved seeing the couple's faces when they first saw a place they wanted to call home, loved their happiness on the day of closing when they had signed all the papers and finally made their dream of being homeowners a reality.

She always sent a special gift to each of her clients on their moving day, a wooden angel six inches high that held a banner reading WELCOME HOME. She'd met the man who carved them at a craft fair at one of the local malls a year before and had fallen in love with the pretty angels. He'd agreed to keep her supplied for as long as she wanted.

One of the angels had a place of honor on her fireplace mantel. Whenever she saw it, it filled her with warmth, with the gratitude that she'd managed to keep this house despite all the adversity she'd faced.

She worked the computer for an hour, then decided to call it a night. She'd just gotten into bed when the telephone rang. Rolling over on her side, she grabbed the receiver of the cordless she kept by the bed.

"Hello?"

There was no reply, although she could tell somebody was on the line. It wasn't the profound silence of a dead line.

"Hello?" she repeated. "Is somebody there?"

She bit her bottom lip as she waited for the caller to speak. The seconds stretched into a minute . . . two minutes. "Who are you trying to reach?" she asked.

Still no reply. Seconds once again passed; then finally there was a soft but audible click and the line went dead.

A wrong number, she told herself. Nothing ominous about it. But if it had been a wrong number, why hadn't the caller hung up immediately? She returned the receiver to the cradle and wondered why a chill danced up her back, pulling goose bumps to the surface of her skin.

Chapter 9

"Where are we in the interviews of the people who attended the art show the night Gallagher was murdered?" Detective Tyler King asked. He and his partner and two other detectives sat in a conference room that in the last couple of days had been transformed into the home base for a small task force.

The death of Andre Gallagher had garnered a lot of heat. He'd been a personal friend of the mayor's, and a philanthropist who had given generously to various organizations.

If his death had put pressure on the detectives to solve the crime, Matt McCann's murder had lit a fire under Tyler's ass, and the man holding the flame was Sam O'Dell, the chief of police.

"We've interviewed everyone on the guest list except four people," Mike Mason said. He flipped open a pad in front of him. "Mr. and Mrs. Devon Chancellor and Mr. and Mrs. Ward Samson have been out of town since the night of the show. The Chancellors are supposed to be back in town tomorrow and the Samsons are to return by the end of next week."

"You follow up with them, and James, I want you to continue talking to all the people McCann represented. Somebody apparently has a hard-on for people in the art world and whoever it is had ties to both Gallagher and McCann."

Clint James nodded. He was a good man, meticulous to a fault. If there was a connection between Gallagher and McCann besides the obvious, James would find it.

"What am I supposed to be doing?" Tyler's rookie partner glared at him. He'd kept her tightly reined, much to her disgust. There was a right way and a wrong way to conduct a murder investigation and Tyler was determined that Jennifer Tompkins would leave his tutelage a smarter, more patient cop.

"I thought you were known as the cop who talked to the dead. Why aren't Gallagher and McCann talking to you and telling us where the fuck to look for the killer?"

James and Mason both appeared to hold their breath. Tyler slammed his fist down on the table and stared at Jennifer. "You use that tone of voice again in this room and I'll write you up for insubordination. I'll have you back to writing traffic tickets so fast your head will spin."

She had the good sense to flush and mutter an apology, although Tyler knew he hadn't scored points by berating her in front of the others. Still, there was only so much a man could take and she'd pushed him to his limit.

"You and I are going to go back to Carrie Sinclair and reinterview her, see if she can think of anyone who might have held a grudge against both Gallagher and McCann."

He directed his attention back to James. "You checked on the bat?"

"Sold at every Kmart and Wal-Mart in the country. I contacted the managers at the stores within a twenty-mile radius of McCann's house and told them I needed to know about the sale of any baseball bats in the last six months. I'm expecting to have those records by the first of next week."

Tyler nodded in satisfaction, although he didn't expect the results to yield anything. The killer was not only vicious but also smart. "What about the paint?" He looked at Mason.

The big man winced and shook his head. "According to the lab, it's ordinary oil paint sold at any place that carries art supplies. They identified the pigments and determined the paint color is vermilion. I spoke to two art supply places and they told me it was one of the most common colors sold."

"What about the murder weapon in the Gallagher case?" He turned his attention back to James. "Anything new?" The sculpture that had been used as a murder weapon on Andre Gallagher had been found in a Dumpster a block away from the art gallery.

"You know it all. No prints left behind. The title of the sculpture is *Destiny*." James shook his head. "Kind of morbid considering what it was used for. The artist's name is Jay Johnson. He lives in the Ozarks and has pieces at several galleries in the Midwest. His alibis for the nights of the murders checked out."

Tyler released a sigh of frustration. Two murders. Two murder weapons. And no leads. "Let's break for lunch and meet back here at two this afternoon."

The two male detectives stood and left the room. "You want to get a burger?" Tyler asked Jennifer.

She shook her head. "I brought my lunch today." She got up from her chair, her gaze not quite meeting his. "Look, I'm sorry about my outburst. Sometimes I let my emotions run ahead of my brain."

"That's something you can't allow to happen in this job," he said gently. "You want to work the murder squad, you need to understand how homicides work."

She looked at him then and her eyes were filled with torment. "I just want to do something, you know? Make a difference. Find this guy and see him put behind bars."

"We all want that," Tyler replied. "Jennifer, this is your first murder case. I don't know what you expected, but most of the work we do is tedious and time-consuming. A homicide investigation is hours on the phone, hours spent reading reports over and over again. There's rarely a hero when it comes to solving murders, and if you're looking to be a hero, you're definitely in the wrong job."

She bit her bottom lip as if to keep herself from saying something that would only piss him off. He pointed toward the door. "Go eat your lunch and be back here in an hour."

She turned and left the room and Tyler went back to the table and sat down, his gaze focused on the crime scene photos tacked to a bulletin board.

Two men brutally murdered, the obvious connection the art world. There was no robbery in either case. Matt McCann had had two thousand dollars in cash on top of the dresser in his bedroom. If it had been a robbery, that wouldn't have been there when the police arrived.

Neither victim had defensive wounds of any kind, indicating that the attack on each man had been a surprise. It appeared from the blood-splatter evidence that Andre had been smashed in the head as he'd entered his office in the back of the gallery. Matt McCann had been hit the moment he'd opened his front door.

Tyler frowned and used two fingers to rub the center of his forehead where a headache throbbed. What they knew about the perpetrator could be placed on a small index card. The killer was obviously intelligent and organized. The paint slash indicated a ritual element to the kills.

The murderer's gender hadn't yet been determined. Although the blows to both men had been devastating, a determined female filled with the strength of rage might have been able to make the kills.

He leaned back in the chair and closed his eyes. It was personal. The killer had wanted the two men dead. *Talk to me.* He mentally willed the victims and what little evidence the police had gathered to speak to him in words that made sense.

He'd gotten the reputation for talking to the dead because of his phenomenal solve rate. It had been a long running joke in the department that Tyler King was the man who talked to the dead.

He was no John Edwards. He couldn't tell anyone where Aunt Ruby had left her ring or where Uncle Albert had stashed his life savings before dying.

He didn't hear voices in his head, didn't dream of talking corpses. He didn't see phantom dead people. All he did was immerse himself in the case, keep an open mind and let the evidence talk to him. He went into each murder investigation believing anything was possible, which allowed him to explore avenues that to others didn't look viable.

The red paint carefully brushed on the chest of each victim implied a ritual, and that worried him. Ritual killers rarely stopped on their own. The police had managed to keep the paint out of the news reports. It was the single piece of evidence they had held back in order to separate the crazy people who loved to confess to murders from the real killer.

At the moment nothing was speaking to him, not the victims, not the evidence, nothing. And what worried him most was that somebody else might have to die before they got a break.

Chapter 10

The bedroom looked as if the fashion police had raided Vanessa's closet and left appalling rejects piled in the middle of her bed.

She'd tried on half a dozen things in an attempt to find the perfect outfit for dinner and dancing with Christian. She'd finally settled on a flirty navy dress with a navy and silver belt, an outfit that would be perfect for whatever dancing he had in mind.

She'd pulled her hair back at the nape of her neck with a silver clasp and added small silver earrings. At six fifteen she gave herself a final once-over in the bathroom mirror, then went into the living room to wait for Christian, who should be arriving to pick her up in fifteen minutes.

Nerves jumped and tumbled in her tummy as she sat on the sofa to wait for him. She couldn't remember being this nervous when she'd first gone out with Jim.

Maybe it was because the stakes felt higher this time around. She was no longer a starry-eyed twenty-one-year-old falling in love for the very first time. She was

a single parent who knew exactly what she would accept and what she wouldn't accept when it came to a
relationship.

She was smarter, but so lonely, and she didn't want the
loneliness to cause her to make stupid mistakes.

She hadn't had time to pick up the house or clean up
the mess in her bedroom, but it didn't matter. She didn't
intend to invite Christian in. She needed to go slow, although whenever she thought about the kiss they'd
shared, slow didn't seem like a reasonable option.

At six thirty she got up from the sofa and moved into
the dining room, where she had a view from the window
to her driveway and the street.

It felt odd, to be waiting for a man to arrive, to be dating once again. She certainly didn't feel guilty. She'd
mourned Jim for a long time and although his life was
gone, hers continued. She wasn't sure if Christian was in
for a long-term relationship, but she had realized in the
last several days that she didn't want to spend the rest of
her life alone.

Six thirty came and went. Six forty arrived and still no
Christian. She started to wonder if she'd been stood up.
Maybe he'd had second thoughts about getting involved
with a single parent raising a ten-year-old boy. Or maybe
he'd just decided he wasn't really interested in her.

At six forty-five his car pulled into the driveway and
he hopped out like a man who knew he was late. As he
approached the door, she watched him, admiring the fit of
his navy dress slacks and long-sleeved blue and gray
dress shirt beneath his opened leather dress jacket. She
smoothed down her navy dress. They'd coordinated their
colors without even knowing it.

She grabbed her purse and coat as the doorbell rang. Before opening the door, she drew a deep breath in an attempt to steady her erratic heartbeat, but it refused to calm down.

"I hate people who are late," he said when she opened the door. "And I really hate it when I'm one of them. I'm sorry, there was a glitch on one of the job sites this afternoon and I didn't get away as quickly as I'd hoped."

"Stop." She held up her hand and laughed at the earnest look on his face. "It was just a few minutes."

"Still, I don't like to keep a beautiful woman waiting and you look ravishing."

She thrilled at his words, at the look that shone from his eyes. "Thank you."

He took her coat from her and held it out for her to put on. Then together they left the house and headed for his car. "You have a nice place," he said as he pulled out of the driveway.

"We put a lot of blood, sweat and tears into it before Jim died. It's cold in the winters and hot in the summers, but it's home." His car smelled not only of his cologne but also of car cleaner, and she wondered if he'd taken the time and trouble to clean the interior just for tonight. The thought pleased her.

"So, where are we going?" she asked.

He cast her a quick smile, then focused back out the front window. "To one of my favorite places. A little hole-in-the-wall called Frank's Place. They serve the best steaks in town and have a little dance floor and a band that plays old standards."

"Doesn't sound like the typical singles club."

"It's not. I tried the popular clubs when I first moved

to town but found the bands too noisy, the dancing too frantic and the people too desperate. They weren't my style."

"Doesn't sound like it would be my style either, although I know Alicia, the receptionist at the office, spends almost every night at one club or another."

"Somehow that doesn't surprise me. She has that kind of desperate look in her eyes that should send any rational man running in the opposite direction."

Vanessa wondered if she had that look in her own eyes. That hungry look she'd seen so often in Alicia's eyes when an attractive man came into the office.

And if she didn't have it now, would she have it in a year, in two years of dating an endless stream of men in an effort to find the one who might mean something to her?

Never, she thought. She knew how to live alone. She knew how not to need anyone, how not to depend on anyone but herself.

"You mentioned you had a problem at work? I hope it was nothing serious," she said. She looked at his profile, noting the bold, classic lines of his face. There was such strength in his features, a strength that inspired trust.

He sighed. "I had to let a worker go, something I hate to do. It got messy. I had to have my security team escort him off the site."

"Sounds tough."

"It was. He's a young guy with a family and this time of year it's rough to find another construction job. But he drank and my foreman and I suspected he was doing drugs. I can't have something like that going on at a site. Too dangerous for everyone."

He waved one of his hands. "Enough about work problems." He flashed her another one of his killer smiles. "Tonight is about good times and slow dances and a steak that will knock your socks off."

His words made her bones turn mushy and she melted back against the seat. "Sounds wonderful."

For a few minutes they rode in silence, but it was not an uncomfortable one. It was as if they were waiting until they reached their final destination to share anything else with each other.

He hadn't been exaggerating when he said that Frank's Place was a hole-in-the-wall. Tucked back from the street next to a tattoo parlor, the restaurant would have been easy to miss if you didn't know it was there.

"How on earth did you find this place?" she asked as they got out of the car and headed for the front door.

"Actually, Andre found it and introduced it to me." A sad smile curved his lips and she knew he was thinking of the friend he had lost. "Andre hated clubbing, but he loved good music. I don't know how he found it, but most Friday nights after the gallery closed he'd come here and drink beer and listen to the band."

As they walked into the dim interior the enticing scent of grilled meat made her mouth water. "Mr. Connor, nice to see you again." The hostess, an older woman, smiled at him.

"Thanks, Madge. You have my table ready?"

"Follow me." She grabbed two menus from a stack and led them to a table near the dance floor. The small stage was empty and piped music played softly from speakers.

"Your waiter should be here in a minute. Enjoy." She left them to settle in at the table.

"The band doesn't start playing until eight," Christian said as he pulled out the chair for her, then seated himself across from her. The table was small, a candle burning in the center to create an aura of intimacy.

"This is lovely." She picked up her menu and opened it.

"I hope you like steak. That's definitely the specialty here." He didn't open his menu. "The fillets are great, as are the strip steaks."

"I'll trust your judgment. A fillet sounds wonderful." She closed her menu and set it to the side. "Other than your problem today, how was your week?" Dating 101: ask questions. She'd read somewhere that most men loved to talk about themselves.

"It was a good week. What about yours?" He turned the conversation back to her so easily she wondered if he'd read the same article.

"It was okay. I have a couple who is making me crazy. I've been showing them properties a few times each week for a month and I can't seem to please the woman with anything."

"Does that happen a lot?"

"Often enough. There are people out there who seem to make it a hobby to look at homes. They have no real intention of buying. They just enjoy looking. We call them looky-dos."

"I'm not a looky-do, but I have a confession to make." He leaned forward, his eyes glittering in the candlelight. "I kind of liked the very first house you showed me, but I didn't want to jump too fast or I wouldn't have had an excuse to spend time with you."

At that moment the waiter arrived at their table, saving

her from making any kind of a reply. Still, she couldn't help the wave of pure pleasure that engulfed her.

"Would you like a glass of wine?" Christian asked as the waiter stood ready to deliver whatever they requested.

"No, thanks. A Diet Coke will be fine."

"You sure? You aren't the designated driver tonight."

She shook her head. "I'm sure."

He ordered himself a glass of red wine; then they placed their meal orders and the waiter departed. He returned almost immediately with their drink orders.

For the next few minutes Christian entertained her with stories about his work, making her laugh as he described the eccentric people who had once worked for him and the struggles he'd encountered when first starting out.

The laughter felt good, and she found his sense of humor as sexy as his physical presence. There was something wonderful about sharing laughter. The waiter bringing their salads interrupted the conversation once again.

As they ate, they talked about where they were in their lives and the loneliness that plagued each of them. "My lonely time is first thing in the morning," he said as he speared a slice of carrot from his salad. "When I sit at the kitchen table to have that first cup of coffee."

"Mine is just after supper, when the dishes are put away and Johnny is busy with his own things. I usually sit at the kitchen table with a cup of tea and unwind. That's my loneliest time of the day."

It was a half-truth. While that time of day between twilight and dark could be difficult, it was at night when the real ache of loneliness often struck her. When she turned over in the king-sized bed and there was nobody on the opposite side.

While she recognized that part of the ache came from the fact that she missed sex, most of it came from wanting something deeper, something far more intimate than sex. She didn't want to just allow a man access to her body; she wanted to give some special person all the parts of her heart and mind.

"Maybe I should call you every evening and talk you through the lonely time," he said lightly.

She smiled. "And I could call you at the crack of dawn. But then you'd know I'm not much of a morning person."

"Ah, one of those. I'll bet you hate people who smile in the mornings."

"Detest them."

"And people who sing with the sunrise?" He quirked up one of his eyebrows, his eyes lit with humor.

"Abhor them."

"I promise to keep that information in mind for future purposes," he replied.

Their steaks and baked potatoes arrived and they dug in, eating and talking as if they'd known each other forever. They talked about grade school and high school, about most embarrassing moments and special days of happiness.

Still, each time his gaze lingered on her across the candlelight a delicious shiver raced up her spine.

They had just finished the meal and had ordered coffee when the band began to play. It didn't take long for several couples to hit the dance floor.

The general crowd in the place was older and it was obvious that some of the couples had been dancing together for years. They danced with a fluid grace, as if able to anticipate each other's movements.

"Shall we?" Christian asked when the third song began to play.

A burst of nerves struck her. "It's been years since I've danced," she protested. "I'll probably step on your toes."

He smiled, leaned across the table and took her hand in his. Standing, he pulled her to her feet. "My toes can handle it," he said as he led her toward the dance floor.

She'd known being in his arms would hold a certain magic and she wasn't wrong. As his hand slid to her waist a heady warmth suffused her. He held her just close enough to be exciting, but not so close to be inappropriate.

He was a strong lead, his hand at her waist and a touch of his thigh guiding her where he wanted her to go. He was surprisingly graceful and made her feel as if she glided in his arms.

"I've been waiting for this opportunity all night long." His breath was warm, teasing her ear and the length of her neck.

"What opportunity?" she asked, her voice half-breathless as her heart beat with a rapid pace.

"The whole time we were eating all I could think about was that as soon as the band began to play I'd finally get the chance to hold you in my arms."

"I hope the anticipation lives up in reality," she said.

He smiled down at her and slightly tightened his grip at her waist. "Believe me, it's a thousand times better than I'd imagined."

Slow, she reminded herself. It was sensible to take things slow. But it would be so easy to forget being sensible and fall into his seductiveness.

They sat out the next dance and sipped on fresh drinks. He had a beer and she had another diet soda. They danced three more times, and each time he held her a little closer. Each time she wanted him to hold her a little closer.

It was almost midnight when they left Frank's Place to head home. "I hope you had a good time," he said.

She smiled. "I had a wonderful time. I'd forgotten how much I loved to dance and the food was delicious."

"And the company?"

She laughed. "Are you fishing for a compliment?"

"Absolutely."

"You dance like a dream, your small talk is fascinating and altogether on a scale from one to ten I'd rate this date an eight."

He shot her a frown. "An eight? Why not a ten?"

"If I gave you a ten now, there would be nothing for you to aspire to in the future."

"Does this mean you'll go out with me again?"

"Only if you ask," she replied. And how she wanted him to ask. As she'd danced with him his breath had warmed her neck and once she thought his lips had skimmed her forehead. The dancing had renewed an ache of desire inside her, the desire for skin-to-skin contact, for hot kisses and sweeping passion.

"I'm asking," he said as he parked in her driveway. He shut off the engine, unbuckled his seat belt and turned to look at her, his eyes gleaming in the light from the dashboard. "I want to take you out again. I want to spend more time with you." He grinned. "Would tomorrow night be too soon?"

A breathless burst of laughter escaped her. "Yes, it would." He took her breath away with his smoldering gaze and handsome features. He made it so hard for her to deny him with his wonderful sense of humor and his aura of caring.

"Okay, then how about you show me some more houses on Wednesday and we'll have lunch and maybe next Friday we can go out again. In fact, I'll cook for you at my place."

She frowned. "I don't know. It seems a little fast for a second date to be at your house."

"Think about it—if you count all our lunches together, it would really be our fourth or fifth date. But if you aren't comfortable with me cooking for you, then we'll go out."

"No, I'd love for you to cook for me." Maybe she was allowing things to move too fast, but at the moment she decided to throw caution to the wind. She eyed him dubiously. "Didn't you tell me you didn't cook? That you are the king of the TV dinner meal?"

"I'll cheat. I'll order in, replate it, and you'll pretend I'm a magnificent chef."

"You've got a deal," she replied.

They got out of the car and walked toward her front door. She hoped he wouldn't ask her to invite him in. She was afraid she'd forget her intentions and agree and things would flame out of control, move too fast.

"I had a great time tonight, Vanessa," he said when they reached her front door. He reached up and touched her cheek with his hand. "Andre was right about you. You aren't just beautiful, but you're smart and funny and strong."

His voice was husky and he released a small laugh.

"You make me feel like I'm seventeen again. It's the most awful, wonderful feeling in the world."

His words, coupled with a hint of vulnerability in his gaze, touched her. "I don't want to make you feel awful," she said softly, and reached up and captured his hand against her cheek.

She knew he was going to kiss her; she saw the intention in his eyes as he stepped closer . . . closer still. She dropped her hand to her side as he gathered her into his arms, so close she could feel the pounding of his heartbeat. Or was it her own?

His mouth took hers in a kiss both demanding and possessive and she felt the power of it right down to her toes. She raised her arms and placed her hands on the nape of his neck and he pulled her closer still as he deepened the kiss.

His tongue swirled with hers, creating a firestorm of pleasure inside her. The hair at the nape of his neck was silky-soft and she twined her fingers through it as a small moan escaped her.

His hands slid from her waist to the top of her hips and he moved her so tight against him she could feel that he was aroused.

A wicked sense of feminine power filled her as she realized she was responsible for his erection; that he wanted her that badly.

And she wanted him. The taste of his mouth weakened her knees and the touch of his hands wreaked havoc on her resolve. But she refused to allow herself to make a mistake by allowing physical desire to rule her actions. With a groan of regret, she softly pushed against his chest.

PAINT IT RED   117

Instantly he released her and stepped back. She leaned against the front door and tried to catch her breath. He raced a hand through his hair and drew in a long, deep breath.

"I definitely think a brutally cold shower is in my immediate future," he said, his voice low and husky.

"I'd invite you in, but . . ."

"You don't want things moving too fast." He shoved his hands in his pockets and smiled. "I've heard that good things come to those who wait. You'll find that I can be a patient man."

She rose up on her tiptoes and pressed her lips against his jaw. "Good night, Christian. I'll see you Wednesday morning at the office." She pulled out her keys and unlocked the door; then she remembered the roses and turned back to face him. "I never thanked you for the roses."

"You're quite welcome, but now I'm a bit upset," he said.

"Why?"

"I obviously have competition, because I didn't send you any roses."

Vanessa's heart fell to her feet. If Christian hadn't sent her the roses, who had?

Chapter 11

Who sent the roses? It was the question that plagued her as she fell asleep that night and the first thing that filled her head when she awakened the next morning.

She drank her coffee sitting at the table and stared at the fully bloomed flowers in the vase. Despite the memories that the peace roses had brought, she'd loved these because she'd assumed Christian had sent them.

But he hadn't.

Who had?

She finished her coffee, rinsed the cup, and then took the flowers from their vase and shoved them into the garbage can. She didn't want to look at them anymore; she would not be able to find pleasure in the delicate pink-tinged blooms when the sender was a mystery.

Vanessa didn't like mysteries. She didn't want a secret admirer. She'd always found the concept creepy instead of romantic. If a man were interested in her, then she wanted him to step up and declare his intentions, not hide behind anonymity.

Roses disposed of, coffee gone, it was time to get her

son back home from her in-laws. Minutes later as she drove the short distance to the Abbott home, her thoughts went back over the evening she'd spent with Christian.

She'd been so young when she'd met Jim. He'd been her first real grown-up relationship. Sure, she'd dated before him, but she hadn't tied herself to any one boy in high school or in her first few years in college. Jim had been her first serious love affair. And she suspected if she let him, Christian might be her second.

She was not surprised to see all the cars in the Abbott driveway when she pulled up. Saturday mornings the clan often gathered for coffee and some of Annette's famous biscuits and gravy.

Dan met her at the front door, his smile vague and distracted. "They're all in the kitchen," he said.

"Thanks, Dan." As she walked through the living room Dan sat on the sofa and punched up the television volume on a morning news show.

Bethany, Steve, Garrett, Dana and Johnny sat at the table and Annette stood in front of the stove stirring a pot of gravy big enough to feed a small army.

"Hi, Mom," Johnny said, the corners of his mouth holding evidence of biscuit crumbs and sausage gravy.

"There she is." Annette pointed a finger at one of the empty chairs at the table. "Sit. I'll fix you a plate."

"So?" Dana looked at her expectantly.

"So what?" Vanessa asked in mock innocence.

"How did it go last night?"

"Yeah, did you have fun?" Johnny asked.

"I had a very nice time. We had a nice steak dinner, then did some dancing."

"Dancing? I didn't know you liked to dance." Annette set a plate of biscuits and gravy in front of her.

"As I recall, Jim had two left feet," Garrett said. He had the red-rimmed eyes of a man who had drunk too much and stayed up too late the night before. "I was always the dancer in the family." He elbowed Johnny in the ribs. "Your uncle Garrett can really get his groove on when it comes to the dance floor."

Johnny giggled and everyone else groaned. "Maybe you should spend less time on the dance floor and more time doing background checks into the women you choose to date," Annette said dryly.

"Ma, you wound me," Garrett exclaimed.

"Where's Brian?" Vanessa asked, deciding a change of topic was definitely in order.

"Working," Dana replied. "Some big project that has to be finished by Monday morning. He told me to not expect to see him until after it was done."

"Aunt Dana brought me a picture Uncle Brian found of Dad's," Johnny said. "It was one of Dad's first drawings."

"That's cool," Vanessa said.

"He was digging around in some old boxes we had packed in the basement and found several of Jim's old drawings. He thought Johnny might like to have the first picture Jim drew that got him noticed by his art teacher," Dana explained.

"Johnny shows every bit as much talent as Jim did," Annette said. She walked over to Johnny and kissed the top of his head. "Our boy here is going to surpass his father's fame. When people talk about Jim Abbott, they won't just talk about how talented he was before his death. They'll also talk about how talented his son is."

Johnny nodded, his little face somber. "I'll make you proud of me, Grandma. You just wait and see."

"I'm sure your grandma is proud of you if you never paint another picture," Vanessa said, and glanced pointedly at Annette.

"Well, of course I am," she hurriedly agreed. "We're all proud of you, Johnny."

Steve stood and looked at his watch, then glanced at his wife, a touch of impatience evident on his features. "Time to move, honey. We've got a store to open and I've got meetings across town."

"How are the plans for the new store coming along?" Vanessa asked as she cut into one of the huge gravy-laden biscuits.

"He's had a migraine for a month," Bethany said. "He's trying to do too much and needs to learn how to relax. I keep telling him it would be nice if we had more than an hour together each day."

"Success takes sacrifices," he replied. A muscle ticked in the side of his jaw. Of all the brothers, Steve was the most high-strung. He was in a perpetual state of movement. He was always the first to be ready to leave when the family got together for any occasion.

"I'm worried about them," Annette said a few minutes later when Steve and Bethany had gone. "She can't get Steve to slow down and I think it's definitely putting a strain on their marriage."

"Johnny, why don't you go wash your face and hands," Vanessa said. He didn't need to hear a discussion about the state of his aunt and uncle's marriage.

"Bethany thinks Steve might be having an affair," Dana said when Johnny had left the room.

"No way," Vanessa scoffed. "There's no way I'd believe that."

Dana shrugged. "I'm just telling you what Bethany told me. She says she can never seem to get hold of Steve when he tells her he's going to be someplace. There are times of the day and night when he doesn't answer his cell phone."

"Not answering a cell phone is a long way from having an affair," Annette said. She joined them at the table, a worried frown creasing the center of her forehead. "I'll talk to Steve, remind him that ambition is fine, but not at the expense of his family."

For the next few minutes the conversation focused on the upcoming week and plans for Christmas. Vanessa ate the biscuits and gravy, then carried her plate to the sink and rinsed it.

By that time, Johnny had returned to the kitchen. "You ready to head home, sport?" she asked.

"Okay. I'll just go get my overnight bag." He disappeared once again and Vanessa turned to Annette. "I don't intend to take advantage of your generosity, but would you mind having him again next Friday night?"

"Another date?" Dana asked with interest. "So this is serious?"

Vanessa laughed. "I wouldn't call it serious. We just had a good time last night and he invited me out again."

Annette reached out and covered Vanessa's hand with hers. "You know I'd love to have Johnny here anytime you need. He's such a good boy and he reminds me so much of his daddy." She sighed and for a moment Vanessa knew she was thinking of the son she'd lost, the man they had all lost.

Vanessa squeezed her hand, then stood. "I've got to get home. This is the first Saturday I've not worked in a couple of weeks and there are tons of things I want to get done."

Minutes later as she and Johnny drove home, she found her thoughts skating back to Christian. Jim had come from such a strong, supportive family, but she suspected Christian didn't have the same kind of relationship with his parents. And yet Christian seemed so wonderfully normal, so completely well-adjusted.

"What would you like to do today?" she asked Johnny as she pulled into the driveway. "You want to go see a movie?"

"Nah, I've got to work on my painting. I have to turn it in next week to the contest committee."

"Wouldn't you rather take off just for a couple of hours and see the new Disney flick?"

"I don't think so. This contest is really important." He smiled with boyish apology. "It's okay if we don't go to the movie, isn't it?"

She leaned over and ruffled his hair. "It's definitely okay." Her smile faded as she looked at her son. "I just want you to know that there's more to life than drawing and painting, Johnny."

"I know that, Mom." He got out of the car and she followed more slowly.

Everyone told her not to worry, that Johnny was doing just fine, that he was well-adjusted and bright. But everyone else wasn't his mother and there were still dark moments in the night when she worried that he'd embraced his father's life, when she was afraid that Jim's obsession had somehow transferred to Johnny.

She shoved her worries away as they went into the house and he bounded up the stairs toward his bedroom. He isn't like Jim, she told herself. He'd never be like Jim. She'd make sure of that.

Although she'd told Annette she had tons of things to do, the day stretched out empty before her. She had just a little housework to do and it wouldn't hurt for her to check the computer for new listings that might have become available, but other than that, she had no plans.

She'd just pulled out her cleaning supplies when Johnny came down the stairs and into the kitchen. "Here's the picture Uncle Brian gave me that Dad drew when he was in third grade." He held it out to her.

It was a landscape with a stream in the foreground and an old barn in the background. The lines and angles were dead-on, showing a maturity that was rare in eight-year-olds. At the bottom right corner he'd written simply *ABBOTT*, a signature that had remained the same throughout his adult years.

"We'll need to get a frame for that and you can hang it in your room," she said, and handed it back to him.

"That would be cool." He looked around the kitchen curiously. "Hey, what happened to your flowers?"

"They were getting all brown and wilted so I had to throw them out." The roses. Who had sent her the roses? Damn, the mystery was driving her crazy.

"Too bad. They were really pretty. Can I take a glass of milk up to the studio?"

"Of course," she said. "Just remember to bring the glass back down when you're finished."

He got his milk and disappeared once again. Vanessa frowned, wishing he hadn't brought up the subject of the roses. It had taken her forever to get to sleep the night before as she'd wondered who might have sent them to her.

She'd thought about Buzz, her coworker. Was it possible he had sent them to her? Certainly he'd shown on more than one occasion that he'd be interested in dating her whenever she felt ready to enter the dating game again.

But Buzz was known in the office as a cheapskate. She couldn't imagine him spending the kind of bucks to get roses in the winter for a woman with whom he'd shared only a working relationship.

The other men in the office were happily married and certainly had never given her any indication that they might be interested in an affair.

She thought about the clients she'd been working with over the past couple of weeks. Had Robert Worth maybe become infatuated with her as his wife had dragged him from house to house?

The last time she'd taken them out, Robert had stayed in the living room talking to her while Kate had explored the other rooms in the house alone.

"Enough," she muttered aloud, and grabbed a dust cloth and the bottle of Orange Glo. She refused to dwell on the mystery of the roses another minute. If she had a secret admirer, eventually he'd show his hand; if he didn't, what she didn't know couldn't hurt her.

She spent the rest of the morning vacuuming and dusting, then moved back into the kitchen to fix some lunch for her and Johnny.

Remembering her vow to do more baking, she decided to make a batch of chocolate-chip cookies. The first batch was cooling on a rack when she heard Johnny's footsteps coming down the stairs.

"Aha! Now I know the secret to getting you to come down for lunch," she said as he came into the kitchen.

He rubbed his stomach and grinned. "I could smell those cookies all the way upstairs."

"A sandwich first." She pointed him to the table. "Ham and cheese or peanut butter and jelly?"

"Ham and cheese, then about a million of those cookies."

Vanessa laughed. "I only baked two dozen." She made them each a sandwich, and then sat with him at the table to eat.

While eating, they talked about the upcoming holidays and what Johnny wanted for Christmas, and they made bets on when they would get their first real snowstorm.

They had just finished their meal when the doorbell rang. "I wonder who that could be." She got up from the table and hurried to the front door.

"Surprise!" The big man on the porch grabbed her and pulled her against him in a bear hug, lifting her feet off the floor.

"Gary, put me down," she said with a laugh.

He set her on her feet inside the entry hall and grinned. "Surprised to see me?"

"I figured you'd turn up here sooner or later. Scott told me you were back in town. Come on into the kitchen and we'll play catch-up."

He followed her into the kitchen and stopped in the doorway. "That big guy at the table can't be Johnny. Last time I saw him he was nothing but a little punk who wasn't dry behind the ears." He pointed toward Johnny. "But that guy is practically a full-grown man."

Johnny grinned. "Hi, Gary."

"How are you doing, kid?" Gary shrugged out of his corduroy coat, tossed it on a barstool at the counter, then flopped into the chair next to Johnny's. "How's life treating you?"

"Good. I'm entering an art contest. Want to see the painting I'm working on?"

"Why don't you let me visit with your mom for a little while. Then I'll take a look at your painting."

"Cool. I'll see you in a little while. Mom, I'm going back upstairs." Johnny got up from the table and left the room.

"Wow. He's grown up so much. How about a cup of coffee for an old friend? It will go well with the cookies I smell."

Gary Bernard had been another one of Jim's artist friends. Supported by a healthy trust fund, Gary was among the fortunate few who had never had to work to live.

Jim had always talked about the fact that an artist with money was an artist with little motivation. He often railed over the fact that Gary wasn't driven enough to enjoy any kind of real success.

Gary enjoyed looking the part of a starving artist. His black hair was pulled away from his face and braided down his back, exposing lean, hungry features that were at odds with his laid-back personality. He wore a pair of tattered jeans and a Southwestern-style shirt with braided ribbon trim that had a hole in the underside of the pocket.

"As I recall, when you left Kansas City you swore

nobody would ever see you again, that you'd find peace and your muse in the red rocks of Sedona." She fixed the coffee and punched the button to start the brew.

"God, I hate people who remember things I say in the heat of the moment."

"Sedona didn't work out?"

"It's a nice place to visit, but I wouldn't want to live there. I thought I'd find inspiration there. I mean, Southwest art is my specialty, but I sat on every one of those magical vortexes in Sedona and all I got for the trouble was air up my ass."

She laughed and poured them each a cup of coffee and pushed the platter of cookies closer to him. "So, tell me what's new with you."

"I got married and divorced." He grabbed a cookie and managed to shove the whole thing into his mouth.

"Jeez, Gary, what does that make? Four?"

He held up five fingers as he finished chewing. "Five if you count that lost weekend in Vegas. But I take great pride in the fact that all my ex-wives have remained friends with me."

"That's because you're so lovable," she said teasingly.

"Absolutely." He grabbed another cookie from the platter. "So, tell me how you've been doing. You look terrific." His chocolate brown eyes studied her face. "Things going okay?"

"Things are good. Work at the realty is going fine. Johnny is doing well and I'm fine."

Gary broke his eye contact with her and stared into his coffee cup. "I should have been here for you. Jim would have wanted me to be here to support you and Johnny, to help pick up the pieces."

He looked up and in his eyes she saw a deep torment. "But I couldn't." He swiped a hand across his whiskered jaw and leaned back in his chair. "What he did, it devastated me. I mean, we all knew Jim was moody, but what he did was so crazy, so wild. I didn't even stick around to go to the memorial service."

"Gary, it's all right."

He sighed and leaned back farther in the chair, which looked dwarfed beneath him. "He was the best of us all, the one with the most talent. He was the one who was going places, and the fact that he destroyed it all made me so damned sad and so damned angry."

Vanessa wrapped her fingers around her coffee mug, seeking the warmth to banish the chill that thoughts of Jim always brought her. "Jim wasn't just moody. He was mentally ill." She'd never spoken those words aloud before, although she'd thought them many times in the past.

She and Scott had certainly talked about Jim being unstable, depressed, but never had she said that he suffered from any real mental illness.

Gary frowned at her. "What do you mean, mentally ill?"

"Needless to say, I'm no psychiatrist, but I think he was bipolar . . . manic-depressive. I tried and tried to get him to go see somebody, but he refused. I think he was afraid that taking medication might interfere with his work."

"Jim was intense, but I never saw signs that he was crazy."

Vanessa sighed. "You and Scott got together with Jim one night a month to talk art and drink wine. On those nights he always managed to pull himself together. But I think if he hadn't jumped off that bridge, his work would have eventually destroyed him anyway."

"The rest of his family doing okay?"

For the next few minutes she caught him up on all the Abbott doings, telling him about the new store for Steve and Bethany, about Brian's rise in the graphic-art firm and that Garrett was still looking for Ms. Right.

"Now, there's a crazy man," Gary said with a grin. "I've never seen a guy more prone to failure than Garrett. He dates the wrong women, drinks like a fish and still depends on his mommy to wipe his butt."

Vanessa laughed, his description of poor Garrett dead-on. At thirty-seven years old Garrett was still a mama's boy. He lived at home and depended on Annette to wash his clothes and fix his meals.

The ring of the doorbell stymied any further conversation. Vanessa excused herself and hurried to the door. A wave of disquiet engulfed her as she opened the door to a man holding a bouquet of pink long-stem roses. "Vanessa Abbott?" he asked. She nodded and he held the roses toward her. "These are for you."

She didn't move to take them, but stared at them with apprehension. Another gift from her secret admirer? The deliveryman's smile fell and he shoved the roses closer, forcing her to take them from him.

Their sweet scent filled her nostrils as she took the vase, thanked the man, then returned to the kitchen, feeling as if she held a live snake in her hands.

"Wow, roses. You must be doing something right in your life," Gary said as she set the vase on the counter. "Who are they from?"

A clear plastic card holder stuck out of the lovely

blooms. It held a tiny white card. She plucked it out and opened it, relief flooding through her as she read what had been written.

I hate competition. Thanks for a terrific night.

It was signed *Christian*. Suddenly the roses that had filled her with such dread looked more beautiful, smelled even sweeter.

"They're from the man I went out with last night," she said to Gary. She tucked the card back in the envelope. She'd put it in her keepsake box.

"Must have been a good date."

She smiled and returned to the table. "It was. It was my first since Jim's death."

"So, you're moving on."

"Life goes on," she replied.

He smiled. "I'm glad. You deserve some happiness. And speaking of moving on, I'd better get upstairs and see what Johnny's working on. Then I've got to get out of here."

"You go on up. I'm going to clean up the lunch mess."

As Gary left the kitchen Vanessa leaned over the vase of flowers and breathed in the rose scent. She felt giddy, filled with a delicious sense of anticipation she wasn't sure she'd ever felt before.

She couldn't wait until Friday night, couldn't wait to be with him again, to see that wonderfully warm sexy smile of his, feel his strong arms around her.

"Hurry, Friday," she whispered to herself.

Chapter 12

"We got your name from the Wests," Regina Walters said to Vanessa as she ushered her into the huge two-story vacant house. "They were so pleased with how quickly you sold their place and spoke so highly of you."

The mini mansion was set up on bluffs, the back of the house overlooking a greenway complete with a large pond and a stand of trees that would be breathtaking in the spring.

Vanessa had gotten the call at the office from Regina first thing Monday morning and had agreed to meet the woman the next day.

"The house is lovely," Vanessa said. Regina's husband, Todd, had been transferred to St. Louis. They'd already moved everything there, leaving this place empty and them eager to get out from under the mortgage. "New carpeting?" she asked, noting the pristine condition of the beige rug.

"Installed a week ago. Everything is in good shape. The house is only five years old." She followed Vanessa into the large, airy kitchen. "All the appliances work fine and, as you can see, the wood floor is in excellent shape."

Vanessa nodded and moved to the glass doors that led out onto a massive deck. "May I?"

"Of course. You need to see the view."

Vanessa opened the doors and stepped out onto the deck. The cold wind whipped her hair around her face and she pulled her coat tighter around her as she took in the view.

"This was our favorite place to sit. On nice days we'd have coffee out here in the mornings and cook out in the evenings."

"It's beautiful," Vanessa said. "The pond doesn't look frozen."

"There must be some kind of a warm spring feeding it. It rarely completely freezes up. We have geese that hang around all winter."

The two women returned to the warmth of the kitchen. "It's perfect for someone who doesn't necessarily want to live in a neighborhood," Regina said. "Our nearest neighbor is down at the bottom of the bluff."

"Would you be willing to sign an exclusive with me for six weeks?"

Regina hesitated only a moment. "Certainly."

Vanessa placed her briefcase on the countertop and opened it. She withdrew a contract and handed it to Regina. "Take this with you and talk it over with your husband. If you agree, then just sign the contract and you can fax it to me at the office." She smiled. "I feel confident I'll be able to move this quickly. It's a lovely place to live."

Minutes later as Vanessa headed to the office, she

thought of the house she'd just left. It was a coup. She had several people pop into her mind who she knew might be interested in just such a place.

"You have some phone messages," Alicia said when Vanessa walked through the front door of the real estate office. Dark gray eye shadow hung on her eyelids, letting Vanessa know instantly that it was going to be one of those days.

"The Worths called and canceled your appointment for this afternoon. Mr. Worth has the flu. The Templetons want you to call them. Apparently they want to make an offer on the Sanders house. And Christian Connor has called twice. I didn't realize part of my job description was to take personal messages for you."

Vanessa hung her coat on the rack and tamped down her irritation. "You know Christian is a client. I'm working on finding him a place to live."

"You're working on something," Alicia replied thinly.

Vanessa walked past the woman and down the hallway that led to the break room. She'd return her phone calls from the phone in there; then she'd take off. She wasn't going to hang around and listen to Alicia's not-so-subtle digs and put up with her foul mood.

"Hey, girl, what's up?" Helen sat at the table in the break room, a cup of coffee in front of her and a McGriddle in her hand.

Vanessa rolled her eyes. "One of these days I'm going to tell Ms. Alicia to get bent." She sat in the chair next to Helen's and released a sigh of frustration.

"Your problem is you're too nice," Helen replied.

"I just don't understand why she has such a problem with me."

"It's nothing but sheer jealousy, honey." Helen took a sip of her coffee; then continued. "A streak of green jealousy and a mean spirit."

"Of all the people in the world, why would she be jealous of me? My husband committed suicide, I'm raising my son alone and I haven't exactly been living on easy street for the last couple of years."

"But you're bright and you're beautiful and everyone adores you. Hell, now that I think about it, I'm jealous of you." Helen cast her a joking grin.

Vanessa laughed, then sobered. "Sometimes I feel such hatred coming at me from her."

"Honey, don't give her too much power over you. She's a bitch and the best way to handle a bitch is to ignore her. However, if you ever get the balls to tell her off, just let me know when and where because I'd love to be a spectator."

"That's probably never going to happen. You know how much I hate drama," Vanessa replied.

"That's the understatement of the year," Helen said. "You'd walk barefoot on hot coals before having a confrontation with anyone."

Vanessa grinned. "I just came back here to return some phone calls; then I'm going to head out for the day. Oh, I think I bagged an exclusive this morning on that house that sits up on the bluffs off 169 Highway."

"The two-story with the greenway in the back? Now I know I'm jealous as hell of you," Helen said dryly.

"Eat your heart out," Vanessa said with a laugh. "I did a walk-through this morning and it's in move-in condition."

"You shouldn't have any problems selling it quickly."

"The sooner the better. I haven't made a sale this month and Johnny gave me his Santa list last night." She got up from the table, deciding to go back to her desk to make her calls. Alicia's foul mood wasn't going to force her away from her desk. "What's on your plate for today?"

"Nothing much. They're closing on the Smith house today and I'm thinking about taking the afternoon off to celebrate."

"Sounds like a plan to me," Vanessa replied. Then with a wave of her hand she left the room and returned to the main office area.

Alicia was on the phone, whispering frantically into the receiver, her pale complexion mottled with splotches of red. "Guy, I've got to go," she said when she saw Vanessa. She slammed down the receiver and stared at the computer screen in front of her.

Trouble in paradise, Vanessa thought as she sat at her desk. Over the last week Alicia had been talking about Guy, the new man in her life. But the past couple of days there had been a lot of whispered phone conversations between Alicia and Guy, most of them ending with Alicia slamming down the phone.

Not my problem, Vanessa told herself. She made her business-related calls first, then settled back in the chair and punched in Christian's cell phone number. Thankfully Alicia chose that moment to go into the break room.

Christian answered on the second ring, his deep voice filling her with that luscious surge of excitement that could very easily become addictive.

"The roses are beautiful," she said.

"More beautiful than the other guy sent you?"

She heard his smile in his voice. "I threw the other ones away."

"That's my girl," he replied. She liked the sound of those words. His girl. She hadn't realized until this moment how much she wanted to be his girl. "Are we still on for tomorrow?"

"I've got you in my official computer appointment book for ten o'clock," she replied. She squeezed the receiver closer to her ear, as if that might somehow get her closer to him. "I have a feeling you're going to be one of those difficult clients."

"Difficult? Me?"

"Oh, yes. I think you might be one of those that I have to take out again and again before we find the perfect home for you."

"Ah, I think you might be right. A man's got to do what a man's got to do to get a lunch date."

She laughed. "I also have a feeling you wouldn't have any problems getting lunch dates if you wanted. I know you're probably busy, so I won't keep you. I just wanted to return your call and thank you for the roses."

They said good-bye and hung up. For the next few minutes she worked on the computer, typing up a flyer that she would use if Regina and Todd Walters decided to give her the exclusive on their house.

When she was finished she got up and grabbed her coat. She needed to go by the Sanders place and give them the offer the Templetons had made. Hopefully the Sanders would accept and she could mark that off as a sale.

After that, she planned on doing a little Christmas shopping. Every day the news announcers were giving the shopping-day countdown until Christmas, and she didn't have just Johnny she wanted to buy for. There was Scott and Eric, her coworkers and all of Jim's family.

By the end of the day she was feeling quite pleased with herself. The Sanders had accepted the Templeton offer and she'd been able to put a SOLD sign in front of the house.

An afternoon at the nearest mall had yielded a perfect china teapot for Annette to add to her collection and a cashmere sweater for Scott, who had a fondness for all things cashmere.

She ordered pizza for dinner and afterward sat up in the studio and watched her son work on his painting. In the first year of their marriage Jim had often encouraged her to sit and watch him work. But after that year he became more and more unwelcoming when she'd come up. She'd finally quit trying to share his work.

"What do you think, Mom?" Johnny asked, and stepped back from the easel to allow her to see what he'd done.

Like his father, Johnny understood angles and how to distort them just enough to be fascinating. Although Vanessa knew little about art, she knew enough to be awed by her son's seemingly natural talent.

"It's great, Johnny."

He grinned at her, a touch of red paint dancing on his cheek with the gesture. "You'd tell me that even if it was awful."

She returned his grin. "You're probably right, but you know you're good. You don't need me to tell you that."

"Do you think Dad would have thought I was good?"

"Your father would have thought you were amazing," she replied.

He nodded as if satisfied by her answer, then turned around to face his easel once again. "Scott says Dad was the most talented artist he's ever known in his life."

"Your dad was talented," Vanessa agreed.

Johnny dabbed a bit of paint on his canvas, and then turned to face her once again. "Sometimes I worry that I'll forget him." He frowned thoughtfully. "Sometimes at night I try to remember how he looked and I can't."

"You know that framed photo of your dad I have in my nightstand? Would you like that to keep next to your bed?" Vanessa asked.

"Okay, that would be good." He turned back to his picture.

It was just after eight when she insisted he stop working for the night and go get his bath.

She went back downstairs and fixed herself a cup of tea. As she sat at the kitchen table and stared at the darkness outside her window she remembered her conversation with Christian about the loneliest time of the day.

She'd told him that it was just after dinner, but she'd been wrong. It was in the hours after Johnny had gone to bed and before she turned in. Even when Jim had been alive they had been lonely hours.

Stirring sugar into her tea, she forced her thoughts away from her dead husband. It was funny, but that part of her life seemed like the distant past of a character in a book she'd read, a book with a tragic ending that she had no desire to read again.

She was ready for a happy ending. She reached out and touched one of the velvety blooms of the pink roses.

There was no way to know if Christian would be a part of a happy ending or not, but this time she wouldn't settle for less than what she deserved.

The phone rang as she was rinsing her teacup. She placed the cup in the dishwasher; then she brought the phone to her ear. "Hello?"

No answer, but she could hear the sound of breathing. Deep. Low. Steady.

"Hello?" she repeated. Her gaze shot in the direction of the window, through which the darkness was profound. "Is anyone there?" she asked impatiently.

The line filled with the sound of rushing water. She frowned, wondering what on earth was going on. Was this some sort of childish prank? She could remember junior high school slumber parties when they'd make prank phone calls just to break the monotony of a Friday night.

"I'm hanging up now," she said.

"No," a soft deep voice replied. "Help me," he whispered. Then the line filled with a gurgling sound, as if he were underwater, as if he were drowning.

Christian finished writing out the checks he intended to give his crew as Christmas bonuses and locked them up in the small safe inside the work trailer.

He twirled the combination lock to secure it, then checked his watch. Almost ten. It had been a hell of a day, one filled with irritating problems that had kept him jumping and putting out fires.

At least he had his time with Vanessa to look forward to tomorrow. He returned to the desk and sat, his head filled with thoughts of her.

He'd known he had a fierce physical attraction to her, but he hadn't expected to like her as much as he did. Her sense of humor jibed with his and although there was a vulnerability about her, there were times when her eyes shone with an inner strength he admired.

Christian had enjoyed a number of romantic relationships in his past but had never had the desire to get married . . . until lately. In the last six months the loneliness of his youth had returned with a vengeance.

His initial worry that Vanessa was part of the upper crust and involved in the art world had been laid to rest. Oh, sure, she had artist friends and her son was pursuing his talent, but there was nothing about her that made him think she was anything like what he'd left behind in Denver.

He cleared off his desk, then stood and stretched with arms overhead. Time to head home. He should have been home hours ago, but had stayed on the site to finish up some paperwork.

Exhaustion weighed heavily on his shoulders as he turned off the lights and stepped out into the darkness of the night. He left the trailer unlocked for Casey McNabb, the private security guard who worked nights keeping the site protected from vandals and thieves.

As he walked toward his car in the distance, he pulled his keys from his pocket, his thoughts once again filled with Vanessa.

He'd told her the truth when he'd said that she made him feel like a teenager again. When he was with her he felt as if all things were possible, was filled with a strange nervous excitement he'd never felt before.

"Hey!"

Christian had just reached the side of his car when the voice rang out. He started to turn to seek the source when something struck him on the side of his head.

The pain exploded, shooting stars across his vision as his knees buckled. He tried to grab hold of something, anything, to keep him upright, but there was nothing. As he slid to the ground the darkness of the night crawled into his head.

Chapter 13

As Vanessa drove to work the next morning she found herself checking her rearview mirror again and again, nervous tension coiled in her stomach like something bad she'd eaten.

She tightened her fingers on the steering wheel and told herself it was silly to let a phone call so unsettle her. Her knuckles turned white as she gripped the wheel and thought of the call.

At midnight she'd been so creeped out she'd thought about calling the police. But what could she tell them? That somebody had called from an anonymous number and had gurgled into the phone? They'd tell her to chill out and get her number changed.

Had it been merely a coincidence that her husband had drowned two years ago and some silly teenagers had chosen her number at random to make that call to? Or had it been something more evil?

She reached out and turned the fan to blow higher, needing the warmth of the heater to take away the chill that had possessed her body since the phone call the night before.

By the time she reached the office, she'd managed to turn her thoughts to the day ahead. She'd see Christian today. Somehow she had a sense that just being in his strong presence would make her feel better.

In any case, a phone call, no matter how disturbing, didn't have the capacity to harm her physically. From now on, she'd check caller ID before she answered and if it showed an anonymous caller, she'd let the machine pick up.

She flew from the car to the office, trying to outrun the icy wind that blew from the north. The forecast was for cold, but still no snow, thank goodness. Nobody wanted to house shop in the snow.

"Whew, it's freezing out there today," she exclaimed as she stepped through the door.

"It's only supposed to get worse. I heard the weatherman say this morning that by next week we'll be in single digits," Alicia said with a friendly smile.

The woman was positively schizophrenic, Vanessa thought as she shrugged out of her coat and hung it up. Yesterday Alicia had shot poison darts out of her eyes every time she'd looked at Vanessa and today she smiled as if they were very best friends.

"Johnny has a school skating party next week at Englewood Park. At least I don't have to worry about the ice on the lake not being thick enough."

"I heard a report this morning that said all the area lakes are safe for skating." Alicia got up from her desk. "I'm going back to get a cup of coffee. Want me to bring you one?"

"That would be nice, thanks." Vanessa watched the slender blonde disappear down the hallway and wondered how long Alicia's good humor would last. It could be minutes, hours or, if she were lucky, a couple of days.

A few moments later Alicia returned, carrying two foam cups of coffee. "One spoon of sugar, right?"

"That's right. Thank you." Vanessa took the coffee from her and sipped the hot brew, enjoying the warmth going down her throat and into her stomach, where a cold knot still remained.

Alicia returned to her desk and looked at Vanessa expectantly. "So, how was your night?" she asked. "Did you do anything special?" She sipped her coffee and eyed Vanessa over the rim of the cup.

"No, nothing, just the usual quiet Tuesday night," Vanessa replied. It was rare that Alicia asked her about how she'd spent an evening. "What about you?"

As Alicia went into a monologue about her wonderful evening spent with Guy, Vanessa's thoughts went to dark places. Was it possible that Alicia and Guy had made that phone call the night before?

She knew the woman didn't like her and yesterday she had been in major-bitch form. Certainly Alicia knew how Jim had died, would have known how such a call might upset her.

If Alicia had done it, it was a wicked, awful thing to do. But Vanessa knew there was no sense in confronting her. If Alicia was responsible for it, she certainly wouldn't admit to it. Vanessa knew that Alicia could lie without batting an eye. She'd seen her do it a dozen times before.

The ring of the phone interrupted Alicia as Buzz walked through the door with Craig Meloni, another of the agents. Vanessa greeted them as Alicia hung up the phone and looked at her. "That was a Mrs. Walters. She said to give you the message that the fax is on its way."

"Terrific," Vanessa said.

"What fax?" Buzz asked, propping a hip on the desktop.

Vanessa told them about landing an exclusive on the Walters home. "And I have several potential buyers in mind, so it should be a quick turnaround."

"Lucky you," Craig said glumly. "Lately it seems like I couldn't sell a furnace in Alaska."

Buzz clapped him on the back. "Winter is always slow, but if interest rates stay down, I'm betting that we're all going to have a great spring."

Vanessa looked out the window, where the stiff wind whipped the hanging Christmas decorations on the nearby streetlamps. She wrapped her arms around her shoulders, a new chill working up her spine. "Spring can't get here too quickly for me."

The phone rang again and Buzz and Craig headed back to the break room. "Vanessa, it's for you. Line one."

Vanessa picked up the phone receiver on her desk. "Hello, this is Vanessa Abbott."

"Mrs. Abbott, my name is Jason Weir. I work for Mr. Connor, and he wanted me to call you to tell you he won't be able to make his appointment with you this morning."

Dismay filtered through her, followed by concern. Why wouldn't Christian be making the call himself? "I'm sorry to hear that," she replied, then, unable to help herself, added, "I hope everything is all right."

There was a long pause, then a deep sigh. "He didn't want me to say anything, but maybe you should know that he was attacked last night on one of the job sites."

"Attacked? Is he okay?" Tears blurred her vision as her heart seemed to skip a beat.

"He's fine," he said hurriedly. "Thank God he has a hard head, but the doctor insisted he stay in the hospital overnight."

Hospital? How seriously had he been hurt? What on earth had happened? "What hospital is he in?"

"St. Luke's North. He probably won't be released until sometime late this afternoon."

"Thank you so much for calling." She'd already grabbed her purse and keys as she hung up the phone.

"Everything all right?" Alicia asked curiously.

"Fine. I'll check in later this afternoon." She wasn't going to share any more personal information with Alicia. Besides, she didn't want to take the time to explain. All she could think about was getting to St. Luke's North and seeing for herself that Christian was okay.

Attacked. He'd been attacked; that's what Jason had said. What did that mean? Who would have done such a thing? If the doctor had insisted he spend the night in the hospital, then it had to have been serious.

The hospital was only a fifteen-minute drive from the office and it was only as she was parking that she wondered if perhaps she wasn't overstepping the lines of propriety. After all, she and Christian had only had one official date and a couple of lunches, yet she was rushing to be at his side like a lovesick teenager.

No, she was rushing to be at his side because she cared, she told herself. And there was nothing wrong with that. By the time she found a parking space, she felt the rightness of being here shining in her heart.

An inquiry at the front desk let her know that Christian

was in room 323. She stopped in the gift shop and bought a helium-filled balloon that read GET WELL, then took the elevator to the third floor.

As she walked the quiet corridor toward his room, she prayed that Jason Weir wasn't the king of understatement and that Christian really was all right.

Although his door was open, she knocked, relieved when she heard his voice say "Come in."

His room was in semidarkness, the blinds pulled shut against the morning sun and only a soft light above the bed illuminating the room. But even the faint lighting couldn't diminish the brightness of his smile as he saw her.

"Ah, I see my foreman doesn't listen to a word I say. I told him not to tell you what had happened."

"Thank goodness he didn't listen to you," she replied, relief flooding through at the sight of him. Although he wore a blue-flowered hospital gown, he looked gorgeous, with no sign of whatever injury had landed him here. She pulled up a chair to the side of his bed.

He smiled and gestured to the balloon in her hand. "Nobody has ever bought me a balloon before."

She would think about that sad fact later. "What happened, Christian? Jason told me you were attacked?"

He touched a button and the head of his bed rose. "I worked late last night at one of the job sites. It was around ten when I decided to call it a night. I had just reached my car when somebody whacked me over the head from behind." She gasped. "Unfortunately I fell to the ground unconscious and didn't find out until later what happened after that."

"And what did?" She leaned forward, fighting the impulse to take his hand in hers and hold it close to her heart. Now that she was closer to him she could see the fatigue that darkened his eyes, the evidence of stress in the lines across his forehead.

"Apparently my security guard saw a man behind me, saw him swing something at my head. He yelled and the man ran off. Casey, my security guy, called 911 and got me loaded into an ambulance and brought here."

"Did he catch the person who did this? Did he recognize the man?"

"When Casey yelled at him the creep ran. He got away and all Casey could tell the police was that it was definitely a man. I'm thinking maybe it was the kid I fired last week."

Her heart pounded as she realized how easily this could have turned into a real tragedy. If the security guard hadn't been there, hadn't seen what happened . . .

"Don't look so scared," Christian said with a soft smile. "I'm fine. The only reason I'm in here is because I live alone and they wanted to check me throughout the night for a concussion. Fortunately I'm as hardheaded as everyone tells me I am."

"You could have been killed," she said, her raspy voice reflecting her emotions as she thought of what might have happened.

"I'll tell you what's killing me, the fact that I'm missing a lunch with you."

She couldn't stand it any longer; she had to touch him, needed to feel the reassuring warmth of his skin. She reached out for his hand and gripped it tightly. "Are the police looking for this man you fired?"

"An officer showed up first thing this morning and I gave him all the information, his name and his address."

He squeezed her hand. "Really, I'm fine and the police will take care of it from here. Now, let's talk about something else. How are things with you?"

She dismissed the very idea of telling him about the creepy phone call the night before. He had enough on his mind at the moment and didn't need to hear about her personal dramas. "Everything is fine with me. I did a little Christmas shopping yesterday. The mall was so pretty with all the decorations." She released his hand and sat back in her chair.

"Did you sit on Santa's lap?"

She grinned. "I wanted to, but there were so many three- and four-year-olds standing in line, I decided to talk to Santa another day."

"I'll dress up like Santa and you can sit on my lap." His eyes gleamed with wicked intent.

"Big promises from a man in a hospital bed wearing a flowered gown." She sobered. "Seriously, what are your plans for Christmas? Are you flying home?"

"No. My parents have a trip planned, so there's no point in me going to Denver." The lines across his forehead seemed to deepen.

"Why don't you plan on having dinner with us the night before Christmas?"

"I wouldn't want to intrude on any family traditions," he replied.

"You wouldn't be. Johnny and I usually spend some time Christmas Day at Jim's parents' house, but Christmas Eve we just have a quiet night at home. You're welcome to come."

"Thanks. That would be nice."

She frowned. "Maybe we should cancel our plans

for Friday night. You may not feel like doing much of anything."

"I'll be fine." His gray eyes held her gaze. "While I've been laying here in this bed the only thing I've been thinking of is that in two more days I get to spend time with you."

"Are you sure you're going to be up for it?"

"Absolutely. In fact I've already got our gourmet microwave meal planned."

A small burst of laughter escaped her once again. "Gourmet microwave meal seems kind of like an oxymoron. I'll tell you what, I'll bring dessert. What's your favorite kind of cake or pie?"

"Black Forest cake, but you don't have to do that," he protested.

"You're right. I don't have to, but I want to," she replied.

A knock on the door halted any further conversation as a police officer walked in. "Mr. Connor, I'm sorry to disturb you, but I have a couple more questions for you."

Vanessa stood. "I'll go so you can talk to the officer." She leaned down and brushed her lips against his cheek, where pale whiskers had appeared at some point over his long night.

It was only after she'd left the room that she marveled at how right it had felt to give him a kiss. Somehow, someway, in a very short span of time Christian Connor had forged a path into her heart.

Telling herself that it was important to go slow was one thing; trying to slow down a relationship that was building fast and furious was something else.

How could a man get to be thirty-five years old and

never have received a balloon? What about when he'd been young? On his birthdays? Special days? She suspected his relationship with his parents wasn't a good one and wondered why.

The wind still howled as she left the hospital, shooting icy air over every inch of exposed bare skin. She pulled her coat more tightly around her as she ran to where her car was parked. She fumbled with her keys, her fingers already numb from the cold.

She finally got the door unlocked and slid behind the wheel. Starting the engine, she prayed it wouldn't take long to warm up. As she sat there waiting for the car to heat up, the crazy, creepy feeling of somebody watching her raised the hairs on the nape of her neck.

She gazed around the parking lot. People were coming and going from cars, but nobody she knew, nobody who paid her any attention.

Still the creepy feeling remained as she pulled out of the hospital parking lot. She told herself it was just a residual effect of all that had happened in the past twenty-four hours. The horrid phone call. Christian's attack. They all played in her head to create a disturbing edge of apprehension.

"That's what it is," she said aloud, as if the sound of her firm voice could convince her.

But it didn't.

The fucker had gotten lucky. Christian Connor should be dead, painted red. But the security guard had interrupted and the bastard had lived.

The killer pulled out of the hospital parking lot ten

minutes after *she* had left, his heart burning with the need for revenge.

He hadn't been surprised when she'd shown up here. She'd come running to her lover's side as if riding on angel wings. But she was no angel. She was the devil in disguise. She was a fucking bitch who deserved pustules of disease to infect her body. She was a fucking whore who deserved to be alone and terrified before she met her untimely end.

He pulled over to the side of the street, suddenly overwhelmed with emotion that swelled in his chest and choked in the back of his throat.

His heart pounded with such a vengeance he wondered if he was having a heart attack. He'd almost gotten caught. That security guard had nearly caught up with him.

It had been easy to find Christian Connor. There were several job sites in the area that had trailers announcing them the property of Connor Construction.

He hadn't planned on attacking him last night. He'd just been watching him, learning his habits, but the opportunity had presented itself and his blood had burned hot with need.

"Fuck," he screamed, and pounded his fist on the steering wheel. He'd wanted him dead. He'd wanted her weeping. He wanted her to suffer like he had suffered the last two years.

As he thought of the aching loneliness he'd felt for the past two years, as he thought of all the dreams that had been shattered, all the hope that had been lost, deep wrenching sobs built up inside him.

He fought against the wild, clawing anguish that was

never far from the surface. Then he simply gave in to it, allowing the deep sobs to explode. He crashed his head down to the steering wheel as tears blinded him and the pressure in his chest increased.

He didn't know how long he wept, but just as quickly as the tears had come, they were gone and he was laughing . . . laughing with a wildness that was freeing.

He'd gotten a taste of revenge now and it tasted as sweet as anything he'd ever eaten, excited him as much as sex. The mental list he had in his head of the people who had been the destroyers was now two shorter than it had been.

Andre was gone. Matt was dead. But there were still so many who had to pay; there was so much to do to exact revenge. And he couldn't wait.

Raising his head, he stared out the window and thought of her. Vanessa. A quick death was far too good. He had an exquisite form of torture for her in store.

A new burst of laughter escaped him as he thought of the phone call he'd made the night before. Although she hadn't said a word, he'd felt her fear radiating across the line just before she slammed the phone down.

Her fear made him hard. Her death would be his ultimate release.

Chapter 14

On Friday night Vanessa drove to Christian's apartment complex with the scent of the freshly baked Black Forest cake filling the car. When Johnny had gotten home from school she'd taken him to Annette and Dan's, then returned home to bake the cake.

When the cake had finished baking she'd taken a long, leisurely bath, relaxing muscles that had kinked with tension throughout the week.

For the past two days there had been no more disturbing phone calls, and other than the frigid weather, life had been good. Christian had gotten out of the hospital Wednesday afternoon and had called to tell her he was fine. Johnny had finished his painting and Scott had taken it that morning to turn in to the contest committee.

And within minutes she'd be sharing dinner with Christian at his apartment. The tension that clutched her stomach now felt good; it was the nervous expectation of being with him, the anticipation of what might happen. This would be the first time the two of them would be truly alone.

The Sunset Hills apartment complex was a twenty-minute drive from her house. She'd heard that the apartments were upscale and lovely.

She pulled into a parking space in front of his unit, a new wave of nervous anticipation fluttering in the pit of her stomach. She checked her reflection in the rearview mirror, making sure her lipstick was still intact; then she grabbed the cake from the passenger seat and got out of the car.

The frigid wind danced up the hem of her dress, chilling her legs and blowing her hair. By the time she reached Christian's front door her fingers and cheeks burned from the cold.

He answered her knock almost immediately, his smile heating her as he pulled her into the warmth of the apartment. "Here, let me." He took the cake keeper from her. "Come on in, I'll just take this to the kitchen."

She stepped from the entryway into the large living room. A bank of windows covered one wall; another held a fireplace that snapped and sparked with flames. She took off her coat and placed it on the back of an overstuffed, masculine-looking black and gray sofa. Then she went to stand in front of the fireplace to take the last of her chill away.

As she held out her hands to the fire she looked around the room. The color scheme was black and various shades of gray. The coffee and end tables were black wood, all oversized and bold. A flat-screen television was set in an entertainment center, along with what looked like a state-of-the-art stereo and several books on motorcycles and architecture.

"Something smells wonderful," she said as Christian

came back into the living room. "Much better than anything I've ever microwaved," she teased.

"I could lie and tell you I've been slaving over a hot
oven all day, but the truth is, Crystal's Catering Service is
the reason for the savory scents." His gaze swept the
length of her. "You look gorgeous."

"Thanks." She smoothed her hand down the skirt of
the cranberry-colored dress. "And you look quite handsome." He wore a pair of navy dress slacks and a navy
sweater that clung to the width of his shoulders and
hugged his slim waist.

"Now that we have the mutual compliments out of the
way, why don't you come into the kitchen with me so I
can finish up?"

The kitchen was stunning, with black granite counter-
tops and appliances. The table in the eating alcove was
set with black plates and napkins and a beautiful bouquet
of red chrysanthemums.

He gestured her to a barstool in front of the island. "I
just need to do some finishing touches." He went to the
refrigerator and pulled out a bottle of wine. "How about
a glass to start the evening?"

She set her purse on the island, then scooted onto the
stool. "No, thanks. But I would take a soda if you have
one."

"No problem." He pulled out a can of Coke and poured
it in a glass of ice for her. He poured himself a glass of
the wine and joined her at the island.

"You don't drink?" he asked.

"No, I don't." Tell him, a little voice whispered in her
head. If you intend to have any kind of relationship with

him, then he has a right to know about your faults as well as your strengths.

She took a sip of the Coke, her throat suddenly dry. Then she opened her purse and withdrew a folded piece of paper. She clutched it in her hand as she looked at Christian.

"I thought I was handling things okay immediately after Jim's death. I started with one drink a night. A gin and tonic just to take the edge off, just to relax me a little."

She took another drink of her soda, surprised to discover how difficult it was to talk about the darkest moments of her life. "Anyway, it wasn't long before one drink became two, then two drinks became three." She broke eye contact with him and instead stared into her glass. "Then I was skipping the tonic and drinking straight gin. I was still getting Johnny off to school in the mornings and going to the real estate classes, but once I was home, the bottle was my very best friend."

She looked at him once again. His handsome features showed neither support nor condemnation. "One early Saturday morning I woke up on the sofa, a bottle of gin cuddled to my chest. Johnny was up, and watching cartoons on the television. When he saw I was awake he couldn't wait to show me what he'd drawn." Her fingers trembled as she carefully unfolded the sheet of paper and handed it to Christian.

She didn't need to look at it to refresh her memory of what Johnny had drawn. The image was etched into her heart, into her very soul. Her son had drawn what he had seen: his mother passed out on the sofa, a bottle in her arms. Her hair was disheveled, her mouth agape. It was the picture of a drunk.

"Do you like it, Mommy?" Johnny had asked eagerly.

She'd hated it. She'd wanted to rip it into a million pieces as if that would destroy what she had become. But she hadn't done that. She'd kept it to remind herself of just how far she'd fallen.

Christian looked at the picture, refolded it and held it out to her. His eyes were soft with understanding as he gazed at her, but he didn't say a word, allowing her to tell the story in her own time, in her own way.

"That was the day—no . . . that was the moment I stopped drinking," she continued. "I've never even had a faint desire to drink again."

She stared at him, afraid that she'd blown it, that the character flaw that had allowed her to fall into the bottom of a bottle might be too big for him to handle.

"I was fifteen when I went through a period of drinking booze and smoking pot and I didn't have a good reason for my actions other than youth and stupidity." He reached out and covered her cold hand with his warm one. "What that tells me about you, Vanessa, is that you're human and you went through a bad time and were strong enough to pull yourself out of it."

Sweet relief rushed through her at his words. "It's not a big deal in my life. I just choose not to drink at all. I don't even like the taste of alcohol."

He removed his hand from hers. "Does it bother you when somebody else drinks?"

"Not at all." She frowned thoughtfully, wanting to make things as clear as possible. "It wasn't the alcohol that was the problem. If I'd had pills to take, I would have done that instead of drink. The problem was that I had taken a leave of absence from life. I just wanted to escape." She smiled. "Now, enough about me. Tell me about your youthful fall into debauchery."

He laughed. "When I was fifteen I went through a three-month period of doing everything I shouldn't do." His smile faded and his eyes took on the cast of distant memories. "I think I was trying to get a reaction from my parents. I'd tried doing everything right to get their attention and that hadn't worked, so I decided to do things wrong."

"Did it work?"

"No, the only person who noticed was the family cook, who threatened to make liver and onions every night until I straightened up."

"That's enough to make any self-respecting teenager shiver in his shoes," she replied.

"It worked on me." He stood and went to the refrigerator. "And now it's time for me to get this meal on the table."

She wanted to ask him about his parents, but it was obvious he'd halted any conversation where they might be the topic. She watched as he pulled out a bowl of salad and set it on the table.

"Crystal herself assured me that this was a foolproof meal. All I had to do was keep things warm before serving." He grabbed a couple of hot pads, removed a foil-covered baking dish from the oven and placed it on the table.

"If you hadn't told me it had been catered, I would have thought you'd spent the entire afternoon cooking," she said.

"I spent the afternoon chatting with the police and arguing with an electrician." He gestured toward the table.

She carried her soda to the table and sat. "Have they caught the man who attacked you?"

He shook his head and pulled off the foil from the baking dish, exposing chicken breasts and wild rice. "He had an alibi for that night. He was in a bar with dozens of witnesses." He joined her at the table. "I'm relieved that it wasn't Ted, but I don't have a clue who else might have wanted to hit me over the head."

"You're feeling okay now?"

He grinned, that wonderfully wicked light shining from his eyes. "At the moment I'm feeling fantastic. I have a beautiful woman seated across from me, a delicious-smelling meal before me and plans for seduction in my near future."

Her heart thumped and banged with a rhythm of anticipation. "Let me know when you get to the seduction part so I'll be prepared."

"If I have to tell you, then I'm not doing it properly," he replied.

"You'd better feed me now. I have a feeling I'm going to need my strength."

He laughed and served her from the baking dish. As they ate they talked about the events of the last week. He told her that he'd been hired to build another strip mall south of town and about his plans in the future to build and own his own shopping mall. She told him about signing an exclusive on the Walters property.

"Is it something I'd be interested in?" he asked.

"Maybe. It's a gorgeous two-story in pristine condition. The back deck overlooks a greenway with a small lake and woods."

"Sounds nice."

"It is and it's in your price range." She gave him a teasing smile. "But I'm definitely beginning to think of you as one of those looky-dos." She sobered and glanced around. "Although this place is so nice I can't imagine why you'd want to leave here."

"It is nice," he agreed. "And I've been relatively happy here. But aside from the fact that a house would be a good investment, I'm ready to put down real roots. I'm ready to have a lawn to mow and to plant flowers. I'm ready for all the joys and the headaches of owning a home."

The rest of the meal passed pleasantly. The chicken was wonderful, juicy and seasoned just right with savory herbs. The rice was cooked to perfection and the salad was an interesting blend of vegetables and fruit with crunchy almonds and a dressing that was sweet and tangy. Dessert was the cake she'd brought, along with a cup of coffee.

The conversation was light and effortless, yet there was a simmering tension between them that was invigorating. After they'd eaten she helped with the cleanup; then they moved into the living room. She sat on the sofa while he added another log to the fire.

"I love a real fire," she said when he joined her on the sofa. "When we were renovating the house Jim wanted to turn our fireplace into a gas one, but I put my foot down."

"It's a mess, but there's nothing that can compete with the scent and beauty of a real fire," he agreed. "You want some music on? I can turn on the stereo."

"That would be nice." Her heart had begun the beat of excitement. Dinner was finished; the lighting in the living room was dim. The stage was being set for seduction and she was ready for it, for him.

He turned on the stereo and soft instrumental music began to play. When he rejoined her on the sofa he sat closer than he had before, close enough that she could smell the enticing scent of him, feel the heat from his body.

"I feel a seduction coming on," she said.

"Am I that obvious?" He pretended to yawn and stretched his arms overhead. Then he plunked one arm around her shoulder. "That was my smooth move when I was in high school."

She giggled. "That was totally lame."

His eyes gleamed hot like molten lead as he gazed at her. "Yeah, but it accomplished what I wanted. I have my arm around you." He raised his other hand and coiled it into her hair. "I've been wanting to touch your hair all evening. Almost as much as I've wanted to kiss you."

"And what has stopped you?" She didn't think it possible for her heart to beat any faster and yet when he leaned closer it did.

"You scare the hell out of me," he said, his mouth mere inches from hers. "I can't remember wanting a woman as much as I want you."

She opened her mouth to speak, although she had no idea what she intended to say. In any case it didn't matter, for his mouth covered hers, making speech impossible.

The kiss seduced with tenderness as his lips nibbled softly and his hand moved from her hair to caress the curve of her jaw, the hollow of her throat.

The kiss was all too brief. Then he pulled her into the crook of his arm and leaned back, seemingly content for the moment to just sit and listen to the music and hold her.

All the tension of the past week melted away as she

settled against him, her head on his muscled chest and the steady rhythm of his heartbeat against her ear. "This is nice," she said.

"One of the things I like about you is that you seem to appreciate quiet moments. You aren't one of those people who feel the need to fill every silence."

"I'm comfortable with silence. There's been a lot of it in my life in the past couple of years."

His arm tightened around her. "I'm sorry for what you went through, but I'm not sorry for whatever fates blew you into my life."

She was afraid to hope that happiness might be as close as this man. She'd been fooled by fate before. Surely there had been enough heartache in her life. Surely it was time that she finally get a chance at joy.

"Tell me about your parents," she said. She felt his muscles tense and she raised her head to look at him. "I've told you so much about my grandpa John. Tell me about the people who raised you."

He sighed and she sat up, sensing that the topic wasn't a pleasant one. But she wanted all the pieces of him. If she intended to allow herself to be vulnerable with him, to continue a relationship with him, she needed to know where he came from and what ghosts might haunt him.

"There are some people who just aren't cut out to be parents. My parents are two of those people. My father is a concert pianist and composer and my mother is besotted with his brilliance and importance. They weren't abusive or anything like that. They were just absent, absorbed with their own lives."

"That's so sad." She reached out and placed a hand on his jaw. His muscles were still tight beneath the skin, but as she touched him she felt them slowly relax and he smiled.

"I made peace with it a long time ago. They aren't bad people. They just weren't capable of giving a child what was needed."

"Now that you're an adult, do you have a relationship with them?" she asked.

She dropped her hand from his face and he pulled her back into his arms. She once again placed her head on his chest as his hand caressed her hair.

"I call them once a week and talk to my mother, who tells me all the wonderful places they've been and are going. She extols my father's talent and talks about the expensive restaurants where they've eaten, the fancy hotels where they've stayed. The conversations are pleasant and superficial and that's as good as it will ever be."

Sorrow swept through her and she burrowed her head into his sweater, loving the scent of detergent and fabric softener and his brand of cologne. "Death robbed me of the chance to have an adult relationship with my parents. I just think it's tragic that your parents are alive but apparently don't want a close relationship with you."

"It is what it is. I think not having that core family unit has made me appreciate other relationships in my life. Like my friends. Like you."

Her heart swelled as he placed a finger under her chin and raised her face. This time the kiss he gave her didn't seduce with tenderness but rather with bold, hot hunger.

She responded with all the desire that had built up inside her for so long. She opened her mouth, allowing his tongue to touch first the edge of her lip, then slide inside her mouth to battle with hers.

Someplace in the back of her mind she knew a decision was going to have to be made, the decision to sleep with him or not. She didn't know what he expected of her, if he expected anything. But she knew she wanted him.

And she tasted his desire for her in his kiss, felt it in the way his hands stroked up her back. She heard his want for her in the slight groan he released as he deepened the kiss.

It didn't seem to matter that she hadn't known him for very long. There was a part of her that felt as if she'd known him forever, as if she'd been waiting for him for a very long time.

This time when he broke the kiss his eyes smoked with desire. "I don't want to push you, Vanessa. I don't want you to do anything that you don't want to do, but I've got to tell you, if we aren't going to take this further, we should probably stop kissing."

He held her gaze with an intensity that seemed to pierce through her. She knew instinctively that if she told him they weren't going any further, he would be all right with it. But would she? A shimmering need flooded through her, the need to be held in his arms, to feel the warmth of his naked flesh against her.

She licked her lips as a new wave of heat cascaded through her. She felt as if her decision had been made that first night that Andre had introduced Christian to her. That night butterflies had fluttered in her stomach and she'd felt electrified by his presence.

"I think we should keep kissing," she said. She knew in speaking that the decision had been made. His eyes flared and he stood, his body taut with a wild energy. He held out a hand and as she took it he pulled her up from the sofa.

Neither of them spoke a word as he led her down a hallway and into the master bedroom. Big bold furniture dominated the room, the focal point the king-sized bed covered in a blue and gold spread.

A hint of apprehension fluttered inside her as she stared at the bed. "Would you excuse me for a minute?" She gestured toward the door to the master bath. "I'll be right back." Escaping into the bathroom, she fought against the burst of nerves that had her feeling half-sick.

She closed the door and stared at her reflection in the mirror over the sink. Her cheeks were unusually pink, her lips slightly swollen by his kisses. Her eyes were a deeper blue than usual, filled with the emotions that swirled inside her.

Jim had been her one and only lover and he'd never seemed much interested in sex, which had on many nights left her questioning her own desirability.

Was she a good lover? She didn't know, but she wanted to be for Christian. She wanted to be everything he wanted, everything he needed.

She turned on the water in the sink and sluiced cool water over her fevered cheeks, telling herself there was nothing to be nervous about. Christian would take the lead and all she had to do was trust him and follow. And she did trust him. As quickly as her anxiety had possessed her, it left.

Coming out of the bathroom, she saw him standing in the exact spot where he'd been when she'd left. "Vanessa, we don't have to do anything," he said, as if he sensed what emotions had driven her into the privacy of the bathroom. "I'll wait for you to be sure. I'll wait however long it takes."

If she'd felt any lingering fear, his words dispelled it. She walked over to him and looped her arms around his neck. "I'm sure."

Whatever control he'd been hanging on to seemed to snap at her words. He lowered his head and took her mouth with his in a fierce kiss that left no energy for doubts. His tongue battled with hers and he pulled her intimately against him, close enough that she could feel his arousal.

His hands caressed her back, sliding over the silky material of her dress and warming her skin beneath. The kiss fired heat through her and stoked a hunger she couldn't ever remember possessing.

The memory of aching lonely nights faded away as she melted against his hard chest. This was where she wanted to be at this moment, in his arms. It didn't matter what tomorrow brought. She intended to savor the night.

His mouth left hers and trailed kisses down the length of her neck, finding the area just below her ear that moved shivers of pleasure through her. Leaning her head back, she gave him access to the hollow of her throat.

She gasped as his hands moved down to cup her buttocks and he pulled her more intimately against him. Sharp sensations spun through her at the sensual contact.

"Vanessa," he whispered against her throat, his breath renewing her shiver of pleasure. "God, I want you."

She closed her eyes, savoring the sound of those words, the husky tone of his voice. When she opened her eyes again she looked up at him. "I want you, too."

His gaze held hers intently as his fingers moved to

the top of her dress zipper. The zipper hissed as he pulled it down, the cool air chilling her back as bare skin was exposed.

With the dress unzipped, he stepped away from her. He walked over to the side of the bed and pulled the spread down, revealing pale blue sheets. He then went to the light switch on the wall and flipped it off, leaving the room illuminated by only the moonlight that cascaded through the bank of windows and the faint glow of light spilling from the bathroom door.

When he looked at her again she slid her dress from her shoulders and let it fall to the floor. Rather than feel exposed beneath his hungry gaze, she felt warmed and aroused.

He unbuttoned his shirt and took it off, the sight of his muscular chest making her weak in the knees. As his fingers went to the fastening of his slacks she took off her panty hose and slid beneath the sheets.

The bed smelled of him, a scent of clean male and cologne, and the depth of her desire for him overwhelmed her. He stepped out of his slacks, his legs long and lean and the white briefs almost obscene as they pulled taut across his obvious hardness.

He joined her beneath the sheets and immediately pulled her into his arms as their mouths met in mutual need. His palms were hot as they moved down her back, flirting first with the hooks on her bra, then moving down to rub across the waistband of her panties.

Each teasing caress was an exquisite form of torment that soon had her gasping. He pulled his mouth from hers and swept his lips down her neck to the very edge of her bra. "I knew your skin would be soft, but touching you makes me wild," he murmured against her.

She raked her hands down the width of his back, the play of his taut muscles only increasing her need. She nearly wept when he unfastened her bra, took if off and captured her full breasts in his hands.

His thumbs grazed the hard tips and she moaned his name, her hands clutching the back of his head, fingers twined in his thick hair.

As his mouth took possession of one of her breasts, her hands moved to his shoulders, where she gripped tightly as he licked and sucked her nipple.

Pleasure tightened in her stomach, building to impossible heights, but just as she was on the verge of explosion, he raised his head, his eyes glittering in the semidarkness.

"I want to take it slow. I want to touch you, to kiss you and make this last a long time." A whisper of a smile curved his lips. "But what my brain wants and what my body wants are two different things. I have a feeling there's not going to be anything slow about this."

"There's always next time for slow."

He groaned then and panties and briefs were removed and the caresses became more intimate. She wrapped her fingers around the length of him, loving the pulsating warmth of him. At the same time his fingers moved between her legs. She gasped as he found the spot where all sensation seemed to be centered.

Moving her hips, she met his touch as a wild tension began to build and build inside her. Mindless with pleasure and the growing need for release, she moved frantically, half sobbing as her release crashed through her in wave after wave of pleasure.

She'd scarcely recovered when he reached into his nightstand and grabbed a condom. He ripped the packet open, rolled it on, then moved between her thighs and slid into her. With his throbbing hardness deep inside her he froze, his features taut with tension, eyes closed, as he drew a deep, shuddering breath.

"God, that feels good," he whispered.

She couldn't speak—words seemed inadequate—so she merely gripped his shoulders more tightly and contracted her muscles around him.

Whatever control he'd fought to maintain snapped and he thrust into her with deep, long strokes that she arched to meet. Faster, more frantically, they moved together until she was once again climbing higher and higher.

When the climax came it crashed through her and at the same time that she cried out he stiffened against her with a deep, guttural moan.

He collapsed just to the side of her, their bodies still joined. A wave of sadness swept through her, sadness that it was over, finished, and all too soon she would leave his arms, get up from his bed and return to her own lonely bed.

"Stay the night," he said softly, as if he'd heard her thoughts. "Stay the night and sleep in my arms."

Why not? Johnny was spending the night with Annette and Dan. There was nobody waiting for her at home, no real reason to rush home.

He rose up on one elbow, his gaze soft and tender as it lingered on her face. He swiped a strand of hair from her cheek. "I can't offer you Crystal's Catering for breakfast." A small smile curved his lips. "But I do have a box of toaster waffles—blueberry."

She laughed. "How can I resist such an offer?"

"So you'll stay?"

"If you want me to."

He traced her lips with the tips of his fingers. "I definitely want."

"Then you have me for the night," she replied. She had no idea where this was going, but she knew already that when it ended she would grieve, for she was perilously close to falling in love with Christian Connor.

What a night, Tyler thought as he stared at the crumpled body of Gary Bernard. The poor bastard had once had a head, but it had almost been taken off with the force of the blows that had felled him in the parking lot of his apartment complex.

Identification had been made from a wallet in his back pocket. The wallet had also contained over a thousand dollars in cash, ruling out a robbery. But Tyler had known in an instant of viewing the body that the motive wasn't robbery. A splash of red paint decorated the front of his shirt like an exclamation point.

"That makes three," Jennifer said from beside him.

Three murders. Three bodies marked with red paint and not a fucking clue to go on. "Cordon off the area," he instructed his partner, his warm breath puffing like smoke in the frigid night air. "I've already called it in, so the crime scene boys should be arriving soon."

He pulled his jacket collar closer around his neck, but the winter air snaked down his back as insidious as the madman who had bashed Gary Bernard's life away. What the hell was going on? Why couldn't he get a handle on this one?

Unlike after the last two murders, there was no sign of the murder weapon, although it was obvious it was some sort of blunt instrument. The ME would be able to give him an idea of what might have been used.

Tyler sighed and stared around the parking lot. At two in the morning it was deserted. Very few lights shone from apartment windows. At this time of night most people were asleep in their beds.

A twenty-three-year-old woman coming home from a night of partying with friends had discovered Gary Bernard's body. She might have been half-drunk when she'd driven home, but the sight of Gary's body had apparently scared her sober.

He glanced over to the police car, where she was seated in the back, tears streaking down her cheeks as she stared straight ahead. She'd have nightmares for a long time to come. God knew, Tyler wasn't a stranger to nightmares.

As part of the murder squad for the Kansas City police force, he'd seen things that were beyond human comprehension. He'd seen children battered to death by the very people who were supposed to protect and nurture them. He'd seen young women beaten by lovers, men shot to death for the change in their pockets.

These crimes were no more heinous than dozens of others he'd investigated, but what bothered him was that he just couldn't get a handle on why these people had been killed.

Even the craziest of serial killers had to have a method to the madness. He stared down at the body, willing it to talk to him, to tell him how he tied in with an art gallery owner and an agent.

But the victim wasn't talking and Tyler was left with the sickening knowledge that there wasn't going to be any holiday cheer until he got this madman off the streets.

Chapter 15

Christian awoke first. Consciousness came in stages. First he became aware of the faint scent of spicy perfume in the air. He was curled spoon fashion around a warm body, a body that fit perfectly against his.

Vanessa.

He opened his eyes to see dawn filtering through the windows, painting the room in a soft gold glow. He leaned his head forward a bit, just enough to nuzzle her hair, and remembered the night they had shared.

It had been amazing. They'd made slow, leisurely love a second time. He'd learned what she liked, all the places to kiss and touch to make her mewl with pleasure. And she'd been a willing participant, giving as well as receiving.

Just thinking about it was enough to make him hard, made him want to repeat it again and again. Her warm, sexy body was tight against him and he drew in the scent of her.

He thought about moving her hair and planting a kiss on the back of her neck, but it was obvious she was sound asleep. Rather than wake her, he gently eased away from her and out of bed.

He grabbed clean clothes from his closet, and then padded down the hallway to the guest bathroom to shower. He didn't want the sound of the water to wake her.

Minutes later as he stood beneath the hot spray, he thought about the night before and the woman who slept in his bed. He was more than a little bit crazy about her. He'd been infatuated before making love to her, but now his feelings went far beyond mere infatuation.

Their bodies had been meant for each other, fitting together as if two pieces of the same puzzle. It was easy for him to imagine making love to her every night of the week and waking in the mornings with her in his arms.

There was just one small problem. Her son, Johnny. Christian had sworn to himself a long time ago that he'd never be a parent, and that included being a stepfather. What he needed to decide was whether he wanted Vanessa in his life badly enough to take on her son.

Thank God no decision needed to be made right now. They were still in the first flush of their relationship, not in a place where any decisions about the future had to be made.

He shut off the shower, dried and got dressed, then went into the kitchen and made coffee. As it brewed he stood at the kitchen windows and stared outside. He didn't need a weatherman to tell him that it was cold and blustery outside. He could feel the cold radiating from the windowpanes, saw the wind whipping errant brown leaves and trash around the small yard.

"Good morning."

He whirled around to see her standing in the kitchen

doorway. She had put on her dress but was barefoot and she looked absolutely stunning. "Good morning. I hope I didn't wake you."

She shook her head. "I smelled that coffee. Then I re-membered that you said your lonely time of the day was first thing in the morning. I figured I'd get up and share that time with you."

His heart swelled. "You ready for some waffles?" He gestured her toward a chair at the table.

"No thanks. Just coffee is fine." She sat at the table, a beautiful smile on her face.

"I thought you were crabby in the mornings." He poured two cups of coffee and carried them to the table.

"It's hard to be crabby when I feel so . . . so satisfied." Her cheeks pinkened just a bit. "Last night was amazing."

"More than amazing," he agreed, and sat across from her.

She frowned thoughtfully. "I worried about it. Before, when I ran into the bathroom. I worried that I wouldn't be very good at it . . . at sex." She broke eye contact with him, the color in her cheeks intensifying. "Jim was never much interested in having sex with me."

"Then Jim was a fool," he said with surprise. What kind of a man would not want to make love with some-body as beautiful as Vanessa? He leaned forward as her gaze met his once again. "Trust me, you're very, very good at it."

She raised a hand to her cheek. "You're making me blush."

He grinned, finding her blush charming. "Drink your coffee before it gets cold."

She wrapped her hand around the mug and leaned

back in the chair. "Grandpa John used to say that mornings were the time to decide where you were going that day, and night was the time to reflect where you've been."

"And where are you going today?" he asked. The sunlight drifting through the window found her face and emphasized the delicate angles.

She took a sip of the coffee, then set the mug back down on the table. "I'm going to pick up Johnny. Then I think maybe we'll spend some time at the mall doing a little Christmas shopping."

He grimaced. "The mall is the last place I'd want to be on a Saturday two weeks before Christmas."

She laughed. "Now you sound like the Grinch." She studied him thoughtfully, a touch of humor lighting her blue eyes. "I'll bet you're the type of man who waits until the night before, then makes a mad dash through the stores."

"Guilty as charged," he replied. "There was never much of a Christmas at my house when I was growing up. The holidays were one of the busiest times of the year for my father. Most Christmases we were in a hotel room in some city or another."

"Grandpa John loved Christmas, couldn't wait for it to arrive each year. We'd put up the tree on Thanksgiving afternoon, and spend the next month decorating the house to gaudy proportions."

"Sounds nice."

"It was nice," she agreed. "He gave me a lot of wonderful traditions to carry on." She raised her mug and eyed him over the rim. "It's too bad you didn't have the same kind of experience."

"Yeah, it is, but you don't miss what you don't know."

He grinned. "I don't have nightmares about it or anything like that. No baggage to speak of from my youth."

They drank their coffee and shared childhood experiences and Vanessa marveled at the fact that despite his cold upbringing, he seemed to be telling the truth about not carrying any baggage. He was the most well-adjusted man she'd ever known and that was important to her.

As they chatted and the sun rose higher, filling the kitchen with light, she found herself thinking back over the incredible night they had shared. She hadn't known that lovemaking could be so magnificent. She'd never dreamed she could feel the kind of intense sensations that he'd wrought in her.

She didn't know what kind of a lover she was, but she knew what kind Christian was . . . demanding yet tender, possessive yet giving. Just thinking about it made a familiar coil of heat reignite in the pit of her stomach.

When he again suggested waffles, she took him up on the offer. Toaster waffles with Mrs. Butterworth's syrup had never tasted so good, and she'd never laughed as hard as she did as he entertained her with stories about his school days.

"I'll admit, I could be ornery as hell," he said as they cleaned up the dishes. "But I like to think I've outgrown most of my orneriness."

"I think you have just enough left in you to be fun," she replied.

It was after nine when she realized it was time to leave. Johnny would be waiting for her and she didn't want to overstay her welcome with Christian. She went into the bedroom and finished dressing, surprised by how much she didn't want to leave.

He walked with her to his door and there kissed her long and deep. He tasted of syrup and a simmering desire that was temptation itself.

"When can I see you again?" he asked when he finally released her.

She thought of the week ahead. "Tuesday night Johnny has a school skating party at seven at Englewood Park. It should be lots of fun. Why don't you come with us?"

A frown line creased his forehead. "Oh, I don't know about that. I'm not really into kids."

It was as if the earth shifted slightly beneath her feet. She stared up at him, her heart beating a dull rhythm of bitter disappointment. "Then what are we doing here, Christian? What are you doing with me? Do you think I'm going to put Johnny up for adoption?"

The words tumbled out of her, backed by a lightning flash of indignant rage as his words echoed in her head. "How nice of you to let me know that you don't like kids *after* you've had sex with me. If you would have mentioned it before, last night would have never happened." She opened the door and started outside, but he stopped her by grabbing her arm.

"Vanessa, wait. It's not like that," he protested. "Please, let me explain."

She jerked her arm out of his grip. "There's nothing to explain." She just wanted out of there, away from him. She now recognized how dicey dating could be when you were a single parent, for she wasn't looking just for somebody to fill the empty spaces in her life, but also in her son's life.

"Look, Christian." She drew a weary sigh. "We're obviously in different places in our lives and want different things. I hope you find what you want." She didn't wait for him to reply, but turned quickly and headed for her car.

The cold air had nothing on the chill in her heart. She didn't even wait for the car to warm up, but instead started the engine and drove off. A glance in her rearview mirror let her know he still stood in his doorway, watching her leave.

She should have known it was all too easy. She should have known not to get her hopes up. After all, Christian had been her first date, her first step toward new life. She supposed she should have realized she'd have several stumbles and falls before finding her real Mr. Right.

Squeezing her fingers around the steering wheel, she tried not to think about how right Christian had seemed. But she would not compromise Johnny's happiness for her own. The man she brought into their lives would not only have to be in love with her but would also have to love her son. That was nonnegotiable.

By the time she reached her house she was resigned to the fact that she'd never hear from Christian again, never see him again. Although she was filled with a million what-ifs, she knew better than to indulge them.

She took a quick shower, changed into jeans and a heavy sweater, then left to head over to the Abbott place to get Johnny.

As usual Dan opened the door and gestured her toward the kitchen before falling back into his recliner and grabbing the remote control.

She found Annette in the kitchen sitting at the table with a cup of coffee in front of her. "Where is everyone?" Vanessa asked.

"Johnny is downstairs with his uncle Brian, and Garrett just went to the bathroom. Steve and Bethany skipped breakfast here this morning and Dana has the flu. And how was your night?"

"It was fine," Vanessa replied as she slid into a seat at the table. She wasn't going to tell Annette that she wouldn't be seeing Christian again. There was no reason she needed to share every aspect of her dating life with her mother-in-law. "What are Brian and Johnny doing in the basement?"

"Going through some boxes that were stored away. Johnny wanted to know if we had any other drawings that his dad had done when he was young, and Brian remembered a box down there. Unfortunately there's a dozen boxes and Brian wasn't sure which one was the right one." She gestured toward the counter. "Help yourself to coffee."

"No thanks, I'm all coffeed out." At that moment Brian and Johnny came into the kitchen.

"Hey, Mom." Johnny walked over to her and placed an arm around her shoulder.

"Hey, son," she replied. She fought her impulse to pull him closer and kiss his downy cheek. He was getting to the age where he didn't like hugs and kisses and she mourned the passing of the little boy who had loved the warmth of his mother's arms around him.

"Brian." She smiled at her brother-in-law as he sat in the chair next to hers. "Annette told me Dana has the flu?"

"Yeah, she woke up puking her guts up this morning," he said.

"Maybe it's morning sickness," Annette said, a touch of hope in her voice.

"Bite your tongue, Ma," he replied. "Two kids are enough." He winked at Vanessa with a teasing grin. "If she had her way, Dana and I would have a dozen kids."

"Speaking of, where are the girls?" Vanessa asked.

"I took them to Dana's mother's place this morning. I've got to go into work this afternoon, so I couldn't watch them and Dana wasn't up to having them today."

"I told you that you could have brought them here," Annette said. "You know I love having my grandkids here." She gestured for Johnny to sit next to her. When he sat she reached out and ruffled his hair. "Did you find some of your daddy's drawings?"

"Nah, we couldn't find them," he replied.

"Why don't you go get your things. We have a lot to accomplish today," Vanessa told her son.

"He reminds me so much of Jim," Brian said thoughtfully as Johnny left the room. "He's got the same drive, the same passion for art that Jim had." His black eyebrows tugged together in a deep frown. "Sometimes I forget he's gone. I expect him to come ambling in behind you and Johnny. I miss him."

"Miss who?" Garrett ambled into the kitchen, his hair tousled and eyes bloodshot.

"Jim," Brian replied.

Garrett's face blanched of color and he rubbed two fingers in the center of his forehead as if to ease a thundering headache. "Can we not talk about him? Every time we get together we end up talking about Jim. It makes me so depressed."

"I'm off for some Christmas shopping," Vanessa said, and stood.

"Ugh, that's even more depressing," Garrett replied. "I hate Christmas. All the stupid music and cheerful little elves running amok in the malls . . ."

Vanessa laughed and leaned over and planted a quick kiss on Garrett's forehead. "You need to sleep more and party less, Garrett. You're way too young to be so cranky."

He gave her a halfhearted grin as Johnny came back into the room. "All set," the boy said.

They said their good-byes and left the kitchen.

"Heading home?" Dan asked.

"To the mall," Vanessa replied.

"Have fun," he replied, his gaze never leaving the television screen.

As she left the house she thought about Dan Abbott. He was a different man now than he had been two years ago. Jim's death had broken something inside him. He kept himself isolated from the rest of the family, lost in sitcoms from days gone by.

"Can we eat lunch at Crazy Ed's?" Johnny asked when they were in the car and headed toward the Metro North Mall.

Crazy Ed's catered to the young crowd, especially those twelve and under. Vanessa hated the place with its multitude of video games and dancing puppets. Johnny loved it.

"Okay, but I'm giving it a one-hour time limit and no more." Crazy Ed's was a place where kids could spend hours.

"One hour," he agreed with a nod of his head. "You think it will snow before Christmas?"

"The weathermen are saying it isn't likely, although it's certainly cold enough."

"Did you have fun last night with Mr. Connor?"

"It was okay." She didn't want to think about Christian. Later she'd have time to kick herself in the butt for falling into his bed without asking some important questions. Live and learn, she told herself. She'd certainly know what questions to ask the next time.

Despite the dull ache of disappointment that thoughts of Christian brought, the day was surprisingly pleasant. The mall was decorated in holiday splendor with carols singing across speakers. Bell ringers smiled, children laughed and mothers and cashiers looked frazzled.

Johnny picked out presents for his grandparents and aunts and uncles and by the time they entered the madness of Crazy Ed's their arms were laden with packages.

They placed their order and bought a handful of tokens, which Johnny took off with in the direction of his favorite arcade game. Vanessa remained in the booth and watched him as he played.

"I'm not really into kids." Christian's words slammed back into her head. Not into kids—what exactly did that mean? He didn't like kids? She would never have guessed that about him.

Certainly she was not exactly objective, but nobody who met Johnny wasn't charmed by him. He was so bright and well-mannered, not precocious or trying at all. He'd been cheated in the father department and he deserved a man who would love him like a dad. If she couldn't find a man to love Johnny, she wouldn't have a man in her life.

It was after four when they arrived home. No messages were on her answering machine and she was vaguely disappointed that Christian hadn't called. Not that she cared. Not that anything could come of it. He'd made his position clear and it wasn't one that was acceptable to her.

For the next two hours she and Johnny wrapped and labeled the presents they had bought. Then Johnny went upstairs to work on his new painting and Vanessa went to her computer to print off flyers for several houses.

She wanted to stay busy. She needed to stay busy to keep thoughts of Christian at bay. Even knowing what she knew now, she wouldn't have taken back the night spent in his arms. Last night had been a reminder to her of what love could be, of how right it could feel.

By nine o'clock Johnny was in bed and Vanessa was headed there. She'd gotten too little sleep the night before and now exhaustion weighed her down, making it difficult to think.

Clad in a pair of warm, flannel pajamas, she crawled into bed and shut off the lamp. Moonlight drifted into the window, and memories of how Christian had looked naked and hungry filled her head.

He'd been beautiful, his skin sleek and tanned, his muscles taut and strong. She'd felt safe in his arms, as if he could keep the ugliness and danger of the world away. But he'd been just another rut life had thrown her way, another in a long line of bumps that had created heartbreak.

She closed her eyes, fighting against an unexpected burn of tears. Jim's family was supportive and loving, but there were times when she still desperately missed her grandpa John. And there were times she wondered, if he hadn't died, would she have still married Jim?

Grandpa John would have liked Christian. "You can tell a man's worth by the lines on his face," he used to say. "There's good lines and there's mean lines. Old man Kruger, he's got mean lines from frowning and squinting and yelling all the time."

"But you have good lines," she'd replied, and placed her hand on his weatherworn face.

He'd smiled, deepening the crinkles around his blue eyes. "That's right, sweetie. When you get big enough to date, you find a man who has good lines on his face."

Jim had remarkably few lines on his face. For a man who had been as emotional as he'd been, those emotions didn't mar the smooth skin on his face.

Christian, on the other hand, had furrows etched beside his mouth and faint spiderwebs radiating out from each eye. Good lines, but he wasn't into kids.

She pulled the spare pillow against her chest, hugging it in lieu of a warm bedmate. Even when Jim had been alive she'd often been in this bed alone. His creative muse didn't work nine to five, but had raged most often through the night.

She should be accustomed to sleeping alone, but for some reason tonight the bed seemed bigger, emptier. Squeezing her eyes closed, she sought the comfort of sleep.

The ring of the phone jarred her from a dream. In the darkness she reached for the receiver, not completely awake but pulled from the pleasant dream.

"Hello?" she muttered.

The rush of water filled the line, like one of those nature CDs that are supposed to be soothing. The sound wasn't soothing to her. Complete consciousness slammed into her.

"Who is this? What do you want?" Her heart raced, palms sweating, as she clutched the receiver tightly to her ear. It was the same kind of phone call she'd gotten before. As if on cue, a gurgling sound violated her ear. Like somebody underwater. Like somebody drowning.

"Prank phone calls are against the law," she exclaimed, not sure if she was angry or frightened. "Stop calling here!"

"Vanessa . . ."

The word hissed through the line like a slithering snake. She gasped and threw the receiver to the center of the bed. Fumbling frantically, she sought the switch on the bedside lamp, needing light.

The lamp came on, casting the bed in soft illumination. She stared at the phone lying on her flowered spread. She clutched a fist to her chest where her heartbeat banged so hard, so fast.

Vanessa.

The caller had said her name. These weren't random prank calls. They were meant specifically for her.

Heart still pounding, she reached out with trembling hands and picked up the receiver once again. She pressed it against her ear.

A dial tone.

Whoever had made the call had hung up.

Chapter 16

Vanessa slammed her front door as she entered the house early Monday afternoon. It had been a bad day. Alicia had been a rip-roaring bitch, a sale Vanessa had thought was in the bag had fallen through and dark gray clouds had hidden any hint of sun that might have shone. She'd endured until noon, but then had decided to call it a day and come home.

It was the thought of that phone call on Saturday night that had kept her on edge all day long, though. Just like the last time, the caller ID had indicated an anonymous caller. She'd spent most of Saturday night on her sofa, curled up beneath a warm blanket, fighting a chill that had gripped her to the bones.

Who would be doing such a thing to her? What was the purpose? To frighten her? It was definitely working. She'd spent the last two days looking over her shoulder, peeking into shadows and battling the feeling that some-body wished her harm.

As she changed from her work clothes to jeans and a sweatshirt, she was aware of the fact that she might be overreacting, that phone calls weren't a physical threat. But being rational had nothing to do with the emotional reaction the phone calls had produced.

As always when stressed, she turned to the kitchen and the comforting tasks of baking. Arranging the ingredients for a loaf of banana-nut bread on the counter, she tried to think of who might hate her enough to want to torment her.

It had to be somebody who knew her, somebody who knew the intimate details of her life. The caller had known exactly how Jim had died. It couldn't be a coincidence that he'd drowned and the calls sounded like somebody underwater, like somebody drowning.

She consciously tried to will away thoughts of the creepy phone call as she measured and mixed. For the first time in a long time she wished she had a close girlfriend. She had Jim's family members and she had coworkers, but she didn't have a woman she considered a close intimate in her life.

When she'd first gotten married she'd embraced life with Jim and had allowed her relationships with friends to be placed on the back burner. They'd been busy renovating the house; then Johnny had come along and life had been so hectic. By the time things had settled down Jim had been so needy, so unpredictable, there hadn't been room for friendships.

It would be nice to talk about what was happening with the phone calls with a friend; nice to talk about what had happened with Christian.

A slight stab of disappointment plunged through her. She hadn't heard from him since Saturday morning when she'd left his house. The emptiness of his absence from her life surprised her. She hadn't realized just how much of her thoughts he had filled, just how much he'd been responsible for a sweet excitement, an edge of anticipation, that was now absent.

By the time Johnny got home from school, two loaves of bread were cooling and two more were in the oven. He flew in, cheeks red from the wintry air, eyes sparkling with a ten-year-old's humor.

"You look like you've had a good day," she said as he placed his book bag on top of the table.

"Billy Martin had Silly String on the bus coming home. He sprayed Mrs. Clinton with it and I think he's gonna get kicked off the bus for the rest of the year."

Vanessa knew Billy Martin was another ten-year-old, twice the size of his peers, and a bully who tormented the kids on the bus almost every day. Johnny giggled. "You should have seen her, Mom. She had red string hanging from her hair and her face was red as the string when she yelled at him."

"That wasn't a nice thing for Billy to do."

"I'm glad he did it," Johnny replied. "I mean, I'm not glad that he got Mrs. Clinton, but if it gets him kicked off the bus, that's fine with me." He eyed the bread cooling on a rack. "Is that for us or is it Christmas presents?"

"A little of both. I thought I'd take a couple loaves to some of the people at the real estate office, but we'll keep one just for us. You want a slice now with a glass of milk?"

He frowned thoughtfully. "Nah, I'll wait until later. I've got to get upstairs and get to work." He walked to the doorway and turned to face her once again. "And don't forget, if you come up to the studio, you've got to knock before entering."

"Got it," she replied. She had a feeling Johnny was working on some kind of special project for her Christmas present. For the last two days he'd been very secretive about his work in the studio.

The art contest he'd entered was on Friday night. At that time they'd find out how he'd done. The young artists' masterpieces would be displayed in a ballroom at the downtown Marriott Hotel. The exhibit was open to the public and ribbons would be placed on the winning work.

She knew Johnny would be disappointed if he didn't win, and she'd been trying to prepare him for that possibility. But disappointment was part of life. Hadn't her experience with Christian reminded her of that fact?

The doorbell rang and she hurried from the kitchen to answer, wondering if maybe Scott had gotten confused and come to sit with Johnny. A peek out the window showed a tall, gray-haired woman in a long black wool coat standing on the porch.

"Mrs. Abbott?" the woman inquired as Vanessa opened the door.

"Yes, can I help you?"

The woman held out a business card. "My name is Freida White. I'm with Child Protective Services. I was wondering if I could come in and speak with you."

Child Protective Services? What was going on? Vanessa opened the door to allow the woman entry. "Speak with me about what?" She couldn't imagine what this was about. She gestured the woman toward the sofa, then sat in the chair nearby, an edge of frightening apprehension fluttering inside her veins.

Freida White looked like a woman without a sense of humor. Her lips were thin colorless slashes in a face devoid of makeup and lacking any warmth. Her eyes were small, dark and slightly accusing as she gazed at Vanessa. "Mrs. Abbott, I'm here to investigate a report about a child in danger."

"A child in danger?" Vanessa's head reeled. "What on earth are you talking about? What report? What danger?" Her heart seemed to stop beating and she drew a deep breath in an attempt to steady herself.

Freida opened the file folder she'd carried in with her. "You have a son? A boy named Johnny?"

"Yes, yes, but this has to be some sort of a mistake. Johnny isn't in any danger. He's fine. We're fine." She couldn't imagine what this woman was doing here. What was going on?

"You understand that my department is obligated to investigate any report that comes in about a child at risk." Again her eyes held a hint of accusation. "Do you drink, Mrs. Abbott?"

If Vanessa's heart had begun to beat again, the question made it stop cold. "What?" The single word fell from her lips in a whisper.

"According to the report that was called in, you have a drinking problem that has put your son at risk. It was indicated that you often drink, and then drive with your son in the car. That he's often without supervision because you've passed out."

"That's ridiculous. Who made such a report?" Her voice was stronger now.

"We're obligated to keep such information confidential," Freida replied. "And please answer the question." Her stern lips pressed together as she stared at Vanessa expectantly.

"No. I do not drink. I don't have a problem. I'm not even a social drinker." She saw no reason to share with this woman her past, no reason to explain that two years ago she'd gone through a dark period that had had her seeking solace in alcohol. "I've never drunk and driven with or without Johnny in the car. I don't pass out and leave him alone. I do not drink."

"Mrs. Abbott, I understand the stresses of single parenting. I know that your husband committed suicide some time ago. It's understandable if you're struggling. We can help." The woman was obviously trying to give the aura of compassion, but the hardness of her eyes belied the attempt.

"I don't need your help," Vanessa replied, and swallowed hard against a well of emotions rising up inside her. "I told you before, I don't have a problem and whoever made that report is lying."

Freida's gaze held hers for a long moment. "Is your son at home?"

"Yes, he's upstairs."

"If you don't mind, I'd like to ask him a few questions."

Hell yes, she minded. This woman's very presence in her living room was an affront. "I'll go get him," she said, and rose from the chair.

As she climbed the stairs to get Johnny, she felt sick to her stomach. A headache banged with nauseating force at her temples. What in God's name was happening here?

Who on earth would have called Child Protective
Services?

The door to the studio was closed and she knocked softly
with a trembling hand on the wood. Johnny opened the door
a crack and she explained simply that there was a woman
downstairs who wanted to ask him some questions.

He followed her downstairs, where she introduced him
to the social worker. "Just answer her questions truth-
fully, honey," she told him. "I'll be in the kitchen."

She sat at the table and stared out the window, tears
burning with the need to be released. She choked them
back. The last thing she wanted was for Johnny to see her
upset.

The murmur of their voices drifted in, too low for her
to hear exactly what was being said. "You've got nothing
to hide," she whispered. Surely the truth would win out
over this crazy false accusation.

Still, even as she told herself this, a fierce fear thinned
her blood, and goose bumps danced on her arms. She'd
heard the horror stories about overzealous social workers.
After several news stories about children lost in the system, children killed by abusive parents, the rule of the day
was now to err on the side of caution.

Dear God, if for some reason she lost Johnny, she
didn't know what she'd do. He was her happiness, her
reason for getting up in the mornings. He was her very
heart.

Freida White spoke with Johnny for twenty long, agonizing minutes. Then she called Vanessa back into the living room. Vanessa smiled at her son and told him he
could go back upstairs, then faced the social worker, her
heart in her throat.

"I'm marking the complaint as unfounded, but I'm recommending that the file remain open for six months," she said.

Vanessa nodded. "Believe me, I'd never do anything that might in any way harm my son."

"I see no reason for any further investigation, but if we receive more complaints or any corroborating evidence that the child is at risk, we'll have to act."

"As I would expect you to," Vanessa replied as they walked to the front door.

It wasn't until the woman pulled out of the driveway that the fear drizzled away and a rich, deep anger took its place. First the phone calls and now this. Who on earth would call Social Services? Somebody was trying to screw with her head. Somebody was trying to screw with her life.

Who in the hell was behind it? Who would be so evil as to call Child Protective Services? Who would want Johnny taken away from her?

And how on earth could she fight back against whoever was responsible? How did you protect yourself against a nameless, faceless threat?

Tyler sat in the conference room, nursing a noxious cup of coffee and staring at the remains of the hamburger in front of him. He should be home in bed. All his team had gone home hours ago. Most of them had families. Tyler had nobody waiting for him. Besides, he knew that the level of frustration he felt would make sleep next to impossible.

He was a man who required very little sleep. When he was younger his mother worried about the fact that her son never slept through the night. "A body needs to rest," she'd say. And he'd always reply that he would rest when he was dead.

He frowned at the sight of the congealing burger, then moved his gaze to the bulletin board at the opposite end of the room. Three dead men all decorated with vermilion paint.

He stared at the latest photographs to make the board of infamy. Gary Bernard. There was a photo of him standing in front of a red rock formation in Sedona, then the crime scene photo, where he was unidentifiable by sight. The police department hadn't released any details of his death yet, although it was just a matter of time before the public knew there was a serial killer working the city.

Over the past couple of days they had learned several things about Gary. He'd been the only child of wealthy parents who had died ten years before. He'd been thirty-four years old at the time of his death. And he'd been an artist, albeit a struggling one. But he'd never had a showing at Andre's Gallery, nor had he ever been represented by Matt McCann.

Connections, connections. Somehow Tyler knew he was missing an important connection, something that tied these men together in the mind of a killer.

He and his team had reconstructed the lives of the victims to the best of their ability. They'd talked to friends and neighbors and loved ones in an attempt to establish a meaningful association between the three.

An art dealer, an art agent and an artist. Art was the obvious commonality. But there had to be something more, something personal.

The murders had been committed with tremendous

rage, the victims beaten, not just to death, but long after death had come. The perpetrator hadn't just wanted them dead—he'd wanted them destroyed.

He. Although Tyler thought of the killer with the masculine pronoun, he knew there was a chance the perp could be female. The ME had been unable to give them an approximate height of the unsub by the angle of the blows. The damage had been so severe and all three men had been beaten after falling to the ground.

Typically, women didn't kill this way, but Tyler couldn't rule out the possibility. At this point in the investigation he had to keep an open mind.

He got up from his chair and walked closer to the bulletin board, so close that if the victims had been real people rather than photographs, he would have been able to see the individual pores on their faces.

Moving from picture to picture, he studied the victims' faces, then the crime scene photos, then turned back again to the victims. "Talk to me," he said softly. But there was no reply.

Chapter 17

It was a perfect night for ice-skating. The wind that had howled from the north for the last two weeks had seemingly blown itself out, leaving behind a cold stillness that was welcome.

Englewood Lake was more pond than lake, a neighborhood body of water and park that was popular for little fishermen and family picnics. During the summer months the water was home to dozens of ducks who feasted on bread crumbs that people threw to them.

Tonight the frozen body of water was ringed, not only by picnic tables and benches, but also by large fire-filled barrels, providing heat for those bold enough to venture out. A local skating rink was supplying shoes for the skaters at a fee and the parents' association from Johnny's school was offering hot cocoa and cookies.

"Have you ever skated before, Mom?" Johnny asked as she angled the car into a space in the already crowded parking lot.

"Never," she replied. "I have a feeling my behind is going to kiss a lot of ice tonight."

Johnny giggled with excitement. "That's funny, Mom."

"Yeah, you won't think it's so funny when it's your behind that's kissing the ice," she replied. She was determined to have a good time despite everything that had happened in the last couple of days.

She turned off the car engine and unbuckled her seat belt. "Before you get out of the car and see all your friends, there's one thing I want to do."

He unbuckled his belt. "What?"

She leaned across the seat and planted a kiss on his forehead. "That."

He grinned and swiped his hand over the place where she'd kissed. "I'm rubbing it in," he said. "And I'm glad you did that now instead of in front of the guys."

"Got your hat? Gloves? Scarf?" She went down a checklist to assure that he wouldn't come home from the festivities with frostbite.

"I've got it all, Mom. Come on," he said impatiently. "Let's go get some skates."

By the time she got out of the car he was already halfway across the parking lot. She watched as he raised a hand, waving at several other little boys who stood by the rental table.

School ended for the holidays at the end of the week and all the kids seemed to be hyped up with holiday energy. Squeals and yells came from the ice, where children were in a variety of positions ranging from skating to falling.

The scent of woodsmoke and hot cocoa hung in the still air, a pleasant mix that promised warmth inside and out. It took only minutes for them to get their skates, put them on and hit the ice. And it took only a minute after that for Vanessa to be on her butt.

Laughing wildly, Johnny tried to help her up but promptly fell as well. The laughter soothed her spirit, which had been sorely tested in the last week.

Between the phone calls and the visit from Child Protective Services, she'd been on edge, unable to get a handle on the nerves that knotted her stomach.

To make matters worse, Gary Bernard had been found murdered outside his apartment building. The news reports had been sketchy, but the fact that three men who had been close to her dead husband were now also dead—murdered—was, to say the least, more than a little bit disturbing.

However, she refused to think about those things tonight. Tonight belonged to Johnny. For the next thirty minutes she and Johnny held hands and carefully made their way around the ice. By the time they'd made one round Vanessa was exhausted and freezing.

"I'm going to take a break and warm up by one of the barrels. Want to come with me?"

Johnny shook his head, his gaze flying around the ice. "Some of my friends are over there. Can I go skate with them?"

Vanessa looked to where he'd pointed and saw two boys teetering precariously on their skates. "Okay," she said. "But stay in this area."

She made it to the edge of the ice where their shoes awaited, and quickly changed from skates to boots and then walked over to one of the flaming barrels to warm herself.

As she held out her hands toward the crackling fire,

she watched her son skating with his friends. His laughter warmed her as efficiently as the blazing barrel. And somebody had tried to take him away from her. Somebody had called in a report that might have seen Johnny ripped from her home, from her life.

"Stop it," she muttered, moving closer to the barrel. She didn't want to think about bad things. She'd exhausted herself over the past couple of days, ruminating on all things bad. Thankfully at that moment one of the other moms joined her at the barrel.

She was still visiting with the woman when she saw him. The width of his broad shoulders beneath the familiar worn leather jacket was unmistakable. What was he doing here? Much to her dismay her heart beat in that familiar rhythm of pleasure.

He stopped at the edge of the lake, his gaze sweeping the area. When he spied her he approached with long determined strides.

"Excuse me," Vanessa murmured to the woman, and she moved away from the fire to meet him.

"We need to talk," he said without preamble.

"I thought we'd said all that needed to be said," she countered. She hated the way her heartbeat quickened at the sight of him, hated that he had the power to affect her on any level.

"I didn't say everything. You didn't give me a chance to explain." He raked a hand through his hair and stared across the ice, where Johnny was skating with his friends. "It's freezing out here. Let's go over there and talk." He gestured toward a nearby barrel that nobody was standing near.

This is ridiculous, she thought as she walked over to

the barrel. There's nothing he can say that will change what I already know, she told herself.

For a long moment he stared out onto the ice, where Johnny and two of his friends were attempting to skate. When he looked back at her his gray eyes were almost black. "The other night when I told you a little bit about my parents, I didn't tell you everything. I lied when I told you they weren't abusive. I didn't tell you that my father wasn't just cold and distant, but he was a miserable bastard. If he wasn't completely ignoring me, he was being overly critical and mentally abusive."

"Christian, you don't have to tell me this," she replied.

"But I do," he protested. He moved closer to her and above the woodsmoke she could smell his cologne, a scent that reminded her of making love to him, of being held tightly in his arms.

"You need to hear it to understand why I said what I did the other morning." He sighed once again. "I decided a long time ago that I wouldn't have kids, that my father had taught me nothing about being a father. That's why I told you I wasn't into kids. I'd never considered even dating anyone who had children. Then I met you."

He held his hands out over the fire and stared into the flames. "I've spent the last four days thinking about you, about how good we are together." He looked at her once again, his gaze intent. "I've always been afraid of the very idea of parenting in any form. I was afraid that because I'd had no good role model in my life, I'd screw it up if I tried to be a father."

"What your father gave you was a role model on how not to parent," she said softly.

"That's what I've come to realize in the last couple of

days. I know what a bad father does. Maybe I can figure out how to be a good one." He hesitated, vulnerability momentarily clinging to him. "You make me want to try."

He sighed with an edge of frustration. "What I'm trying to say is that I don't want to stop seeing you and I'd like to get to know your son. Please, tell me it isn't too late."

Although her immediate impulse was to throw herself into his arms, she suddenly realized the question she needed to ask him. If he gave her the wrong answer or if she sensed any deception in his answer, it was way too late for the two of them.

"Did you call Child Protective Services on me?"

He was either the best liar in the world or he was genuinely puzzled by the question. "Child Protective Services? Why would I do that?"

"Somebody called and reported that I was a drunk and that Johnny was in danger."

"What?" His features radiated shock. "Why would somebody do that?"

"I wish I knew." It was her turn to hold out her hands toward the warmth as a chill seeped through her bones.

"Vanessa, I would never do something like that. Jesus, how could you even think I would?"

"I'm sorry. I had to ask. I'm trying to make sense of what's been happening lately."

"Has something else happened?"

"Nothing important," she replied, not wanting to get into the phone calls and how she felt like somebody was watching her. Tonight wasn't the night for fear. It was a night for laughter and she didn't want to ruin things.

"You never answered my question."

"What question?" She looked at him curiously.

"Is it too late? Will you give me another chance?"

She felt his desire radiating from him and her heart swelled with a renewed burst of excitement, a sense of hope that had been dashed the last time they'd been together. "Do you ice-skate, Christian?"

"I've never had on a pair of skates in my life."

She grinned at him. "Then we're going to change that tonight. Come on, we're going to hit the ice."

Within minutes the two of them wore ice skates and joined Johnny. It took Christian several minutes to keep his feet beneath him, but once he got the hang of it, he showed a certain amount of natural talent on the skates.

She watched the interaction between her son and Christian. Johnny seemed to accept Christian's presence as if he were accustomed to his mother having men around. Although it was initially obvious that Christian was trying too hard, eventually he mellowed out and seemed to enjoy himself.

They remained on the ice for another half an hour; then the three of them got hot chocolate and cookies and found a bench near the edge of the ice, where they sat to enjoy the hot drinks and watch the other skaters.

"I'm entered in an art show on Friday night," Johnny said to Christian. "You want to come to the show with me and Mom?"

"I'd love to come, although I have to confess, I don't know anything about art," he replied.

"That's okay. Neither does Mom." Johnny sipped his hot chocolate. "Scott says I should win first place with no problem."

"It doesn't matter whether you win or not. What's important is that you did your best," Vanessa said.

"I've got to win. I'm the Abbott hope," he replied with a touch of fervor.

Vanessa frowned. "Who told you that?"

"Grandma and Uncle Garrett. They say I'm the Abbott hope for being famous with my painting, just like Dad was."

She was going to have a talk with Annette and Garrett. They probably weren't aware of the pressure they were putting on Johnny, pressure too great for a little boy to wear.

"Johnny, honey, all you need to worry about is being a good boy and being happy. That's all," she said.

He cast her a sly grin. "I'd be happy if I could go get another cookie."

She laughed. "Go. Knock yourself out." He jumped up from the bench and hurried toward the table in the distance.

"He's a nice kid," Christian said.

She nodded. "He's a good kid, although I worry sometimes that he's too much into the art stuff. He rarely plays video games, would rather paint than see a movie, and I don't like the idea that my in-laws are impressing on him that he needs to be successful for the family."

"My dad wanted me to follow in his footsteps and be a concert pianist, but to his dismay I had big, clumsy fingers. When he realized I wasn't going to be a mini him, that's when he decided I wasn't worth his time or attention."

"It's terrible, isn't it, what parents can do to their children? Jim wasn't a great parent either. Most of the time he was pretty unavailable to Johnny." And me, she mentally added.

"Is it all right with you if I go to the art show with you Friday night?" he asked.

She smiled. "I think it would be wonderful if you went with us." She suddenly felt as if the world had been set right again, as if she could handle whatever fate brought her way. With the warmth of Christian next to her and Johnny's face wreathed with a smile as he came running back, cookie in hand, she felt as if she could take on the world.

"And will you show me that place you told me about tomorrow and have lunch with me?"

She thought of her schedule the following day. She was once again taking the Worths out in the afternoon, but she had nothing on her agenda in the morning. "All right. Why don't you meet me at the office at ten."

The rest of the night passed quickly. They hit the ice one last time, clinging to one another for support and laughing when one of them fell.

At nine o'clock the skating party was officially over. Christian walked them to their car and they said their good-nights.

It was obvious the fresh air and exercise had exhausted Johnny. She got no arguments from him when she sent him directly to bed.

As he headed up the stairs she went to the kitchen, thinking maybe a nice hot cup of tea would be welcome before bed.

It was almost ten when she finished the tea, rinsed the cup, then walked back through the living room to go upstairs for bed. She halted in her tracks as she saw the dark, well-worn jacket flung across the back of the sofa.

For a moment her brain seemed to freeze as she stared at the garment. How many times had she nagged Jim to hang his jacket in the coat closet rather than toss it over the sofa? How was it possible Jim's jacket was now there, where it had so often been when he'd been alive?

On leaden feet she moved closer. It was definitely Jim's jacket. She recognized the dark brown wool with the worn pockets, could almost smell the familiar scent of her husband lingering in the air.

How had it gotten there? Who had put it there? The temperature of the room seemed to plunge by a hundred degrees as an icy chill gripped her.

Maybe Johnny had pulled it out of the closet when he'd been getting his outerwear for the skating party. She clung to that explanation. Yes, surely that was it, for nothing else made sense and she desperately needed to make sense of this.

She didn't want to hang it up. She didn't even want to touch the jacket. She left it where it was and went around the house, checking to make sure all the windows and doors were locked tight.

As she climbed the stairs to her bedroom she tried to remember if maybe she'd accidentally pulled it out of the closet and had unconsciously thrown it to the side as she and Johnny had prepared for the skating party.

Any other explanation was simply too horrid to contemplate.

When she asked Johnny the next morning if he'd pulled the jacket out of the closet and hadn't hung it back up, he told her he couldn't remember. He'd had to dig through the various items in the closet for boots and gloves, for the neck scarf and his heavy winter coat.

"I don't remember doing it," he said. "But I was excited and in a hurry. If I did, I'm sorry that I left it out instead of putting it away."

Vanessa didn't hang it back in the closet, but instead put it in a box out in the garage and told herself it had to be her son who had placed it on the sofa, for Jim's ghost certainly hadn't done it.

She then dismissed the whole thing from her mind as she dressed to meet Christian to show him the Walters house.

She still had no idea where her relationship with Christian was going, but she'd seen his effort with Johnny the night before, how hard he'd tried to connect. One thing she knew for certain. She was falling in love with Christian. It was a helpless feeling, knowing that there was no certainty for any future.

Happily Alicia was in a good mood when Vanessa walked into the office. She greeted Vanessa with a friendly smile. "You look nice today," she said as Vanessa took off her coat and hung it up.

"Thanks." The turquoise sweater was one of Vanessa's favorites.

"I've got to go shopping. Guy and I are going to a New Year's Eve ball and I don't have a fancy dress to wear. I also don't have a lot of spare cash to waste on a dress I'll probably only wear once."

Vanessa sat at her desk. "I've got a red Dior, if you'd like to borrow it. Jim bought it for me years ago, but it has classic lines that never go out of style."

Alicia pursed her lips together thoughtfully. "I'm not really a red kind of girl, but thanks for the offer."

"No problem." Eventually Vanessa needed to box up the Dior and take it to a charity. In fact, after the holidays she needed to go through Johnny's clothes and sort out the ones he'd outgrown.

"You all ready for the holidays?" Alicia asked.

"Almost. I've just got a few more things to pick up and some baking to do."

"I hope you're bringing some of those awesome muffins for the party on Friday."

Vanessa smiled. "You mean the cinnamon and rum ones? Yeah, my plan is to make a double batch Thursday night." The office party was on Friday afternoon and everyone always brought goodies.

"I guess we aren't going to have a white Christmas. The forecast is for cold and dry," Alicia said.

"That's fine with me. Nobody wants to go out looking at houses when the ground is covered with snow."

At that moment Christian walked through the door. His hair was wind tousled in charming disarray and the smoke of his eyes warmed her to her toes.

"Good morning," he said to Alicia before turning his attention to Vanessa. "And a good morning to you."

Was this how love was supposed to feel? she wondered. This sweet breathlessness and pleasure at his very sight? She couldn't remember it ever being this way before, feared somehow that it would never be the same with any other man.

"Ready to go?" she asked as she stood.

"Definitely."

Minutes later they were in her car heading for the big

house on the bluffs. "I had a good time last night," he said once they were on their way.

"So did we. Johnny thinks you're nice."

He grinned. "I'm a nice kind of guy."

"I know." She shot him a quick glance. "Christian, just because your father was a bad one doesn't mean that you would be."

"Logically I know that, but emotionally I've always worried that I wouldn't or couldn't live up to a kid's expectations."

She smiled. "That's the wonderful thing about kids. The only expectation they have is of being loved. If you meet that one, everything else falls into place."

"How did you get to be so smart?" he asked with a teasing tone.

She laughed. "Believe me, whatever smartness I've gained has been a result of a thousand mistakes I've made along the way."

"Isn't that the way it always is? Life is nothing more than an educational process."

When they arrived at the Walters place she pulled her cell phone from her purse and called the office. "Alicia, I'm at the Walters property. I'll let you know when we're leaving." She dropped the phone back in her purse.

"The setting is certainly nice," Christian said as they walked toward the front of the beautiful house. There were no city sounds up here, nothing but the quiet rustle of the wind.

"It's definitely isolated. The bulk of the property takes up the whole hilltop, so there will never be any neighbors." She unlocked the front door and they went inside.

"It's warm in here," he said, and shed his leather jacket

and placed it on the floor just inside the door. She did the same and made a mental note to check the thermostat. Some heat was necessary at this time of year to keep pipes from freezing, but it felt as if the furnace was working overtime.

Once again as they walked through the house Christian focused on the woodwork and the general construction. "Nice," he murmured when they entered the kitchen. "Awesome," he exclaimed as he saw the oversized microwave, making her laugh.

Upstairs he looked in every bedroom, every closet. When they reached the master suite he walked over to the bank of windows and stared out where the little lake glittered in the winter sun and the thick stand of trees looked like a tangle of skeletal arms rising up in the air.

"You mentioned this area back here is a greenway?"

"Yes. It's protected property, so nobody will ever be able to build back there."

He turned away from the window to face her, his features taut with a stark hunger. "It's crazy," he said as he took a step closer to her. "It's crazy how much I missed you in the last week."

Her knees suddenly felt weak. "It's crazy how sad I was when I thought I wouldn't see you again," she admitted.

He stopped mere inches in front of her, his gaze lingering on her lips, which parted as if of their own volition beneath the visual assault.

"I can't tell you how much I want to kiss you right now," he said, his voice deep and huskier than usual.

"What's stopping you?" she replied. The words barely left her mouth before he took hungry possession of it. In an instant she was filled with a desire that knew no boundaries, that was almost frightening in its intensity.

As he kissed her, his hands slid up beneath her sweater and she wanted his touch on her back, on her breasts. She needed his touch anywhere and everywhere.

And she wanted to feel his skin. With their lips still locked together she fumbled with the buttons on his shirt, wanting him naked and inside her.

She had no fear of discovery. She had the only key to this house and the owners lived out of town. There was nothing to stop them from making love right here, right now, except their inhibitions and she'd shed hers the moment his mouth had crashed down on hers.

The last of his shirt buttons undone, she tore the shirt off his shoulders at the same time he pulled her sweater off. Eyeing each other with bold primal intensity, they stripped off the last of their clothing and fell to the soft carpeting.

She was ready for him, mindless with need, frantic with want. He slid into her and raised her hips with his hands to deepen his thrusts. He took her with short, fast strokes, the cords of his neck taut and his eyes like chunks of charcoal on fire.

She was lost in a maelstrom of sensation with the nap of the carpet beneath her, his hot hands on her bottom and his hard length filling her up inside.

It took no time at all before she felt the building tension that had her gasping and crying out his name. Her climax slammed through her with the force of a spring storm. She clung to his shoulders as if he alone kept her grounded to earth.

She was still gasping in the aftermath when from the

window she heard the distant sound of geese. Their honking sent an irrational fear rushing through her, bringing memories of her dreams.

She clung tighter to Christian and as he cried out her name and stiffened against her, she fought terror.

Chapter 18

The Marriott Hotel in downtown Kansas City was bedecked for the holidays. Outside multicolored lights outlined the eighteen-floor building, and inside the lobby sported a twelve-foot tree laden with blue and gold ornaments and tinsel to match the decor of the room. Christmas carols drifted softly in the air, background noise that added to the festive aura.

Christian, Vanessa and Johnny entered the lobby a half an hour before the art show was to open to see most of Jim's family standing in a knot near the bar. Vanessa introduced Christian to them and tried not to feel awkward. *It isn't like you're cheating on Jim,* she mentally reminded herself.

"Where's Brian and Garrett?" she asked as she noticed the two missing family members.

"Brian is on his way," Dana said. "He had to work late but called me on my cell about ten minutes ago and said he was en route."

"And Garrett should be here any minute, too," Annette

said. "He left the house two hours ago and said he had a couple of errands to run before meeting us here."

Within minutes both Brian and Garrett had joined them. Garrett went directly to the bar to order a drink.

"Tonight's the big night," Brian said, and smiled at Johnny. "Are you ready to be met by your adoring fans?"

Johnny ducked his head with embarrassment and grinned. "You're silly, Uncle Brian."

"I personally find him irritating as hell," Garrett said as he rejoined them, drink in hand. Vanessa had a feeling it wasn't his first of the evening. Already his eyes held the bleary glaze of a man who was half-lit.

Steve looked at his watch in obvious impatience. "What time does this thing get started?"

"They're supposed to open the doors at seven," Vanessa replied.

Bethany gave her husband a dirty look. "Just for one night can you not think about business?"

"Children," Annette said firmly. "Let's not forget what we're doing here tonight. We're here to support Johnny." She smiled at her grandson. "Who looks as handsome as I've ever seen him tonight. Is that a new tie?"

Johnny nodded and fingered the bright red tie. "Yeah, we bought it last night to go with my suit."

"You know red was your daddy's favorite color," Brian said.

"It's my favorite color, too," Johnny replied.

At that moment Scott and Eric flew into the lobby. "Thank goodness we aren't late," Eric exclaimed. "Somebody decided he needed to go for a run an hour before we were supposed to leave."

"What? I'm a man—it didn't take me fifteen minutes

to shower and dress. I was ready in plenty of time." Scott turned to Johnny and gave him a soft punch on the arm. "How you doing, kid? Got butterflies?"

"A little," Johnny admitted.

Vanessa made the appropriate introductions again and for the next few minutes they all visited. "Mommy, I got to potty," Brian's four-year-old daughter, Diane, said.

"Me, too." Diane's six-year-old sister, Amy, said.

Dana smiled apologetically. "We'll be right back. Duty calls."

Vanessa watched her sister-in-law take her two daughters to the nearby bathroom and a faint yearning filled her. She'd always wanted another child, had never intended for Johnny to be her only one.

She looked up at Christian, so handsome, so tall beside her. He smiled down at her, a secretive smile that sent a sweltering warmth through her. Was he remembering those crazy moments in the Walters house when they'd gone at each other like two animals in heat?

Afterward as they'd dressed again, they'd laughed about how wild it had been and how good. She'd asked him then if that was why he was interested in her, because the sex was hot.

He'd taken her into his arms, any hint of laughter gone. "I'm interested in you because you make me laugh, because you are smart and caring and you bought me my first balloon. The hot sex is merely icing on the cake."

His words and the tenderness in his eyes had pushed her over the edge. Until that moment she'd known she was falling in love with Christian. But in that very moment she recognized she was in love with him.

The impulsive sex wouldn't result in an unexpected

pregnancy despite the fact that they'd used no protection. She'd been on the pill for years and hadn't stopped taking it when Jim had died.

Just as Dana returned with her daughters, one of the hotel employees indicated that the ballroom was now open. As the rest of them started down the long corridor toward the art exhibit, Vanessa grabbed her son's arm and held him back, wanting a few words in private with him.

They had been told that the winning exhibits would sport ribbons and she wanted to prepare her son for his painting not having a ribbon.

"Johnny, I want you to understand before we go inside that my pride in you has nothing to do with your skills at painting. I don't care whether you come in first or last. I don't care if you never pick up a paintbrush again. I'm proud of you no matter what."

Johnny smiled, an adultlike gleam in his bright eyes. "I know that, Mom. I'm fine. Really."

She studied him for a long moment. There was a steadiness in his gaze that reassured her. "Okay then, let's go look at the exhibits." They caught up to where Christian had waited for them.

"Okay?" he asked Johnny. He placed an arm across Johnny's shoulder as if in support. Johnny leaned into him as if hungry for the touch. Vanessa's heart swelled as she saw that her son obviously trusted the man she loved.

Their time spent together at the skating party had started a bond between the two men in her life. Or maybe Johnny just sensed how important Christian was to his mother, so had opened his heart to him.

The ballroom was filled with people. There had been an enormous amount of publicity concerning the event.

The exhibits were divided into groups by the age of the entrant. The entries of the five- through nine-year-olds were located as the visitors first walked through the door. The ten- through fifteen-year-olds' were at the back of the ballroom.

They made their way through the throng of people toward the area where Johnny's painting would be displayed. Vanessa couldn't help the nervous thumping of her heart. She wanted her son to do well, not for her, but because he wanted it so much for himself.

She knew the moment she saw the rest of the Abbotts' faces that Johnny hadn't won his division. Instead of the coveted gold ribbon, a blue decorated the bottom edge of his painting. Third place. She glanced at Johnny. His eyes darkened with fierce disappointment.

"I don't know who the judges were, but they obviously don't know crap about talent," Garrett exclaimed before knocking back the last of his drink.

"Well, there's always next year," Annette said, disappointment thick in her statement.

Christian touched Johnny's shoulder. "You want to come with me and take a look at some of the other entries?"

"Sure," he replied. He looked at his mom.

Vanessa heard a touch of relief in her son's voice, as if he needed some space from his family. "You two go ahead," she said. "I'll stay here with everyone else."

She watched as the two men she loved with all her heart walked away, Christian's hand once again on Johnny's shoulder.

For a few minutes Christian said nothing, waiting to see if Johnny was going to say anything. "There are a lot of entries," Christian finally said as they moved from one exhibit to another. "And you were one of the youngest in your division."

Johnny grinned up at him. "You don't have to try to make me feel better. I'm okay. I mean, I really wanted to win, but I didn't and that's all right."

The kid was something else. In the brief time Christian had spent with him, he'd found Johnny to be surprisingly grown-up and levelheaded for his age.

"You know, I don't know much at all about art, but I thought your painting was awesome and I'm not just trying to make you feel better."

"Thanks."

They stopped in front of a clay sculpture of some sort of a dragon creature. "I tried to do a sculpture once," Johnny said. "Mom bought me some clay and I worked it and worked it, but after all my work it still just looked like a clump of clay."

Christian laughed. "I think probably a monkey could paint a picture better than I could."

Johnny giggled. "Mom can't draw or paint either."

They wandered the aisles, looking at the various offerings, and finally reached the painting that held the coveted gold ribbon.

Johnny studied the landscape for a long time, a little frown furrowing his forehead. "It deserved to win," he finally said. "It's better than mine."

Christian said nothing, sensing that Johnny had more to say. "I like the way he did his shadows. See the way he put shadows on the left sides of the trees and in the water? I'm going to have to ask Scott to show me how to do that."

His shoulder muscles tensed beneath Christian's hand. He sighed, a troubled expression on his face. "I just wanted to win to make him proud."

"Who? Scott?" Christian dropped his hand from Johnny's shoulder.

Johnny shook his head. "No. My dad." He forced a laugh. "Dumb, huh? I mean, he's dead and all, but I thought maybe he'd look down from heaven and finally be proud of me."

For a moment Christian wasn't sure how to respond. There was such longing in Johnny's voice, a longing that made Christian wonder about the relationship Jim Abbott had had with his son, a longing that he could remember feeling himself years ago.

"Johnny, I'm sure that your dad was proud of you every day that he was alive," he finally said.

"I guess," Johnny replied without conviction. "Most of the time I'm not sure that he remembered he had a son. He just painted. That's all he ever did." He sighed, and in the weight of the sigh Christian heard himself and all the longing of a fatherless little boy. All his own father had ever done was play the piano.

"We'd better go find Mom," Johnny said.

As they went in search of the rest of the Abbotts Christian found himself wondering what kind of a man Jim Abbott had been. Vanessa hadn't shared much about him and he now realized there might be important things she hadn't told him.

He looked at the boy beside him. It would seem that he and Johnny had far more in common than he'd realized. He knew what it was like to feel invisible in the eyes of the man you most needed to see you. He knew all about that aching need for acceptance, for love, from the man who had sired him.

Christian stopped walking and looked at Johnny. "You know, there are some people that don't make great dads. Mine was one of those. I never did manage to get his attention or feel like I made him proud."

"Was he an artist?" Johnny asked.

Christian smiled. "Not like you and your dad. He was a musician. He played the piano."

Johnny studied him for a long moment, his dark eyes searching Christian's face as if seeking answers to important questions. "Do you have any kids?"

"No. I've never been married and I don't have any kids. Why?"

"I think you'd make a good dad."

The words spoken by an innocent boy melted something deep in Christian's heart, a core of bitterness he hadn't even realized was there until it cracked apart and fell away.

"Thanks, Johnny. That's a nice thing to hear. I know that if I were a father, I'd certainly try hard to be a good one." He put a hand on Johnny's shoulder and steered him through the crowded room toward Vanessa.

Vanessa saw them coming through the crowd and a wave of relief swept through her. She was ready to get out of here. She'd had enough of the well-meaning but tiresome Abbotts bitching and moaning about the fact that Johnny hadn't won first place.

"It's a conspiracy," Garrett exclaimed, his eyes flashing angrily. "They probably think Johnny entered one of Jim's paintings and that's why he didn't win."

Steve nodded, tapping his fingers restlessly against his thigh. "Bunch of idiots—that's what the judges are."

Brian laid a hand on Garrett's shoulder. "Let's all calm down. We don't want to make a scene and embarrass Johnny."

Vanessa flashed him a grateful look. "Are you ready to call it a night?" she asked when Christian and Johnny rejoined the group.

"We're taking the girls out for ice cream and we were going to invite Johnny to come along," Dana said. "He could spend the night."

"Don't worry, Johnny. We won't force you to play with the girls," Brian added with a grin. "I thought maybe I'd give you a butt kicking at chess."

Johnny looked at his mom. "Can I?" Vanessa hesitated, then nodded, unable to deny her son. Johnny looked at his uncle with a grin. "And we'll see who kicks whose butt tonight."

Minutes later as Vanessa and Christian left the hotel, she was grateful to Brian and Dana for inviting Johnny to go home with them. If anything could take away the disappointment of the art show, it would be spending the night with them.

"Jim's family is interesting," Christian said as they got into his car.

Vanessa laughed at his attempt at political correctness. "They're loud and opinionated and fiercely loyal to me and Johnny."

"And you wouldn't have them any other way," Christian said. He started the engine and turned to face her. "Johnny seemed to accept his third place okay."

"I know he was terribly disappointed."

"Not so much for himself, but for his dad."

Vanessa frowned at him with confusion. "For his dad? What do you mean?"

"I don't want to betray Johnny's confidence, but I think you should know what he told me while we were walking around the exhibits. He thought that somehow by winning, his dad would smile down at him from heaven and finally be proud."

A wave of sadness swept through her and her heart clenched as she thought of the relationship that had been nonexistent between father and son. "Even though Jim was in the house, most of the time he was an absent father. There didn't seem to be enough room in his life for anything but painting."

He reached out and caught her chin between his cold fingers. "Including his wife?"

She took his hand in hers and pulled it away from her face. "The past is gone, Christian. There's no point in rehashing it."

He gazed at her for another long moment, then reached out and started the heater, which thankfully blew a stream of welcome warmth into the interior of the car. "You want to go someplace and get a cup of coffee?"

She was grateful that his tone was normal, letting her know she hadn't offended him. There were places in her past she didn't want to revisit. All she wanted was a clean slate, a fresh start, with nothing from the past to haunt her.

"You can get a great cup of coffee at my place," she said.

A grin slowly spread across his face. "That's the best offer I've had all night."

She returned his grin. "That better be the only offer you've had all night."

As they drove to her house silence fell between them. It wasn't an unpleasant silence, but it was one that made her think of unpleasant things . . . like phone calls and social workers and the inexplicable appearance of a jacket on the sofa.

She hadn't told Jim's family about the social worker coming to the house. She hadn't wanted to worry anyone and it seemed the matter had been settled. But she couldn't help wondering who might have made that call, couldn't help but realize it was somebody who knew her intimately.

Most of the people at the real estate office had known her when she'd gone through the darkness of her alcoholic binges.

"What are you thinking?" Christian asked. He shot her a quick glance. "I can feel tension coming from you."

"Sorry. I was just wondering who might have made the call to Social Services about my drinking."

"I hope you don't entertain any doubts about me making the call."

"To be honest, you're about the only person in my life that I really trust right now," she replied.

"I hope you always trust me," he said. "I want to be the man you turn to when you need somebody."

His words cast the badness away, at least for the time being. She wasn't going to allow bad thoughts to interfere with an evening with Christian.

She'd planned on inviting him back to the house anyway and had spent most of the afternoon cleaning. A sense of pride filled her as he stepped into her foyer and looked around with interest.

"Beautiful woodwork," he said. "Original, isn't it?"

"Yes. We spent months sanding it. The people who owned the house before us had painted it all black."

He winced. "Why do people do that? Cover the natural beauty of wood with paint?" She took his coat from him and hung both his and her own in the entry closet.

"Follow me, I'll put the coffee on." She led him through the living room, aware of him looking around as they passed through.

She was proud of the hunter green sofa with the beige and green–striped accent pillows. Celery green curtains hung at the windows, their cool soothing color complementing the darker tones.

Jim had never had any interest in decorating other than his work space in the studio. She'd had a free hand in the rest of the rooms to choose the colors and styles she loved.

The kitchen was a burst of yellow, bright and cheerful and warm and inviting. She gestured him to the round oak table while she went to the counter that held the coffeemaker.

"I can see why you love this place," he said. "It feels like home, like a lot of care and love has gone into it."

"I was so afraid I was going to lose it when Jim died."

"You mentioned that he didn't have any life insurance? That's odd for a man who has a family."

"I didn't know he didn't have any until he was dead." She busied herself filling a filter with coffee. "He didn't tell me he'd canceled it the year before." She turned back to the counter to pour the water into the coffeemaker.

"Besides, I don't even know if it would have paid out, since he committed suicide."

She'd been devastated when she'd discovered what Jim had done. But it hadn't been the first time she'd been devastated by his unpredictable behavior.

"While this coffee is brewing, do you mind if I run upstairs and change clothes?" she asked.

One of his eyebrows danced up and down in a Groucho Marx imitation. "I can only hope you're slipping into something more comfortable?"

"Yeah, a pair of sweatpants and a sweatshirt."

"There's nothing I find sexier on a woman than sweatpants and a sweatshirt."

She laughed. "Stop looking at me that way. We are going to sit at the table and drink coffee like two adults."

"And after coffee?"

"And after coffee it's quite possible you're going to get lucky, sailor." She danced out of the room, laughing at the expression on his face.

Oh, it felt good to see that light in his eyes, to share the laughter. She practically floated up the stairs, the shine of Christian's eyes warming her heart.

She knew they would make love again tonight. She couldn't resist any opportunity to be in his arms. Johnny was safe at his uncle Brian's and she had a feeling Christian would be sharing coffee at her kitchen table in the morning.

Maybe she'd surprise him and instead of putting on a pair of sweatpants and a sweatshirt, she'd pull on her short red silk summer nightgown. She grinned at the thought. If she did, she had a feeling there would be no coffee drinking going on anytime soon.

She flipped on the light in her bedroom and froze. For a moment she couldn't comprehend what she was seeing. For a moment she couldn't move. Couldn't breathe.

The red Dior dress was laid out in the center of the bed, as if waiting only for her to pull it on over her head. But nobody would ever wear the dress again. The skirt had been slashed to ribbons and a knife protruded from the bodice of the gown.

Right where her heart would be if it were on her body.

The stunned shock that had gripped her and held her inert cracked and she backed out of the room with a scream.

Chapter 19

She turned away, unable to catch her breath, terror making her hyperventilate as she started down the stairs. She nearly stumbled and would have fallen if Christian hadn't caught her by the shoulders to steady her.

"What's wrong?" he asked.

For a moment she couldn't speak, couldn't find the air to force out any words. He gripped her shoulders more tightly and gave her a small shake. "Talk to me, honey. What's the matter?"

"On my bed. My dress. Somebody's been in the house." Fear riveted through her as a new thought struck her. "They may still be here." She clung to him, terror icing her veins. "It's Jim," she whispered, her fingers biting into his arms. "He's alive. Oh God, he's alive."

Christian looked up the staircase toward the master suite. "Honey, you aren't making sense. Show me what's wrong."

She nodded, her entire body trembling. He put an arm around her shoulder and together they walked down the hallway and back to her bedroom.

"Jesus," Christian hissed as he saw the dress on the bed. He tightened his arm around her shoulder. "Come on, let's call the police."

"He could still be here," she whispered. She couldn't get past the terror. It ripped inside her as her gaze darted around the room. Suddenly every shadow looked ominous; every cupboard and closet in the house might hide danger. "We need to wait outside. We need to get out of here." Her voice rose with a touch of hysteria. "Please, get me out of here. I need to get out."

"Okay. Okay, we'll wait in my car. Come on, let's get downstairs."

Her legs felt like frozen weights as they went back down the stairs. He guided her to the entryway closet, where he grabbed their coats. "My cell phone is in the car. We'll call the police from there."

She nodded, just wanting to get out . . . out of this house. The cold night air had nothing on the cold wind that blew through her. She slid into the passenger seat of Christian's car and locked the door. The trembling of her body intensified as she stared at her house.

Christian started the car engine, grabbed his cell phone from the glove box and dialed 911. He gave the dispatcher her address and reported an intruder.

"He's alive," she said when he'd made the call and hung up. "It's Jim. It all makes sense now. The roses, the phone calls, the jacket and now this."

She closed her eyes and rocked back and forth, fighting a fear as great as any she'd ever known. He's alive. He's alive. The words reverberated around and around in her head.

"Vanessa, what are you talking about?" Christian

grabbed her hand and held it between both of his. "Honey, Jim is dead. He's been gone for a long time."

"No." Her eyes snapped open. "They never found his body. We thought he drowned, but he didn't. He's back and he's tormenting me."

"Tormenting you how?" He removed one hand from hers to flip on the heat. He adjusted one of the vents so the warm air was blowing directly on her. But there wasn't enough warmth in the world to fight the icy cold in her veins.

"It started with the roses. You remember, I thought they were from you. They were peace roses, the kind Jim always sent me after we'd had a fight. Then the phone calls started." She swallowed hard, her heart beginning to slow to a more normal rhythm as the flare of initial adrenaline ebbed.

"What phone calls?"

"I answer and hear the sound of water, like the rush of a river or a fast-moving stream. Then there's the sound of gurgling, like somebody is drowning."

Christian gasped softly. "Why didn't you tell me?"

"When I got the first call, I thought it was just a stupid prank. Kids having fun. I tried to forget about it. Then I got the second one, just like the first, only at the end of the call he said my name. 'Vanessa.'" She shivered as she remembered the shock of hearing her name whispered across the line.

"Then the night after the skating party his jacket was tossed over the back of the sofa. It had been hanging in the closet since his death, but there it was, on the sofa. Now the dress. Jim bought it for me. It was his favorite.

Oh God, Christian, he's alive and he's coming after me."
Tears blurred her vision as she stared at him.

"Honey, that doesn't make any sense," he protested
gently. "If it was Jim, why would he be angry with you?
Why would he want to torment you?"

Her heart began to thump again in a quickened
rhythm. She was going to have to talk about it. She was
going to have to go back in time and think about what
things had been like in the months and weeks leading up
to Jim's dive off the bridge.

"He must have known," she said more to herself than
to Christian. She stared at the front of the house, dis-
cernible only by the light burning from a nearby street-
lamp. "Somehow he must have known. That's why he's
doing all this. That's why he's so angry."

"Known what?"

She looked at Christian once again, her heart beating
so hard she felt as if the sound of it filled the car. "I was
going to leave him. I was going to take Johnny and go as
far away from him as I could get."

A headache exploded in the center of her forehead and
she rubbed at it with two cold fingers. How was this possible? How was it possible that he was alive? Had he been
watching them for the last two years? It didn't seem possible and yet nothing else made any kind of sense.

Aware that Christian was waiting for her to continue,
she dropped her hand into her lap and gripped the edge of
her coat as if needing to hang on to something.

"He was sick, mentally ill, and getting more ill every
day. I tried to get him to see a doctor, but he refused. I
tried to be supportive, but it got so bad I knew we

couldn't stay. If nothing else, I had to get Johnny away from the craziness."

Christian tightened his fingers around her hand and his eyes gleamed with a hard edge. "Was he abusive? Did he hurt you?"

"No, no, he never physically hurt me. Jim's abuse was mostly self-inflicted. He'd go days without sleeping or eating. He'd hole himself up in the studio and demand that he not be disturbed. We'd hear him up there, ranting and raving. One minute he'd be laughing wildly. Then the next he'd be sobbing. After that, he'd fall into bed for a couple of days of sleeping. When he got up, things would be relatively normal for the next day or two, but then I'd feel his manic energy building again."

She broke off, surprised that talking about it, about him, had brought an odd cathartic relief. She'd never told anyone how bad things had been with her husband.

"He often bought things we didn't need, things we couldn't use or afford. He'd go to the mall and come home with jewelry and small appliances and I'd spend the next couple of days taking everything back to the stores." There were so many other things; there was so much of Jim's behavior that had been nearly impossible to live with, that at times had frightened her just a little bit.

"Johnny and I were prisoners to his mood swings and I'd made up my mind to end my marriage when he jumped off the bridge and disappeared."

"We'll straighten everything out," Christian said. "Everything is going to be okay, Vanessa."

At that moment a police car pulled to the curb in front of her house and two officers got out of the car.

As she and Christian left his car to speak to the officers,

Vanessa wondered how anything was going to be okay. All she could think about was that Jim was back . . . and he was pissed.

It took the officers a half an hour to clear the house and assure them that there was nobody inside. When Christian and Vanessa returned to the house the policemen walked with her through the rooms, wanting her to indicate if she saw anything missing.

Everything was in its place and when they returned to the living room she sank down to the sofa, afraid that her legs wouldn't hold her up.

"There's no sign of forced entry," Officer Albright said. The other policeman, Officer Ricci, was upstairs bagging the dress and knife. "Who might have keys to your house?"

"My in-laws have keys." Vanessa frowned, finding it difficult to concentrate. "A couple of friends, but I can't imagine any of them doing something like this."

"Is it possible you left the door unlocked? You said you'd spent most of the evening away from the house."

She thought back to those moments when Christian had arrived to drive her and Johnny to the art show. He'd pulled into the driveway and Johnny had raced out of the house. Had she locked the door before she'd pulled it shut behind her? It was one of those automatic actions people did by rote.

"I don't know. I guess it's possible I didn't lock it," she finally said.

"Do you have any idea who might be responsible for this? Somebody you had a fight with, somebody who might not like you?"

"I think it might be my husband," she finally said.

Officer Albright looked from her to Christian, and then back again. "Your ex-husband?"

A burst of hysterical laughter threatened to erupt and she stuffed it back down. "No, my dead husband." As calmly as she possibly could, she explained about Jim and saw the skepticism in the officer's eyes.

"No offense, but I think you'd be smarter to look among the living than the dead to find out who's responsible for this," he replied.

At that moment Officer Ricci came down the stairs, the dress and knife bagged and in his hand. "The knife is one of your own steak knives, Mrs. Abbott," he said. "I noticed the incomplete set in the wood block in your kitchen. I dusted the handle for prints, but there was nothing there. I'd guess whoever got in here was wearing gloves."

"There's nothing much more we can do here," Albright said. "My recommendation would be that you change the locks on all your doors and don't give anyone a key."

"Thank you for coming out," Christian said as he walked the two men to the door. Vanessa remained on the sofa, not having the strength to move.

"Of course they didn't believe me about Jim," she said when Christian came back into the living room.

He sat beside her on the sofa and pulled her into his arms. She leaned her head against his chest. For the first time since seeing the dress, she felt safe with the strength of Christian's arms surrounding her, the steady beat of his heart against her ear.

"You have to admit, it does seem a little far-fetched," he replied. "If it is Jim, if he somehow managed to survive the river, then what's taken him so long? I mean, why is he back now, after two years?"

"I don't know," she admitted wearily. "I can't think anymore." She didn't *want* to think anymore. "Tomorrow I'll have the locks changed on the house."

"You might want to think about a security system as well. If you want, I often work with a security company. They're reasonable and their systems are state-of-the-art."

"Maybe that's a good idea. And after that, I want to go and talk to Detective King. I want him to know what's going on. I need to ask him if he had any doubts whether it was Jim who jumped off the bridge."

He tightened his arms around her. "Do you want to go to my place for the rest of the night?"

She considered the option and a small knot of anger formed in the center of her chest. "No. I won't be put out of my house." She raised her head and looked at him. "I'll change the locks and I'll get an alarm system, but this is my house and I'll be damned if I let anyone scare me away."

"That's my girl," he said, and rubbed the flat of his thumb against her cheek.

Tears once again burned at her eyes as she gazed at him. "This isn't what I had in mind for tonight. I was going to surprise you and put on my sexy little summer nightgown."

He smiled, a gesture of tenderness that cracked the core of ice inside her. "There will be other nights." His smile disappeared. "Tell me what I can do to help."

She snuggled closer to him. "You're doing it right now. Just hold me."

"As long as you want me," he replied.

She laid her head back on his chest. As she closed her eyes, her head filled with questions. Had she accidentally left the door unlocked when they'd left that evening? Or did somebody who had a key use it to get inside and slash her dress?

Was Jim alive? Had he been waiting for the last two years, plotting revenge because he'd somehow known she was leaving him?

She'd never really felt true fear of physical harm from him, but there had been moments when he'd been in the midst of a wild manic meltdown when she'd wondered what he might be capable of.

Christian smoothed her hair with his hand, the gentle touch soothing. She'd thought the bad times were behind her, had believed she was finally in a place to reach out and grab happiness.

But somebody didn't want her happy. Somebody wanted her afraid. And she was. Afraid of what might happen next. Afraid that a dead man had risen from his grave to wreak his own special brand of vengeance on her.

A deep weariness overtook her and with Christian stroking her hair and his arms surrounding her, she gave in to the weariness.

"Never leave me." Jim's arms tightened around her, holding her too tight. His dark, intense eyes bored into hers with a frantic need. "You can't ever leave me. I need you so much."

He held her so close she felt suffocated, smothered by the raging madness in him. The need that shone from his eyes in a frenzied desperation was too great for her to fill, too great for anyone to fill.

Help me, she thought as she fought to get free from him. *Somebody please help me.*

They stood together in the darkness on the edge of the bridge. A cold wintry wind whipped around them, and the river beneath frothed and churned as if waiting to taste them.

"Let me go, Jim," she begged, fighting to free herself from his grasping arms.

"Never. I can't survive without you." There were tears in his eyes. "I'm sorry." He looked down at the water beneath them, then back at her, tears streaming down his cheeks. "I'm sorry, but I can't go on."

He tightened his arms around her and threw himself over the side of the bridge railing, taking her with him. Together they fell, the wind buffeting them as they plunged down . . . down.

She didn't feel the impact of the water, felt only its icy grasp as she plummeted into the depths. She fought, flailing arms and kicking feet, until she surfaced.

Gulping the sweetness of the night air, she began to swim toward the shore. Hands grabbed her and Jim surfaced next to her.

"Come with me." He pressed on her shoulders, dunking her beneath the surface.

Couldn't breathe.

No air.

She fought him wildly, but he held her tight. Drowning her. Drowning himself. No! No! Her lungs burned, needing air. Bubbles spewed from her lips. Darkness closed in and just before she was about to lose consciousness she heard the raucous sound of geese honking in the distance.

"Vanessa!"

The voice pulled her from the undersurface of the water, from the depths of her dreams. She opened her eyes to see Christian's worried gaze. "I had a nightmare." She burst into tears. The night, the dream, all too much for her to handle.

He held her tight, soothing her like one would soothe a frightened child. "It's all right," he whispered against her ear. "Everything is going be okay. I won't let anything hurt you."

She wanted to believe him. But what she feared was that nothing and nobody could protect her from the man she'd once thought she'd loved, the tragic artist she'd thought dead. A man who had flirted dangerously close with insanity and in the past two years might have gone over the edge.

Chapter 20

Christian and Vanessa sat side by side in the police station reception area, waiting for Detective King to see them.

It had been a busy morning. Upon awakening, Vanessa had called Dana to see if Johnny could spend the day with them. Thankfully her sister-in-law had indicated that it wouldn't be a problem.

Vanessa hadn't wanted her son at home while the locksmith worked to change the locks, and the new security system was installed. She didn't want him to be afraid.

Besides, despite the fact that she'd managed to sleep the night through after her nightmare, she didn't feel ready to face Johnny and pretend that everything was all right.

She glanced over to the man seated next to her. Christian smiled at her and reached out to take her hand. "Are you doing okay?" he asked. His deep voice held a strength and a deep caring that should have comforted her, but didn't.

She hesitated a moment, then nodded. She wasn't sure

how she would have gotten through this without him. They'd slept together in the spare room. She'd been unable to face her own room even after the dress had been taken away.

He'd held her through the night, his warmth, his nearness, keeping any further nightmares away. As soon as he'd awakened he'd gotten on the phone and arranged for the men from the security company to come immediately and get started on installing a system. He'd then contacted the locksmith, who had arrived within a half an hour.

Vanessa had sat at the kitchen table, nursing a cup of coffee and fighting a sense of vulnerability she'd never felt before. She'd been so strong. Even with the roses, the phone calls and the creepy feeling she'd had that somebody was watching her, she'd managed to handle it all.

But seeing that dress slashed to ribbons on the bed, the knife stuck into the bodice, had shattered her strength, leaving her with a sense of overwhelming doom.

She had a feeling Detective King would think she was as crazy as the officers the night before had thought. She suspected even Christian was merely indulging her, that he didn't really believe her theory that Jim was alive. But it made an awful kind of sense. It was the only thing that made *any* kind of sense.

Detective King appeared and motioned them to follow him. Christian released her hand as they stood and in that disconnection, Vanessa found her strength once again.

If it was Jim that was responsible for things, then Detective King would get to the bottom of it. If Jim was still alive, then she'd obtain a divorce. Even discounting any past they might have shared, she could easily divorce him on grounds of abandonment and not have to go into anything else.

She'd get a restraining order against him, do whatever she had to do to protect herself and her son from whatever danger he might pose. If he was still alive. If it was him who was tormenting her.

Detective King led them into a small interview room and motioned them into chairs. "What can I do for you today, Mrs. Abbott?" he asked.

He looked weary. Deep lines were etched into his attractive face and his blue eyes were bloodshot. He looked like a man who hadn't slept for days.

"I want to talk to you about my dead husband," Vanessa said. "Because I don't think he's dead."

The detective leaned back in his chair and stared at her blankly for a moment. "What are you talking about?" He looked at Christian, and then back at Vanessa. "As I recall, there was an eyewitness who saw your husband jump off the bridge that night."

"But could he have survived?" she asked.

He frowned thoughtfully. "I suppose anything is possible. What's going on to make you think he's alive?"

She told him everything, about the roses, about the phone calls and finally about the dress. "Is it possible he didn't die in the river that night? Couldn't he have survived the fall and the river?"

"I can't imagine that being the case," he replied. "He'd have had to have been one hell of a good swimmer. Have you seen him? Have there been any odd charges on your credit cards? Any unusual withdrawals from your bank account?"

"No, nothing like that," she admitted.

"Do you believe his family would have helped him? Given him money? Known he was alive and not told you?"

Vanessa frowned, remembering the grief that still tore through the family members whenever Jim's name was brought up. "No, I can't imagine any of them knowing he's alive and keeping it to themselves."

Detective King leaned forward. "Where would he have been over the past two years? What would he have been doing? Why all of a sudden now would he decide to torment you? And why would he be doing all this? As I recall at the time of his death you told me there were no problems with the marriage."

"I don't know. I've asked myself all those same questions and I don't have any answers," she replied. "I just can't make sense of why all this is happening."

"Look, I suggest you look to those close to you, people who might know that kind of information about you, and see if one of them might have a grudge. I'd be more apt to believe whoever is doing these things to you is among the living and that your husband is still among the dead."

Christian leaned over and covered her hand with his. "Vanessa, there's really nothing the police can do at this point."

"I'll make some inquiries," Detective King said. "You filed a report last night?"

"Yes, two officers came out and took the report. They also took the dress and the knife when they left," Christian said.

"What were their names?"

"Albright and Ricci," Vanessa replied.

Detective King scooted his chair back. "I'll look at the report, but Mr. Connor is right. There's little we can do at this point. But maybe there's something you can do for me."

"What?" she asked curiously.

"I'll be right back." The detective left the room.

Vanessa leaned against the straight-backed chair and fought against the sharp edge of fear that sliced through her. Every time she thought of the dress with its lacerated skirt and the knife protruding from the breast, a sickness churned in the pit of her stomach.

Detective King returned to the room. "I want to know if this means anything to you." He shoved a photo across the table to her.

Curious, she picked up the photo. It was impossible to discern what was in the background, but at the forefront of the picture was a red flourish of what appeared to be paint.

"Paint it red," she murmured, more to herself than to anyone else.

"Excuse me?" Detective King leaned forward, his dark gaze intent as it held hers.

"I said, 'Paint it red.'" She gazed back at the picture. "This reminds me of what Jim used to do to the paintings he wasn't happy with. He'd take a brush thick with red paint and slash it down the picture he was working on. 'Paint it red.' That's what he always said when he didn't like something or didn't want it anymore."

She raised her gaze to once again look at the detective. "What is this?"

A muscle ticked in his jaw and Vanessa felt the overwhelming desire to take back her question, to tell him she didn't want to hear the answer.

"That splash of paint was on Andre Gallagher's, Matt McCann's and Gary Bernard's bodies."

A gasp ripped from the very back of her throat. For a brief moment a blackness of horror obscured her vision and she reached blindly for Christian's hand. The blackness passed only when his hand firmly grasped hers.

"It's him. It has to be him." Her throat sounded scratchy, as if she'd been screaming for hours and nobody had heard her cries. She was screaming . . . inside, where nobody could hear. "It has to be Jim. Don't you see? He has to be alive."

"And what motive would he have for killing these men?" Detective King asked.

The question stopped the screaming inside her. What motive, indeed? Andre had been instrumental in gaining Jim visibility. Matt had furthered his career. Gary had been nothing but a friend and support. So why would Jim kill them?

She released Christian's hand and instead rubbed two fingers in the center of her forehead, where an ache blossomed with nauseating intensity.

"I don't know," she finally said. "God, I don't understand why any of this is happening."

"We're doing everything we can to get to the bottom of this," Detective King replied. "But I'm not convinced that two years ago your husband crawled out of the river, went into hiding for two years and has suddenly resurfaced to commit the murders of his friends." He took the photograph from her. "I need to ask you to please keep the information about this paint signature to yourselves. We haven't released that piece of information to the public."

"Is Vanessa in danger?" Christian asked.

"I can't answer that," Detective King replied. Then he frowned thoughtfully. "There's no indication that anything odd was happening in the lives of the men that were murdered. No strange phone calls, no slashed clothing, nothing like that. It's possible that whatever is happening in your life has nothing to do with the murders. However, that said, I recommend that you stay wary and on guard."

Vanessa stood, needing to get out of the police station. She'd hoped somehow to get reassurance, to get some answers, but instead she felt numb and the need to escape from the station, the detective and that damned picture that whispered of a dead man.

"Thank you for your time, Detective King," Christian said.

"Look, if anything else happens, give me a call," he said, but she suspected he said it just to placate her.

"So, what do we do now?" Christian asked as they left the police station.

"I don't know. I guess we wait to see what happens next," she replied. She raised her collar against the cold slicing wind and wondered if she would ever be warm again.

Tyler King remained in the chair in the quiet little interrogation room after Vanessa Abbott and Christian Connor had left. His mind raced with everything he had just heard.

He tapped his blunt fingertips against the tabletop, allowing his thoughts free rein. He'd initially thought that

Vanessa Abbott's theory was nuts, that she was trying to raise a husband from the dead for some crazy reason. Now he wasn't so sure.

Did he believe Jim Abbott was still alive? He didn't know, but it was an interesting possibility. Tyler knew few could take a plunge from the Broadway Bridge and survive. But he also knew it was possible.

So what motive could Jim Abbott have to hide out for two years? And what triggering event had brought him out of hiding?

An edge of excitement fluttered inside him. The art show? Was it possible that the idea of his wife cashing in on his talent one final time had forced him out of hiding, and he was seeking some sort of revenge against her?

He remembered the initial investigation into the suicide. Vanessa Abbott had insisted that she and her husband weren't having problems. But just now he'd gotten the impression that perhaps all had not been paradise in that marriage.

But what caused the rivulet of excitement to whisper through him was the realization that Jim Abbott just might be the connection he'd been looking for in the murder cases that had been haunting him.

It had been Abbott's work for sale the night that Andre Gallagher had been killed. Matt McCann had been Jim Abbott's agent, and Gary Bernard had been his friend.

Paint it red. She'd said that Jim used that term whenever he wanted to destroy something, that he'd make that same slash of red on paintings he'd screwed up. Paint it red.

He left the interrogation room and went in search of

his partner. He found her in the break room sipping a diet soda and munching on a bag of chips.

"Find Officers Albright and Ricci and get me a copy of the report they took last night at the Abbott residence," he said. "Then go down to records and pull the report on Jim Abbott's suicide. It happened two years ago."

Maybe Vanessa Abbott wasn't so crazy after all. His killer was either a man who'd crawled out of the Missouri River two years ago or somebody who had been very close to him.

A tingle of electricity sizzled in his veins, a familiar, welcome feeling. It meant he was on to something, that this might just be the break he needed. It meant the dead were finally going to speak.

Chapter 21

"**Y**ou look like shit," Alicia announced on Monday morning when Vanessa came through the door.

"Thanks," Vanessa replied dryly. Today was the last day she would work before the holiday officially began with Christmas Eve on Thursday night. She took off her coat, hung it up, went to her desk and sat, fighting the bone weariness that had been with her since Friday night.

"You feeling okay?" Alicia asked.

"Just tired. I haven't been sleeping well the last couple of nights. I've been having bad dreams."

"Bad dreams? Really?" Although Alicia's face held the appropriate look of concern, her eyes shone with a touch of glee. "What kind of bad dreams? I'm sort of an expert in dream interpretation." Vanessa eyed her with a touch of disbelief. "It's true," Alicia exclaimed. "I've done all kinds of reading on the subject. So tell me, what kind of dreams are you having?"

Vanessa saw no reason not to tell her. "Geese. I dream about geese."

Alicia frowned thoughtfully. "What are the geese

doing? That's important in a dream. If they're swimming, then it means a gradual increase in fortune. If they're standing around in the grass, that means assured success."

"They're honking," Vanessa said. "Honking so loud I can't hear myself think."

"Ohh, that's not good. That means death."

Vanessa stared at her, wondering if she was joking, if this was just another of Alicia's attempts to get under her skin.

Alicia stood. "I'm going to get a cup of coffee. Want one?"

"No thanks." She watched the shapely blonde disappear into the back room.

Despite the fact that Vanessa believed Jim was behind all the troubling events that had happened over the last couple of weeks, she wasn't one hundred percent convinced. She certainly didn't trust Alicia as far as she could throw her, although she found it difficult to believe the woman could be behind all the things that had recently happened.

There were only two people she trusted without reservation at the moment: Christian and Johnny.

She'd dropped Johnny off that morning at the Abbotts', indicating to Annette that she was hoping it would be a short workday.

Vanessa booted up her computer to check her schedule for the day. While she waited for the machine to upload she thought of the weekend that had passed.

Andre. Matt. Gary. All connected to Jim and now all dead, murdered and wearing red paint. The news had been beyond horrific.

Had it been Jim who had called Social Services to report her as a drunk? Had he somehow been working to get Johnny taken away from her so he could swoop in and take custody of their son?

No matter how many ways she twisted everything around in her mind, it didn't make sense. She could understand if Jim was angry with her, if he'd somehow known that she intended to take Johnny and leave him. But that didn't explain the deaths of those men who had been his friends.

Christian had offered to move in with her until the police got to the bottom of things, but she'd declined his offer. She was old-fashioned enough not to want to give her son the impression that it was all right for a man and a woman to live together unmarried. Besides, the new locks and alarm system had returned her sense of security.

She suppressed a sigh as she realized she had a ten o'clock appointment with the Worths. She wasn't sure she was in the mood for the preppy couple today.

Alicia returned to her desk and sipped her coffee, eyeing Vanessa over the rim of the foam cup. "Ready for Christmas?"

"As ready as I'm going to be. I just have a few last-minute things to pick up. What about you?" Vanessa fought for some semblance of normalcy.

"I shopped all weekend for a dress for the New Year's Eve ball and couldn't find anything I liked. Is the offer of your red Dior still good?"

Vanessa's heart clunked. Crazy suspicions flew through her head as she stared at the blond receptionist. She'd been so adamant last week in declining the offer of the dress. Did she know what had happened to it? Did she want somehow to prompt Vanessa to tell all the horrid details so she could inwardly gloat at what she'd done?

"I'm afraid the dress was ruined this weekend," Vanessa replied.

Alicia's eyes narrowed. "Honestly, Vanessa, if you've changed your mind about letting me borrow it, it isn't necessary for you to make up some story about it getting ruined."

"Alicia, I'm not making it up," Vanessa protested.

Alicia whirled her chair around to face her computer. "Whatever," she exclaimed.

Vanessa sighed. All she had to do was get through this day; then she'd have two weeks before she'd be back in the office. She needed two weeks without Alicia's moods, without thinking about property and sales.

Despite everything that had happened, she was hungry for sleeping in and holiday traditions and time spent with Christian and Johnny.

The day seemed to last forever. She spent the morning taking the Worths to see three different properties, but none of them appealed to Kate Worth.

She dropped the Worths off at their car at one thirty, then grabbed a fast hamburger for lunch and met her next clients, a retired couple who were looking to downsize.

The Perricios were a delightful couple and what Vanessa had planned as a short afternoon became much longer than she'd anticipated.

It was almost six when she finally pulled into the Abbott driveway to pick up her son. The day hadn't exactly been a success. Alicia had been a raving bitch after the dress discussion and Vanessa had just been glad to leave the office behind, knowing she wouldn't have to return for two weeks.

As she got out of her car she tried to put work and Alicia, and everything bad that had happened, behind her. Let the holidays be good ones, she mentally prayed as she walked to the front door. She just wanted peace and love and all the clichés of Christmas.

After she got Johnny, the two of them stopped by the local mall to finish up the last of their Christmas shopping and by nine o'clock Johnny was in bed and she sat in the living room listening to the silence of the house.

When the phone rang her stomach clenched with nerves until she picked up the receiver and saw Christian's familiar number on the caller ID.

"You doing okay?" he asked as she answered.

"Fine, especially now that I'm talking to you."

"How was your day?"

"Long and tiring and I really made Alicia mad." She related the events of the day to him.

"By the time you get back to work in two weeks she will have forgotten all about the dress," he said when she'd finished telling him what had happened.

"I'm sure you're right." She got up from the sofa and carried the cordless with her into the kitchen. "And how was your day?"

As he told her, she put the kettle on to boil and got things ready for a cup of tea. "You're planning on being here Thursday night?" she asked.

"I wouldn't miss it. I can't think of two people I'd rather spend Christmas Eve with than you and Johnny."

"We'll plan to eat dinner around six."

"Sounds like a plan," he agreed. "Are you sure you're doing okay?"

She sighed, the sound lost beneath the shrill whistle of the teakettle. She quickly pulled it from the heat and poured the water into the awaiting cup. "I'm really okay. I'm determined not to let anything ruin the holidays. I'm even sleeping back in my own bed tonight."

"I wish I were there with you," he replied.

She smiled and pressed the receiver more tightly against her ear. "Me, too. I hope you understand my feelings about you staying here. You know, with Johnny and everything."

"I completely understand," he assured her. "And I respect you for it."

"A little respect, that's all a woman really wants," she said lightly, then sobered. "Thank you, Christian."

"For what?"

"For sticking around despite all the problems."

"Vanessa, don't you get it? I'm in love with you."

A sweet ribbon of warmth wrapped around her heart at his words. "You just gave me the best Christmas present I could ever receive," she replied softly.

"The next time I get you alone, I'll give you the second-best Christmas present," he replied with a husky growl.

She laughed. "On that note, I'd better hang up. Otherwise I'll have to go take a cold shower."

"Sleep well and call me if you need anything. Even if you just want to talk or you have a bad dream or whatever."

"Christian? I love you, too."

"We're going to get through this," he said softly. "We're going to have a wonderful life together, the three of us."

She hung up with his words singing in her heart, making her feel strong enough to face whatever might happen. They were going to get through this and be together for the rest of their lives.

He stared at the three-story house where she lived. Johnny would be in his room with the blue wallpaper and the collection of stuffed bears he'd stopped collecting when he'd turned nine.

He'd be sleeping the dreams of the innocent, the gifted. Perhaps he'd be dreaming of colors. Cerulean blue. Umber. Cadmium orange. Yellow ochre. Vermilion.

Artist colors. The boy would dream the paint colors of his genius and that genius must be preserved and protected at all costs. If given enough time, she would destroy that genius, just as she had done with *him*. But he wasn't about to let that happen.

Disappointment welled up inside him. He'd hoped the call to Child Protective Services would yield better results, that Johnny would have been removed from his mother's custody. But the bitch had managed to dodge that particular bullet. Just like her lover had managed to escape the killing blows of his bat.

God, how he wished he'd been there to relish her expression when she'd seen the dress on her bed. Had she screamed? He closed his eyes and tried to imagine the sound of her scream in his head.

He'd heard her scream only once before. It had been at a Halloween party and somebody had jumped out of a closet dressed like a zombie. He dug into his memories to seek that sound, that delicious sound of pure terror.

Would she have spied the dress and released a high-pitched scream or a whimpering mewl of terror? The thought filled him with a pleasure that shuddered through him and made him hard.

He rubbed the back of his hand against his hard cock, thinking about her, about taking his bat and hitting her in the head, in the face, until she no longer existed.

He narrowed his eyes as his gaze swept the house with its cheerful lit wreath on the door and candy canes lining the walk.

She loved Christmas, always decked out the house like a gaudy present. The tree would be in the corner of the living room, garish with sparkling ornaments, flashing lights and shiny tinsel. Stockings would hang on the fireplace. One for Johnny and one for herself. There should be three. Dammit, they had been a family of three.

He'd give her Christmas. More importantly, he'd give Johnny Christmas with his mother. He hoped they had a wonderful holiday. It would be their last together.

Chapter 22

The house smelled not only of the turkey that had been roasting all day but also of pumpkin bread and the baking yeast rolls. Vanessa checked the table one last time to make sure everything was ready for dinner.

Christian would be arriving in the next fifteen minutes or so and she didn't know who was more excited, her or Johnny. "You think Christian knows how to play chess?" Johnny asked from the living room.

"I don't know, maybe," she replied. She checked the rolls in the oven, then walked to the doorway to see Johnny seated in front of the tree, staring at the presents beneath.

"No peeking," she said with mock sternness.

He flashed her a happy smile. "I'm not. I'm just looking." He moved away from the tree and onto the sofa. "Mom?" He looked at her seriously.

"What, honey?"

"I like Christian."

She smiled. "I like him, too."

Johnny didn't return her smile, but instead looked more troubled. "Can I tell you a secret?"

"Always." Vanessa sat down next to her son. "What's wrong, Johnny?"

His dark eyes gazed into hers. "I like Christian better than I liked Dad. Is that bad?"

"No, that's not bad." Vanessa pulled him into her arms.

"When I'm around Grandma and Uncle Brian and Uncle Garrett and Uncle Steve, they always talk about the good stuff Dad did, like his art and silly things he did when he was young. But I mostly only remember bad things. I remember him cursing and crying and telling me to get lost. He never acted like a real dad."

"I know." She tightened her grip around his shoulder. "I know your dad loved us as much as he was capable of loving, but I also know it wasn't enough. He had problems, Johnny, a sickness that made it impossible for him to really love anyone. You never did anything wrong. It was never about you."

He was silent for a long moment. "Would it be all right if I didn't paint so much? I don't want to make everyone mad, but I'm kind of tired of it."

"Oh, Johnny, I've told you a million times that I just want you to be happy. You have the rest of your life to paint if that's what you want to do. But you're only young once and you should be doing all the things that are fun."

"Christian wants to teach me about football. I think that would be fun." His eyes lit with a sparkle that warmed her heart.

She released her hold on him and got up from the sofa. "I've got to check on my rolls." She was almost out of the room when Johnny called to her. She turned back to look at him.

"I love you, Mom."

Her heart felt too big for her chest. "And I love you," she replied.

Minutes later Christian arrived, clad in a ridiculous Christmas sweater with a red-nosed Rudolph on the front. He carried in an armful of presents and a smile that filled every dark corner of the house.

"Something smells delicious," he exclaimed as Johnny helped him stack the presents beneath the tree.

"Mom's been cooking all day," Johnny replied.

"And I'm putting it all on the table right now," she said from the kitchen doorway.

"Do you play chess?" Johnny asked Christian as they came into the kitchen.

"I haven't played for years, but I imagine I could whoop some ten-year-old butt after dinner," Christian replied.

As they ate, Vanessa marveled that Christian might have ever doubted his ability to be a good parent. He didn't just pretend to listen to Johnny; he really listened. He had the patience of a saint and a good humor that had Johnny giggling throughout the meal.

It was magic, watching the man she loved interacting with the boy of her heart. It was magic seeing the secret glances that Christian cast her way, letting her know she was loved by this wonderful man who had come into their lives.

There would never be a repeat of the magic of the first Christmas they spent together, hopefully the first of a lifetime of Christmases together.

After dinner she shooed the men out of the kitchen, insisting they battle each other at chess while she cleaned up the mess.

As she worked, the sounds of their yells, their groans and their laughter filled her soul like it hadn't been filled since Grandpa John's death. When she finally had the kitchen all clean she joined them in the living room, where the two were stretched out on the floor in front of the fireplace, the chessboard between them.

She curled up on the sofa, watching them as they strategized their moves, fierce concentration on their faces. This was what Johnny had lacked in his life, the attention and care of a male. And that had been part of the reason she'd decided to leave Jim two years before.

If it had been just herself involved, she might have tried to hang on to her marriage. Certainly Grandpa John had believed that the marriage vows were forever and had instilled that belief in her. But it hadn't been just her she was concerned about. She'd been worried about Jim's effect on Johnny. And as Jim's mood swings had gotten progressively more disturbing, she'd known she had to leave for the well-being of her son.

She gave a little shake of her head, as if to dislodge any thoughts of Jim. Tonight wasn't the time to dwell on bad things.

"Checkmate," Johnny said triumphantly.

Christian sat up, a stunned look on his face. "I can't believe the little man beat me."

"His uncle Brian plays with him pretty regularly," Vanessa explained.

Christian stood and gave Johnny a noogie on his head.

"Before I play with you again I'm going to have to sharpen up my skills." He joined Vanessa on the sofa.

"Should I go get the book?" Johnny asked his mom. "Is it time to read the story now?"

"Johnny always reads ''Twas the Night Before Christmas' on Christmas Eve," she said to Christian, and then nodded to Johnny. "Yeah, honey, you can go get the book."

As Johnny raced up the stairs to his room, Christian looked at her. "It's so much easier than I thought it would be."

"What is?" she asked curiously.

"Caring about Johnny."

She smiled and touched the Rudolph in the center of his sweater. "That's because you have a loving heart and you're very good with him."

"All I have to do is remember all the things I wanted from my dad and give them to Johnny."

At that moment Johnny raced back down the stairs, book in hand. "Before you start, we need to go get a cup of hot chocolate," Vanessa said. "It's tradition."

A few minutes later, with hot chocolate in hand, they all cuddled around the crackling fire and Johnny read the story that had been entertaining children and adults alike for years.

A sweet peace swept over her as she sat next to Christian, listening to Johnny. This was what the holidays were supposed to be like, this feeling of contentment and, yes, happiness. She embraced the emotions deep inside, wanting to hold them close forever.

After the story and hot chocolate, it was time to exchange presents. Johnny had picked out a wallet for

Christian, a handsome brown leather with his engraved initials.

"See," Johnny said as Christian opened it. "*CC.* That stands for 'Christian Connor,'" he said proudly.

Christian turned the wallet over in his hands and smiled. "I think this is the finest wallet I've ever owned."

Then it was Vanessa's turn to open her son's gift to her. She carefully ripped the paper off the canvas to reveal a portrait of her grandpa John.

She caught her breath as she looked at the face of the man she had loved so deeply. "Oh, Johnny. You've captured him wonderfully."

"Scott helped me. We've been working on it for about three months in secret. Didn't you notice that I took the picture of him off your dresser?"

"No, I didn't notice." She ran a finger down the face, tracing the wrinkles that radiated out from the eyes, the tuft of silver hair that stood slightly askew. "I love it, honey. It's the best thing you could have done for me."

Johnny smiled proudly, then slyly eyed the gifts Christian had carried in. Christian caught his gaze and laughed. "Okay, now it's my turn." He grabbed one of the presents and handed it to Johnny. "This one seems to have your name on it."

"Thanks." Johnny tore at the paper, yelping with delight as he revealed a football game for the PlayStation.

"I figured we could play and you could learn the rules. Then next season we'll all go see some of the Chiefs' games together," Christian said.

"Awesome!" Johnny exclaimed. Vanessa wasn't sure who was more surprised, Christian or she, when Johnny threw his arms around Christian's neck.

Christian's eyes met hers, startled, and then his strong arms enfolded the boy and hugged him tight. If there had been any doubt in her heart about how she felt about Christian, that doubt was laid to rest in the moment of seeing the happiness on her son's face.

"And now, I think there might be something for your mom," Christian said as Johnny released him. He handed Vanessa a gaily wrapped present.

Vanessa opened it to reveal a beautiful blue sweater. "Just the color of your eyes," he said.

"You'd better open yours from me," she said with a laugh. He unwrapped his to find a smoke gray sweater. "Just the color of your eyes," she said, and they all laughed.

The rest of the evening passed quickly. They drank more hot chocolate, sang Christmas carols, and then played a game of rummy at the kitchen table.

It was just after ten when she told Johnny it was time for bed. "You don't want to be awake when Santa Claus arrives," she said.

Johnny grinned. "Mom, I'm a little old for the Santa Claus stuff."

"What? What are you saying? Are you trying to tell me there's no Santa Claus?" Christian looked stricken, making Johnny giggle.

"Off to bed," Vanessa said. "We have an early morning at your grandparents'."

Johnny walked over to Christian and hugged him. "Good night," he said. "And thanks for the game. I can't wait to play it with you." He then went to his mom. Vanessa kissed him with a loud smack on the forehead.

He raised a hand and rubbed the spot. "I'm not wiping it off. I'm rubbing it in."

She slapped him on the bottom. "Upstairs with you."

A half an hour later she snuggled into Christian's arms, the only light in the room the twinkling glow of the Christmas tree and the crackling flames of the fire.

"I wish this night could last forever," she said.

He tightened his arms around her. "Me, too." He ran a hand through her hair, his fingers twirling the strands as if he were memorizing their softness. "You know what I really wanted to get you for Christmas?"

"What's that?"

"A ring. An engagement ring."

Her heart stuttered and she rose up slightly to look at him. "I know, I know," he said hurriedly. "I'm rushing things. But it's just that when I'm certain of what it is I want, I tend to go after it. And I want you, Vanessa. I want you and Johnny in my life forever."

She moved out of his embrace and worried a hand through her hair. "I want that, too. But with things the way they are right now, I couldn't have accepted an engagement ring, not now, not until I know if Jim is still alive." She forced a smile to her lips. "I can't be married to one man and engaged to another."

His dark gaze held hers for a long moment. Then he reached out a hand and laid it on the side of her face, warming her skin with his touch. "Keep in mind that it might not be Jim. I don't want you to be so certain that it's him that you don't watch the other people in your life. I don't want you to let your guard down."

"I won't." She moved back into his arms and he held her tight, felt the beating of her heart against his own. "At least so far, everything that has happened hasn't been physically threatening. Just roses and phone calls and a stabbed dress."

Since the moment they had found that red dress, he'd fought a bad feeling in the pit of his stomach. Christian had never experienced real fear before in his life. Even the night he'd been hit over the head, there hadn't been time for him to be scared.

But he was afraid for her, afraid that he'd finally found somebody he wanted to spend the rest of his life with and a dead man wanted to destroy her.

Christmas Eve and Tyler King was spending it with dead men. He'd sent the rest of his team home hours ago, knowing that most of them had families to go home to.

In the last couple of days they'd checked every resource available for signs that Jim Abbott was still alive. DMV, Social Security, Internal Revenue—he'd had Jennifer hitting the computers in search of a dead man. But they'd found nothing to indicate that Jim Abbott was alive.

They'd learned that Gary Bernard had left Kansas City for Sedona, Arizona, days after Jim's dive off the bridge.

They'd followed Gary's trail, speaking to his landlord in Sedona and the local authorities there, and finally finding a woman who'd been briefly married to Gary during his year in the dusty town. But there was no reason to suspect that somehow Gary might have aided his friend in setting up a new identity or that Gary had in any way harbored Jim Abbott.

Dead ends. Nothing but dead ends.

One thing was certain. Somebody was killing people

who had been close to Jim Abbott. And Tyler's gut instinct told him it wasn't the dead artist himself.

He reached for his cup of coffee and took a sip, his thoughts racing. The murders were personal, filled with rage. He closed his eyes and conjured up a picture of Vanessa Abbott in his mind.

Was it possible she was their killer? That she was somehow seeking vengeance against people who had wronged her husband? Was it possible she'd made up the phone calls, had slashed the dress herself, in an effort to derail any sort of suspicion that might fall on her?

Although possible, it didn't feel right. There was absolutely nothing in Vanessa Abbott's life to indicate that she might be capable of such things.

But if the killer wasn't Jim Abbott, and it wasn't Vanessa Abbott, then it was somebody close to them. Tyler and his team had begun investigating anyone and everyone who'd had anything to do with the couple, both when Jim had been alive and after he'd jumped off that bridge.

Wearily Tyler stood and stretched with arms overhead. Unfortunately the faces staring at him from the bulletin board weren't the only victims in his life screaming for justice.

Two days earlier the body of a young woman had been found in a Dumpster behind a beauty salon on the north side of town. She'd been tortured and mutilated and thrown into the trash like the wrapper off a cheeseburger.

He checked his watch, surprised to see it was a minute past midnight. "Merry Christmas," he muttered to the empty room, then grabbed his coat to head home.

Chapter 23

The doorbell rang at nine the next morning, just as Vanessa had finished dressing for the day of festivities at her in-laws' house.

She peeked through the tiny hole in the door to see Scott and Eric standing on her porch. She hurriedly opened the door. They came in on a blast of frigid air, singing an off-key rendition of "We Wish You a Merry Christmas."

"Enough," she exclaimed with a laugh, her hands over her ears in protest. She gave them each a hug, then gestured them into the living room.

"Where's the kid?" Scott asked.

"Getting dressed to go to Annette and Dan's," she replied.

"Ah yes, the family thing," Scott said, and wrinkled his nose. He set two packages on the coffee table. "We weren't sure if we'd catch you both in bed so early on a holiday."

"Are you kidding? Johnny was up at the crack of dawn to see what Santa had brought him." She pulled two gifts from beneath the tree and handed one to Scott and one to Eric.

"You shouldn't have," Eric protested.

"But we're glad you did," Scott added with a teasing grin. "Have you opened Johnny's gift to you yet?"

"Last night, and it's now hanging in my bedroom."

"It came out great. That kid continues to amaze me with his talent." Scott shook his head. "I think he's even more talented than his dad was."

"Talented or not, he's decided to take some time away from painting and I'm encouraging him to take a break," she said.

Scott looked at her in surprise. "Is this because he didn't win the art contest?"

"No, not at all." She sat next to Scott on the sofa. "I think maybe he's realized he's been driving himself and obsessing about painting for all the wrong reasons."

"What do you mean?" Eric asked.

"He's been painting to please Jim's family and to somehow try to fill his father's shoes. He's finally realized he just needs to be a kid and not worry about others' expectations. There will be time for him to paint, if that's what he decides he wants to do, when he's older."

"Wow, I have to admit, I'm stunned," Scott said. "I just always thought Johnny had the same passion, the same hunger, that Jim had."

"Well, I think it's terrific," Eric said. "He needs to play ball and catch frogs and chase girls like other boys."

"Whoa." Vanessa laughed. "I'm with you about playing ball and catching frogs, but he's way too young to chase girls." She couldn't help but notice that Scott seemed upset.

"Does this mean he doesn't need me anymore?" he finally said.

"Of course not," Vanessa quickly replied. "He needs you as a friend. I need you as a friend. You always have a place in our lives. It just means you might not be teaching him for a while."

Scott nodded, as if somewhat mollified by her words. They visited a few more minutes; then Johnny came down the stairs. They opened presents and hugged Merry Christmas. Then the two men left.

It wasn't until Vanessa and Johnny were on their way to the Abbotts' that she thought about Scott. Christian had told her to look closely at the people in her life.

Scott would know about the roses, about the red dress that had been Jim's favorite. Scott would even know about her brief flirtation with the bite of gin. He'd had a key to the house, although she hadn't given him one since she'd changed the locks.

Scott? But why would he want to hurt her? Why would he want to torment her?

Was it possible he somehow blamed her for Jim's death? There had been a time early in her marriage to Jim that she'd wondered if perhaps Scott felt more than friendship for her handsome husband. But she'd never had any indication that her husband was anything but fiercely heterosexual.

Still, she couldn't help but wonder. Then it irritated her, that she had to be suspicious of friends, of relatives and coworkers. It pissed her off that somebody was messing around in her life and scaring her.

The day passed as all holidays did at the Abbott house. Annette spent the day in the kitchen and Dan sat in front

of the television. Brian, Steve and Garrett looked as if
they'd rather be anywhere else in the world and the little
kids screamed and tore through the place with holiday
energy.

They all ate too much, Garrett drank too much and by
three in the afternoon both Brian and Steve had made
their escapes, pleading work despite the fact that it was
Christmas Day.

After they left, Bethany, Dana, Annette and Vanessa
sat at the kitchen table and talked about men and children
and life in general.

Vanessa found it difficult to concentrate on the mun-
dane conversations swirling around her. Instead she
found herself thinking about her brothers-in-law. Was one
of them behind everything that had happened to her?

She simply couldn't imagine any of them having anything to do with it. These were men who had shared her
pain, shared her grief when Jim had died. What would
possess any of them to suddenly decide to frighten her?
To attempt to take Johnny away from her?

The suspicions haunted her throughout the holidays.
When Garrett called to see if Johnny wanted to go with
him to see the latest action flick, she made an excuse to
keep Johnny at home with her. When Brian called to see
if he wanted to spend the night, she once again made up
an excuse.

Every time she left the house she looked for Jim or for
somebody lurking in the shadows. She hated feeling
afraid, hated fearing for her son and herself. And she
hated the person responsible for her fear.

She and Christian spent New Year's Eve together. She
agreed to let Johnny spend the night with a friend whose

parents she knew and trusted. She and Christian rang in the New Year by making slow, leisurely love.

All too quickly it was time for Johnny to go back to school and her to return to work. The holiday had been idyllic, but it was time to once again get back to real life.

As she drove to the real estate office, the clouds hung low in the sky and the air smelled of the approach of snow. Scott had been on her mind for the past week— Scott, who had been fiercely loyal to Jim—Scott, who would know all the intimate details of her life with Jim. Was it possible he was behind all the things that had been happening to her? Worse, was it possible he had killed Andre and Matt and Gary?

Even though her heart wanted to deny any such possibility, her head couldn't quite let it go. Who else could be responsible? If it was true that Jim hadn't survived his jump into the river, then Scott was a logical suspect.

But what if Jim had survived? This thought haunted her, caused her heart to slide into her throat. By the time Jim had made his leap off the bridge, he'd frightened her with his irrational thoughts and behavior. If he was alive, what twisted thoughts might fill his brain?

The minute she walked into the real estate office she knew it was going to be a bad day. Thick gray eye shadow clung to Alicia's eyelids and she didn't even pretend to smile when Vanessa came through the door.

"I suppose your holiday was just stupendous," she said, her voice low and filled with simmering resentment.

"It was okay." Vanessa hung up her coat and moved to her desk. "What about yours? Did you have a nice Christmas?"

"I had a crappy Christmas, not that you care," she retorted.

Enough, Vanessa thought. She'd had enough of Alicia's snide comments and foul moods. She was about to let her temper rip when the door flew open and Helen blew in.

"Whew, it's colder than a witch's tit out there," she exclaimed. She looked at Alicia, then at Vanessa, and must have felt the tension in the air, for she walked over to Vanessa, grabbed her by the arm and pulled her up out of her chair.

"Come on to the back with me and we'll have a cup of coffee and talk about the after-holiday letdown."

Vanessa allowed herself to be led back to the break room, where she sat, and Helen poured them each a cup of coffee. "One sugar, right?" Helen asked.

Vanessa nodded, trying to tamp down the anger that had risen far out of proportion. Helen handed her the coffee and she murmured her thanks. "I think you just performed a tremendous community service," she said.

"Really? What's that?"

"You prevented the murder of one foul blond receptionist."

Helen grinned. "I figured as much. The tension in the air between the two of you was sharp enough to perform surgery."

Vanessa smiled as the anger seeped away and instead she was filled with weariness. "Bad holidays?" Helen asked.

"Actually, the holiday was wonderful. I spent the entire time with the two men I love most."

"Ah, so things are going well with the new man in your life."

Vanessa took a sip of her coffee and relaxed against the chair. "I didn't know it could be this way. I didn't know love could be so easy. With Jim everything was so hard, but with Christian it just feels so natural and right."

"Then what's got you on edge?"

Helen's question made Vanessa realize the older women knew her better than she'd thought. After a moment of hesitation, Vanessa shared with Helen everything that had been happening. She told her about the phone calls, the dress and the murders that all tied to Jim.

When she was finished, Helen's face radiated the horror that had simmered just beneath the surface in Vanessa. "My God, Vanessa. What's being done about all this?"

"The police are working on the murders. I've had a security system put in at my house and there's nothing else that can be done."

"And you have no idea who might be doing all this? I mean, besides Jim?"

Vanessa shook her head. "I've thought and thought about it. I've suspected friends and family until I'm sick with it." She lowered her voice and leaned closer to Helen. "I even wondered if maybe Alicia was behind the things happening to me."

She'd expected Helen to pooh-pooh the very idea, but instead she frowned thoughtfully. "Alicia certainly seems to have a bone to pick where you're concerned. I think she's capable of making prank phone calls, sending you flowers and even getting into your house and tearing up a dress she knew was important to you. But I can't imagine her killing those men."

"I can't either," Vanessa confessed.

"Do you and Johnny need a place to stay for a while? You know you'd be welcome to stay with me for as long as needed."

Tears stung at Vanessa's eyes at the generosity of her friend's offer. She reached across the table and covered Helen's hand with hers. "No, we're fine. But you'll never know what it means to me that you asked."

Helen squeezed her hand, then got up to refill her coffee cup. "You know, you're a different person now than you were when you were with Jim."

"What do you mean?" Vanessa asked curiously.

Helen returned to the table. "You never talked about your life with Jim. You were the most private person in the office. You always seemed so terribly alone."

"I was." For the first time she remembered just how alone she'd been in her marriage. She'd not been able to talk to any of the Abbotts about the problems she had with Jim. She'd been married to a man who was mentally ill, a man revered and indulged by his family for the genius of his talent.

Jim's instability had made it impossible for her to reach out to others. She'd been afraid to foster friendships, unsure what mood swing might possess Jim if she invited anyone into their home.

It wasn't until this moment that she realized how much she'd been a prisoner to a man she'd no longer loved. And she refused to be a prisoner to the fear that had threatened to grip her so tightly in its insidious claws.

"I've got to get to work," she said, and stood. "I've got a ten o'clock appointment with the Worths, and if they don't find anything that strikes their fancy today, then I'm going to tell them to find another Realtor. I've wasted enough of my time on those two."

Helen grinned. "You go, girl."

Vanessa finished her cup of coffee, then went back to her desk, studiously ignoring Alicia while she waited for the Worths to arrive.

Scott Warren had been depressed since Vanessa had told him that Johnny wanted to take a break from painting. Teaching Johnny had been a way to somehow keep Jim alive. Watching Johnny develop his talent had been a way to assuage the deep ache of absence Jim's death had created in Scott's life.

Scott loved Eric with all his heart, all his soul, but Eric didn't know about art. Eric couldn't understand the passion, the drive, that artists felt. Jim had understood.

He now pulled a crocheted afghan more closely around him and reached for the nearby box of tissues. To add to the depression was the fact that he'd caught a rotten cold over the last couple of days.

He couldn't remember the last time he'd taken a sick day, but he'd called in sick that morning when he'd awakened feeling as if his head had been stuffed with cotton and with chills that made it impossible for him to stay warm.

"I'm off." Eric walked into the living room, where Scott was curled up on the sofa.

Scott couldn't help but notice how handsome he looked in his three-piece power suit. "You look nice," he said, his nasal tone making him wince.

Eric smiled sympathetically. "And you look like hell."

"I'm relatively certain I feel worse than I look," Scott

replied, and blew his nose. He tossed the tissue into a trash can he'd placed next to the sofa for that purpose. "You'll pick me up some cold medicine?"

"And orange juice," Eric replied. "I'll try to run them by here around noon, unless I get hung up in court."

Scott nodded and reached for another tissue. "Have a good day."

Eric left the house and a moment later Scott heard the rise of the garage door opening. He cuddled down deeper into the sofa cushions and picked up the remote for the television, not particularly looking forward to a day of sneezing, snorting and soap operas.

Eric had been gone only about fifteen minutes when the front door opened and then quickly closed. "Eric?"

There was no answering reply. "What the hell?" Scott pulled himself up and off the sofa, the afghan drawn tight around him. "Hello?"

There was nobody in the entry. But he was positive he'd heard the door open, positive that somebody had come in. "Eric?" He peered down the hallway toward the bedrooms. Had Eric forgotten something and come back?

He'd taken only two steps down the hallway when he was struck. Pain exploded on the side of his head and he reeled backward, the afghan falling to the floor as his attacker stepped out into the hallway.

He had a moment of confusion as he recognized the person wielding the bat. But before he could ask why, before he could even utter a word, the bat swung again, catching him in his chest and crashing him to the floor. His head smashed into the door frame and he lost consciousness.

The attacker raised the bat to strike again, wanting . . .

needing to destroy, to punish, to kill, but before he could strike again he heard the front door open.

"Scott? Hey, I decided to go ahead and get you the orange juice and medicine so you wouldn't have to wait until noon." Footsteps sounded in the entry and he froze, bat overhead, and listened to hear the sound of the refrigerator door opening.

He threw the bat aside, flew down the hallway and out the front door, running without looking back, pulling in air that was cold enough to slice through his lung tissue. Sobs ripped through him, deep wrenching sobs.

Let him be dead, he mentally screamed. Had the blow to Scott's head been hard enough to kill him? Had he cracked his head hard enough on the door frame to permanently scramble his brains?

He hadn't even gotten a chance to paint him red. Damn. Damn. He didn't stop running until he reached his car nearly a block away.

He got inside and started the engine. Then, not waiting for it to warm, he pulled away from the curb. Fucked-up. It was all fucked-up. If Scott Warren wasn't dead, everything threatened to explode. Scott could identify him.

"Make him dead. Make him dead. Make him dead." The sentence repeated itself over and over in his mind until the words ran together with manic energy.

"Makehimdeadmakehimdead."

Slowly the adrenaline began to ebb. It couldn't end now. It couldn't end yet. He couldn't get caught until she paid. He had to make Vanessa pay.

Chapter 24

Vanessa sat in the quiet hospital room watching Scott breathe and fought against the wealth of emotion that attempted to crawl up the back of her throat.

She'd just gotten home from work when Eric had called to tell her that Scott had been attacked and was in the hospital. She'd immediately called Christian, who had come over to stay with Johnny so she could go to Scott's side.

He was in the intensive care unit and hadn't regained consciousness since being admitted. The bandages that covered half of his head couldn't cover the dark bruising and swelling on the side of his face, a face as white as the bedsheets that swathed him.

Scott. Her heart ached, not only from her fear for his life, but also with guilt. She'd seriously believed he might be behind all the things that had happened. She'd wondered if perhaps he'd been the murderer and now he was fighting for his life.

According to Eric, who had gone to get something to eat, even if Scott survived the attack, there was no guarantee that he wouldn't suffer brain damage. The doctor had been quite clear with Eric that they wouldn't know the extent of any damage until Scott regained consciousness.

"Wake up, Scott," she whispered softly. "Wake up and be okay." Tears squeezed from her eyes.

She sensed somebody standing just behind her and turned to see Detective King in the doorway. She immediately got up and joined him in the hallway. "Please tell me you caught whoever did this," she said.

Detective King looked like a haunted man. Dark circles shadowed the area beneath his hollow eyes and a muscle ticked in his heavily whiskered jaw. "I wish I could tell you that."

She wrapped her arms around herself. "According to what Eric told me, if he hadn't decided to come back home when he did, Scott would be dead."

"What I need from you is a list of anyone else who was friends with your husband at the time he took that dive off the bridge." His words were delivered in a brisk tone, the tone of a man on the edge. "I need names of anyone Jim might have been in contact with before his death: friends, coworkers, whatever."

"Do you still think he's dead?" she asked, her heartbeat pounding at her temples.

He raked a hand through his short dark hair, causing it to stand up at odd angles. "To be perfectly honest, Mrs. Abbott, I don't know what in the hell to think. All I know is that I've got too many dead bodies and a man in there fighting for his life and they all have ties to your husband and to you."

"There's nobody left," she said, stunned to realize it was the truth. Andre, Matt, Gary and Scott had been integral in

Jim's life, but he'd had no other business associates or friends. "Jim didn't have many friends, but he had his family, his brothers."

Was it possible that Brian, Steve and Garrett might be in danger as well? She told Detective King Jim's brothers' names and by that time Eric had returned.

"I'm assigning an officer to sit out here in the hallway until Scott regains consciousness," Detective King told Eric.

Eric raised a trembling hand to his throat. "You think whoever did this might come here?"

Detective King's dark eyes narrowed slightly. "Who knows? All I know for sure is that right now Scott is our hope for finding out who's behind the murders. Pray that he wakes up and can give us a name, describe a face."

"I just pray he wakes up," Eric replied.

Suddenly Vanessa wanted to be home. She needed to hug her son close to her heart, feel the warmth of Christian's love surrounding her.

"You'll call me if there's any change or if you need anything?" she asked Eric.

"Of course." He leaned forward and kissed her on the forehead. "Thank you for coming."

Minutes later as she got into her car to drive home she checked her rearview mirror, looking for whom? Looking for what? She didn't know whom to be afraid of, but she was afraid.

Maybe it will all be over soon, she told herself. Scott will wake up and he'll be able to tell Detective King who attacked him. Detective King will make an arrest and it will finally all be over.

She held on to that thought the rest of the drive home.

It was possible that before this day was over the guilty party would be behind bars.

"That's the thing about life," Grandpa John used to say. "It's filled with all kinds of wonderful possibilities."

And terrible possibilities, she thought. But nothing stayed bad forever. Life wasn't static. Things changed, circumstances changed and murderers sooner or later got caught.

She walked into her house to the sound of Christian and Johnny yelling and cheering as they played a game of video football. The minute Christian saw her he paused the game, his expression somber as he stood to greet her.

"How is he?" he asked.

"Still unconscious."

"And how are you?" He pulled her into an embrace.

She allowed herself to relax against him for a long moment, then stepped out of his arms. "So, who's winning?" She gestured to the video game.

"He is, right now," Johnny replied. "But I'm still learning how to play. I figure by next week I should be able to beat him."

"Bring it on, little man," Christian teased.

Later, after Johnny was in bed, Vanessa and Christian sat on the sofa in front of a crackling fire. She'd called the hospital twice to get an update on Scott, but Eric had told her there was no change.

"Maybe you should take some time off," Christian said as she cuddled into his arms. "Just until the police get a handle on the murders."

"I'd go crazy just sitting around here thinking about everything," she replied. "Besides, I don't think I'm personally in any danger." She rose up and looked at him. "If the person responsible for all this had really wanted to hurt me, then there wouldn't have been a knife through a dress on my bed. He could have hidden in my closet and waited until I was alone and asleep and then killed me."

Christian's arms tightened around her. "Don't remind me."

A sudden thought struck her and she held his gaze intently. "Is it possible you were an intended victim? That night when you were attacked."

His gray eyes darkened. "I hadn't thought about it."

"I think you need to call Detective King and tell him about the attack. He probably doesn't know about it, since he didn't take the report."

"I'll call him first thing in the morning," he replied, then pulled her back against his chest, his fingers stroking through her hair. "It's going to be all right, Vanessa. We'll get through all this together."

She closed her eyes and listened to the steady beat of his heart, hoping, praying, that he was right.

Chapter 25

When Vanessa left for work the next morning, dark gray clouds hung so low in the sky it looked as if they threatened to engulf the earth. The wind that had been blessedly absent for the last couple of weeks was back, blowing at near gale force straight from the north.

The forecast was for snow by late afternoon, but she was hoping to be home long before the first flurries began to fly. Morning had yielded no change in Scott's condition, good news in that he was no worse and bad news in that he was no better.

Salt and sand trucks passed her on the street, hurrying toward the interstates to spray down a layer of grit for the arrival of the predicted storm.

She had two appointments today, one at ten and one at twelve thirty. The ten o'clock appointment was with the Perricios, the pleasant older couple she'd taken house hunting before the holidays. The twelve-thirty appointment was with a middle-aged couple who had just transferred to the Kansas City area from California.

She'd told Johnny that morning that she'd be home

when he got off the school bus at three forty-five. Hopefully the snow would wait until after then to begin falling. If it snowed as much as the weathermen predicted, Johnny would be home from school for the next couple of days and she'd stay in as well.

They'd bake cookies and watch movies and she might even play a game or two of that video football with him. She smiled at the thought of her son.

Over the holidays there had been a subtle transformation in Johnny. He seemed less intense, less adultlike. He hadn't gone up to the studio since he'd announced to her that he wanted a break from painting. She had a feeling much of the change in him had to do with Christian's presence in their life.

It was as if Johnny had surrendered the need to be his father in return for being a little boy and allowing Christian to be the man of the house. It was healthy and good to see.

What wasn't good was Alicia's mood when Vanessa walked through the realty office's front door. "For God's sake, shut the door. It's freezing in here," she exclaimed.

She wasn't just wearing gray eye shadow; she was swathed in gray, from the top of her turtleneck sweater to the bottom of her gray plaid skirt.

Vanessa was grateful that she had appointments that would keep her out of Alicia's way. There was enough going on in her life without her dealing with Alicia's foul moods.

She hung up her coat and went into the break room for a cup of coffee. She poured herself a cup, sat at the table and waited for the chill of the outdoors to leave her body.

Despite everything that had happened, she couldn't

help the core of happiness that shot through her whenever she thought of Christian. They had talked about marriage last night. They had pretended that the possibility that Jim was still alive didn't exist and they'd planned their wedding and their future.

"We'll take turns with the cooking," he'd said with that sexy, teasing light in his eyes. "Every other night I'll fix us a gourmet microwave meal that will knock your socks off."

"I have a better idea," she'd replied. "Why don't I do all the cooking and you do all the cleaning?"

"How about we eat out every night and hire in a cleaning crew?"

"Now, that's a real plan," she'd said with a laugh.

Even after he'd left for the night, the warmth of their plans, the love she'd felt radiating from him, had stayed with her. She'd slept without dreams. Unfortunately the light of dawn had brought back cold, stark reality.

There would be no marriage until they discovered if Jim was still alive. She certainly didn't want to have a wedding with the dark cloud of danger that seemed closer than ever.

Maybe in the spring. She sipped her coffee. God, she was ready for spring. Spring had been Grandpa John's favorite season. She'd watch him working soil between his fingers, readying it for a new flower or plant, and while he worked he'd tell her all about the wonderful things that happened in the spring.

"Birth, honey," he'd say. "That's what spring is about. Birds have babies, flowers raise their heads. Spring is for birth and new beginnings."

She was ready for a new beginning, a new life with

Christian and Johnny. She was ready to grasp at the happiness that seemed to flirt with the very end of her fingertips.

"Your clients are here," Alicia said from the break room doorway, then disappeared.

Vanessa quickly swallowed the last of her coffee, then went to meet with the Perricios for a morning of house hunting.

It was not only a pleasant morning but a successful one. She showed the Perricios a total of three houses, and the third one they fell in love with.

"Look, honey, there's a peach tree in the backyard," Mrs. Perricio had said to her husband. "Remember that peach tree we planted on our first anniversary?"

Mr. Perricio had joined his wife at the window and placed an arm over her frail shoulders. As they softly spoke together Vanessa had the feeling that the two were just as in love with each other today as they had been forty-two years ago on their first wedding anniversary.

Vanessa wanted that in her life, the kind of simmering passion and total commitment that would last through the years. She truly believed she'd found it with Christian, if fate would just be kind enough to let them survive the madness that had gripped their lives.

At noon she grabbed a burger to take back to the office and ate in the break room alone. Alicia's mood hadn't seemed to change during the course of the morning and Vanessa wasn't about to give herself indigestion by eating at her desk, where she could see the sourpuss look on Alicia's face.

It was while she was eating lunch that she realized how right Helen had been about her, how much she hated confrontations of any kind. She'd never really thought about it before, but she realized she'd go out of her way not to have terse words with anyone.

Her need to escape confrontation was what had kept her in her marriage for as long as she'd stayed. It was what had her spending every single holiday with her in-laws when there were times she'd prefer to simply stay at home. And she was eating lunch in the break room because she didn't want an ugly confrontation with Alicia.

Her twelve-thirty appointment was right on time, but they insisted they drive their own car and follow her in case the weather suddenly turned ugly. And it looked as if it could turn ugly at any moment.

"I'm taking the Brenners to see the Jenkins, Black and Walters places," she said to Alicia. "I'll check in from each." Alicia merely blinked her heavily shadowed eyelids in response.

The clouds were darker than they had been and the air definitely had the smell of impending snow. She kept her eye on the Brenners' car behind her as she drove to the first house she intended to show.

The Brenners had money to burn and were looking for an upscale home. The Jenkins place was a lovely two-story, complete with three-car garage and a great room that boasted a twelve-foot ceiling. It was obvious they liked it, but they weren't crazy about it.

The next stop was the Blacks' home. The house smelled of freshly baked bread and cinnamon. Alice Black knew how to show a house and always had something baking and everything in pristine condition when Vanessa brought people to see the place.

Again, the Brenners were impressed but not over the

moon. It was just after two when she drove up the hill to the Walters place, the Brenners following behind her.

Flurries had begun to dance lazily in the air and as the Brenners got out of their car, Lisa Brenner lifted her face to the frozen precipitation. "Isn't it wonderful?" she asked, cheeks pink from the cold.

"She's never seen snow before," Terry Brenner explained. "And we'd better take a fast look here before this wonderful stuff starts to pile up. It's been years since I've driven in snow."

The house was warm and Vanessa shrugged off her coat as they entered the kitchen. She took them from room to room, her saleswoman spiel falling effortlessly from her lips. She tried not to think about the last time she'd been in the house, especially when they came to the master suite, where she and Christian had made love on the floor.

"It's beautiful," Lisa said as they came back down the stairs and into the kitchen. "It's perfect for entertaining with this kitchen and the large dining room."

Terry moved to the door that led out onto the huge deck. He peered outside, where the snow flurries were a bit more earnest in their attempt to cover the ground. He opened the door and stepped outside, looked around and then came back inside.

"I don't know. It's pretty isolated up here. That road coming up here is pretty steep. How does snow removal work in the winter?" he asked.

"The city does a great job with snow removal, but I wouldn't be honest if I told you that hill would never be a problem," Vanessa replied.

"But I do so love the house," Lisa exclaimed.

Terry put an arm around his wife's shoulder and smiled at her with obvious indulgence. "I need to think about it." He looked at Vanessa. "We'll get back to you in a couple of days." His gaze shot out the window once again. "But I think the best thing right now is to get home. It looks like the storm they predicted for this evening is moving in more quickly than they'd thought."

Vanessa walked the couple to the front door. "If you decide that this place isn't right for you, I have other properties to show you."

"We'll be in touch," Terry said.

After saying good-bye, Vanessa watched as they got into their car and headed back down the hill. Time for her to get home. She checked her watch. It was almost three. Given the deteriorating weather conditions, she had to head home to meet Johnny.

She climbed the stairs once again, needing to check to make sure no lights had been left on upstairs. She paused for a moment just outside the master suite, allowing herself to fall back into memories of how the passion between her and Christian had exploded so out of control.

She'd never felt that way before. She'd never felt that intensity of emotion like she did whenever she was with Christian. He fed something inside her that had been nearly starved. It wasn't just physical; he fed her heart, her soul, as well as he fed her body.

A glance out the window showed her the snow was falling at increasing speed, no longer dancing lazily down from the sky but rather pinging slightly against the windows, indicating an icy core to each flake. Time to get home.

She headed back down the stairs and walked into the

kitchen, where her purse and her coat sat on the counter-top. As she rummaged in her purse for her cell phone she realized she smelled something odd, something familiar.

Paint.

Oil paint.

She turned around, heart thudding with a dreadful anxiety. Then she saw it. A splash of red paint on the pantry door.

Chapter 26

Christian stood at the window in his apartment kitchen and watched the snow fly. Work would be spotty now with the full brunt of winter upon them. The ground was too frozen for excavating and the last of the work on the latest strip mall had been completed.

He turned away from the window and sat at the kitchen table, where partially finished blueprints of his pet project were laid out.

He was at a place in his life, in his career, where he was ready to take risks, ready to jump into building the upscale shopping mall that had been only a dream up to this point.

Leaning back in the chair, he stared up at the ceiling and contemplated the fact that he was ready to take all kinds of risks. It was amazing how love could make you feel invincible, capable of any and all things.

Falling in love with Vanessa, he'd risked his heart as he hadn't risked it since being a child. Realizing that she loved him back had made the risk more than worthwhile. Loving Johnny had been an added, unexpected bonus.

He grinned as he thought of the boy. Johnny made it so easy to love him. The boy led with his heart, obviously hungry for a man, for Christian, in his life.

In feeding Johnny's needs, Christian had been surprised to discover the scars from his own past healing. He was determined to be to Johnny what Christian's father had never been to him . . . a loving support and mentor, a soft place to fall when the world got too hard.

His gaze once again went out the window, where a stiff wind was blowing the snow sideways and visibility was deteriorating quickly. It made him cold just looking out the window.

He focused back on the blueprints. It was a perfect day to sit inside and work on the plans. When he finally had them all finished he intended to talk to Vanessa about finding a good commercial location.

It was after four when his phone rang. He glanced at the caller ID and saw Vanessa's phone number. He grabbed the receiver to answer.

"Christian?"

The sound of Johnny's voice surprised him. "Hey, buddy, what's going on?"

"Mom told me this morning she'd be here when I got off the school bus, but she's not here and I've been home for a while. She doesn't like me to be home by myself."

Christian heard a faint tinge of worry in the little boy's voice. "You know, the roads are getting pretty nasty out. Maybe it's just taking her longer to get home than she thought it would," he said, trying to appease some of Johnny's worry.

"So I should just stay here by myself?" Johnny's voice held a slight quiver.

"How about if I come over?" As Christian talked he grabbed his car keys off the counter. "I can be there in about fifteen minutes or so." It would probably take longer, but he didn't want Johnny to know that.

"Would you? I mean, I don't want to bother you or nothing, but I don't like being here alone."

"I'm on my way right now. I'm sure by the time I get there your mother will be home, and if she isn't, then we'll play some football while we wait for her. Keep the door locked and don't open it to anyone but me, okay?"

"Okay." That single word held a wealth of relief.

Christian hung up, grabbed his coat and headed for the garage, trying to ignore the edge of concern that whispered through his veins.

Surely it was just as he'd told Johnny. She'd gotten hung up somewhere and was just running late. There was nothing to be worried about.

As he pulled out of his driveway, icy pellets pinged on the windshield, and his tires spun a moment before grabbing pavement. Snow was bad enough, but ice created all kinds of problems.

He hoped like hell that Vanessa wasn't off the side of the road in a ditch somewhere. Steering with one hand, he reached for his cell phone with the other. He punched in her number, but it went directly to voice mail. Wherever she was, she wasn't answering her phone.

He tossed his cell phone on the seat next to him, then turned on the radio in time to catch a news update. Snow ordinances were in effect. The news announcer reminded people no parking was permitted on snow routes, chains or snow tires were required and if anyone was involved in a fender bender, he was to get the appropriate information from the other driver and make a report at the nearest police station.

Road conditions were going from bad to worse and the forecast was for near-blizzard conditions in the next couple of hours.

Christian tightened his grip on the steering wheel, hoping, praying, that when he got to Vanessa's she would be there safe and sound.

She's been held up by the weather, he told himself again. That's all it is. Nothing more nefarious than slick roads and diminished visibility.

Yet even as he told himself this, he couldn't help the icy chill that invaded his heart, a chill that had nothing to do with the weather outside.

Chapter 27

Paint it red.

Vanessa stared at the paint, her heart crashing so hard she felt as if the frantic beats might break a rib. It didn't make sense. Her mind worked desperately to wrap around the presence of the paint.

Somebody is in the house!

The thought screamed through her fog-filled head. Somebody was in the house! Was it Jim? Had he come to punish her for imagined sins? To get revenge because she'd secretly been planning on leaving him?

Sheer panic forced a gasp from her as she fumbled in her purse, seeking her phone. It wasn't there. Had she left it in the car? God. Oh God. She had to get out of here.

"Vanessa."

She froze at the sound of her name, her hand still in her purse. Shock sizzled through her as Brian stepped into the kitchen.

"Brian. What are you doing here? Is everything all right?" She strove for a tone of normalcy, as if she didn't notice the bat he held in one hand.

"Everything is perfect," he replied. He *thunk*ed the end of the bat on the floor.

Thunk.

Thunk.

The hollow sound of the bat hitting the floor was horrifying and oddly hypnotic. She fought to stay calm, her mind screaming to make sense of things. Her fingers closed around the can of pepper spray in her purse.

"Brian, what's going on?"

"Justice. That's what's going on." He made no move toward her, but there was no denying the threat that radiated from his eyes.

"Justice? What do you mean?" Keep him talking, a little voice whispered in her head. As long as he was talking he wasn't swinging that bat at her.

Thunk.

"For Jim. It's all been for Jim."

"What are you talking about? Brian, what have you done?" Her body tensed and she watched him intently, knowing that the danger she'd felt surrounding her for so long now stood in front of her.

"What have I done? I've punished the people who killed my brother."

"Brian, Jim killed himself. He jumped off a bridge. Nobody else killed him. He was ill, Brian. He was mentally ill."

"Shut up! You shut up, you lying bitch." He took a step toward her, his eyes orbs of burning rage. "There's no mental illness in my family. Jim wasn't crazy—he was a genius. A fucking genius, and all he needed was people who understood him."

He might think there was no mental illness in his fam-

ily, but Vanessa recognized the shine of irrational right-
eousness that burned in his eyes, the kind of mindless fervor that had often lit Jim's eyes.

"He was going to make it," Brian continued, and the
bat thunked faster against the floor. "He was going to be
famous. He was going to have it all. But everyone ruined
it for him. Andre and Matt, they were like vultures, sucking the blood out of him to feed themselves." *Thunk.*
Thunk. "And Gary, that piece of worthless shit, didn't
even stick around to mourn Jim." *Thunk.*

The whole time he was talking, she was considering
her options. He stood between her and the doorway leading to the front of the house. If she was going to escape
him, there was only one way out and that was through the
door that led to the balcony.

He took another step toward her and her fingers tightened on the can of spray. "But you, you were the worst of
them all," he said. His features were contorted with his
rage, holding little resemblance to those of the brother-in-
law she'd always liked, had always trusted.

Thunk. Thunk.

The sound made her feel as if she were losing her
mind. Brian. Not Jim. Brian had killed those men,
smashed their heads in without pity, without remorse.

She stared at him in horror. This was the man who had
taught Johnny to play chess, the man who had come to
her house in the middle of the night last year when the
pilot light on her furnace had gone out. How was it possible that he now stood before her with a bat in his hand
and death in his eyes?

"Brian, I tried to help Jim. I did everything I could to
help him."

"Liar!" he screamed, the cords of his neck popping out as the bat once again slammed to the floor. "If you'd been there for him, if you'd been everything he needed, then he wouldn't have killed himself." Tears filled his eyes. "You destroyed him, just like you'll destroy Johnny."

He laughed, a deep rumble of laughter that chilled her to the core. "But I won't let you ruin him. Johnny is the Abbott hope. He has even more talent than his father had. He will be saved."

He raised the bat and rushed her. With a cry she pulled the pepper spray from her purse and aimed for his face.

He screamed and dropped the bat, his fingers scrubbing at his eyes.

Vanessa wasted no time. With tears stinging her eyes, she scrambled to unlock the back door. With a sob she ripped the door open and ran out onto the balcony. The wind whipped her hair, the cold slicing through her with a hot fire. The blowing snow nearly blinded her as she backed up against the deck railing.

A howl of rage resounded from the kitchen and he appeared in the doorway, eyes red and watering, but bat once again in hand.

"This is for my brother," he screamed. "This is for Jim!" He exploded out of the doorway, bat held as if he were about to hit the winning run out of Kauffman Stadium.

Vanessa had a single instant to realize she was trapped. Her instinct had been to escape, but in running out the back door, she'd sealed her own death warrant.

There was only one way out and that was down. She'd cheat him of his chance to deliver death. Without giving herself time to wonder if the fall would kill her, having no time to assess any other option, she grabbed hold of the railing and vaulted over it.

By five thirty Christian knew something was terribly wrong. Vanessa would never leave her son home alone for two hours without even a phone call.

She was in trouble. He felt it in his heart, in his soul. She was in trouble and he didn't know where she was.

He tried to call the real estate office, but nobody answered.

Johnny stood at the front window, staring out into the wintry mix, his back rigid and his fingers white as he gripped the window frame. "Where could she be?" He turned around to look at Christian, his face as pale as the snow flying outside the window. "Why isn't she home?"

"I don't know, buddy. But I'm sure she'll be here any time." Christian forced a smile of reassurance to his lips.

As Johnny turned back around to look out the window, Christian walked into the kitchen and punched in the number for the police department. This wasn't about the weather conditions. The fear that ripped through Christian had nothing to do with snow and ice. It was time to talk to Detective King.

The dispatcher who answered the call told him that Detective King wasn't in. "Please, this is an emergency," Christian said. "Have him call me as soon as possible." He gave the dispatcher Vanessa's phone number; then hung up and returned to the living room.

Once again Johnny turned from the window and looked at Christian. "Mom's in trouble, isn't she?"

"What makes you think that?"

Johnny frowned. "I'm not stupid. She put new locks on the door and the alarm thing and all those people we know have been murdered." Tears shone in his dark eyes. "I'm scared."

Christian crouched down next to Johnny and drew him into an embrace. "We'll find her, Johnny. I'll do everything I can to see that she comes home safe."

Johnny clung to him, his slender body trembling. Christian held him tight, his mind racing. Where was Vanessa? Dammit, what had happened to her?

The phone rang and he released Johnny, hoping the call was either from Vanessa or Detective King. He hurried into the kitchen to answer. It was the detective.

"Vanessa Abbott is missing," Christian said. "I know you-all don't consider missing-persons reports until the missing person has been gone for more than twenty-four hours, but considering the circumstances, I had to call you."

"I'm just getting ready to leave the hospital," Detective King said. "Scott Warren has regained consciousness and gave us the name of his attacker. It was Brian Abbott."

"Brian?" Shock gripped Christian. "Have you arrested him?"

"We can't find him. He's not at work and he isn't at home. I've got a dozen men out searching for him, but so far we don't have a clue where he might be."

"He has her." Terror gripped him, twisting his stomach into hard knots. There was no time to consider why Brian might want to kill her, no time to delve into the mind of a man who had already bludgeoned to death three men. "Jesus, we've got to find her."

"I'm heading back to the station."

"I'll meet you there." Christian didn't wait for the detective to protest, but instead hung up. As he pulled on his coat he wondered what he should do about Johnny.

He hated to take the boy with him out into the storm, but he had no other options. He could drop him off at the Abbotts', but considering the circumstances, he couldn't, wouldn't do that.

"Come on, Johnny. We're going down to the police station. They're going to help us find your mom."

Within minutes he and Johnny were in the car, driving the snow-packed streets toward the police station. Each minute, every second, that passed was sheer agony.

"The roads are bad," Johnny said, a small glimmer of hope in his voice. "Maybe she just had problems driving home."

"Maybe," Christian said.

Let her be okay, he prayed. Let us have our future together.

Tyler King met them at the door and saw on Christian's face the same kind of dangerous tension that coiled inside him.

"Why don't I have my partner take care of the boy while you and I have a talk." He ignored Jennifer's pointed glare of displeasure. He didn't have time to make nice with his partner. He had a killer to catch. "Detective Tompkins, why don't you take the young man here to the break room and get him a soda and some chips."

He gestured Christian into the closest interview room. "Any word on Brian yet?" Christian asked.

"No. We've got officers at his house and at his parents'

home. Now tell me about Vanessa." He motioned toward one of the chairs, but Christian didn't sit.

"She'd told her son she'd be home from work when he got off the bus this afternoon. When she didn't show up by four he called me and I went to her house. Now it's almost six and nobody has heard anything from her."

"And where does she work?"

"The Wallace Realty, but I already tried there. Nobody answered. I imagine everyone went home when the snow started falling." He paced, back and forth, nervous energy rolling off him. "I know she had two appointments for today, one this morning and one early afternoon, but she should have been home by now."

"So nobody knows if or when she left the office?"

Christian stopped pacing and stared at Tyler. "The receptionist would know exactly where she went throughout the day. They have a system. When she takes out a client she calls in to the receptionist, who keeps tabs on where she is."

"And what's the receptionist's name?"

Christian frowned. "Alicia." He slammed his hand down on the table. "I don't know her last name."

"Wallace Realty, right?" Tyler grabbed his cell phone. "Dave Wallace is the owner." It took only minutes for Tyler to connect with Dave Wallace, who gave him the name and number of the receptionist.

"Now let's hope Ms. Richards is home," Tyler said as he punched in the number. He didn't want to tell Christian, but he had the horrible feeling that if Brian had Vanessa, then it was already too late for the beautiful woman. He'd seen what Brian was capable of, knew she wouldn't have a chance against him.

Alicia Richards answered on the second ring. Tyler identified himself. "We're looking for Vanessa Abbott and we understand the last place she would have been seen was at the real estate office. Do you have any information on where she might be?"

"She took clients out just after noon and never returned to the office," she replied.

"Let me talk to her," Christian said to Tyler, a sense of urgency in his voice. Tyler handed him the phone.

"Alicia, this is Christian Connor. Where was Vanessa taking her clients? What houses was she showing this afternoon?"

Christian's hand tightened on the phone as he heard her reply. "What do you mean you don't know? It's your job to know." His eyes flashed with anger. "How could you neglect to write it down? Jesus Christ, Alicia. If anything happens to her, I'll personally—"

Tyler snatched the phone away and ended the call. Christian sank down into one of the chairs at the table, his head hung in defeat. When he looked back at Tyler his eyes were those of a dead man. "You've got to help her," he said, his voice a tortured plea. "We've got to find her."

"We'll find her," Tyler said with forced confidence. He just didn't know if they'd find her alive . . . or dead.

Chapter 28

She landed on her butt, the fall forcing all the air from her lungs. She looked up to see Brian staring down at her from the balcony, his face contorted with fury. It was there only a moment, then gone.

He's coming. The words screamed through her head. She pulled herself up to her feet and looked around wildly. No place to hide. To make matters worse, the snow that had been nearly blinding before had suddenly stopped.

The world was white and a preternatural silence hung in the air. Run! She couldn't go back toward the driveway. That was the direction from which Brian would come. There was only one way she could run—across the greenway, around the lake and through the trees. If she could make it, there was a housing development on the other side. Help. She could get help there.

The cold bit at her face and as she ran, and the air she drew into her lungs burned like fire. Her teeth chattered like castanets and her entire body shook. It took her only three steps to lose her high heels in the snow, and only several steps after that for her hose-encased feet to become numb blocks of ice.

The only sound was her breathing—a harsh rasping noise. She glanced back once, a harsh sob ripping from her soul as she saw Brian following her tracks.

She picked up her pace, stumbling to one knee and then rising again to run . . . run. She was halfway to the lake when the snow began to fall again, coming down with blinding fury. She welcomed it.

Hide me! Hide me, she thought.

"Vanessa!"

The cry was filled with venom. She glanced back once again, just barely able to make him out in the whirling snow. She could hear him now, not just his voice, but deep grunts of determination as he strode steadily through the storm.

Thank God she had decided to wear a light beige sweater and beige slacks today. If she was lucky, the pale colors would blend with the snow and he wouldn't be able to see her.

Her face and fingers had burned but now were frighteningly numb. She stifled a cry as she stumbled and slid face-first into the snow. She couldn't run much farther. Her body was beginning to give up, her blood freezing in her veins.

She reached the stand of trees and spied a fallen trunk. There was no way she would ever reach the housing development that might mean help. In fact she was becoming disoriented, unsure in what direction to run.

Finding it difficult to think, she crawled behind the downed tree trunk and curled up in a fetal ball. Cold. So cold.

Somewhere in the distance she heard the whack of wood against wood. Brian, hitting tree trunks with that bat and screaming her name.

"Vanessa! Vanessa, you bitch. I'll find you."

Whack. Whack.

She burrowed deeper into the snow, surprised to find it warming her. "Cover me," she whispered.

"Vanessa!"

Whack. Whack.

The voice seemed farther away and she began to relax. She felt as warm as if Christian's arms surrounded her. Christian. She smiled at thoughts of him. They were going to have a wonderful life together. She would finally have the kind of husband she'd wanted and Johnny would have the kind of father he deserved.

Sleepy. She was so sleepy. Maybe she'd just close her eyes for a few minutes. It was then that she realized she might be dying and she heard the sound of geese, honking discordantly from someplace overhead.

Tears oozed from her eyes, burning as they froze on her cheeks. She squeezed her eyes closed, unable to fight the sleepiness that overwhelmed her.

"Here!" Christian pulled up Vanessa's appointment book on her computer.

Alicia Richards stood at the front door. Detective King had managed to talk the woman into meeting them at the real estate office, in hopes they'd find something, anything, that would let them know Vanessa's route for the day.

"Her twelve-thirty appointment was with the Brenners. There's a phone number here." Christian read the number off and Tyler punched it into his cell phone.

Christian had never wanted to hit a woman in his life, but as he looked at Alicia Richards he wanted to put his fist into her face. They'd lost precious time because she hadn't done her job.

It took only minutes for Detective King to learn from the Brenners that the last time they'd seen Vanessa had been at a big house on a bluff overlooking a greenway.

"I know where it is," Christian said with urgency.

Within minutes they were in Tyler's car and headed to the house. As he drove, Tyler used the radio, checking in to see if Brian Abbott had been picked up. He hadn't been.

"There's no guarantee she's there," he said to Christian.

"She's there. She has to be." Christian's heart slammed against his ribs. He couldn't consider that she might not be there, that they'd rush to the house and still wouldn't know where she was.

The going was slow. The snow came down in torrents and night had fallen. Night. Christian couldn't imagine enduring much longer without finding Vanessa. He wouldn't make it through a night without knowing she was safe.

"Can't you go any faster?" he exclaimed.

"I'm going as fast as I dare," Tyler replied.

Frustration etched pain through Christian. "Why would Brian do something like this?"

"Hopefully we'll find out before this is all finished." Tyler cursed as the back end of the car threatened to skid out. "Right now I care less about why he did it and more about getting him into custody, where he can't hurt anyone else."

God, were they going to be too late? The Brenners had indicated they'd left her just before three.

When they reached the road that led up to the house, it was obvious the car wasn't going to make it. Tyler parked at the bottom of the hill and got a couple of flashlights from his trunk; then together the two men trudged toward the house.

Christian's heart threatened to explode as he saw Vanessa's car in the driveway. She was here! The front door was unlocked. "I'll take the downstairs," he said as Tyler took the stairs.

"Vanessa!" Christian screamed as he looked first into the garage, then raced through the living room. "Vanessa!" He flew into the kitchen, where her coat and purse were on the countertop. He stopped short at the sight of the red paint on the pantry door. "No." The single word fell from his lips with a horrifying dread. "Detective!"

"She's not upstairs," Tyler said as he entered the kitchen. His face paled as he saw the paint. He used his radio to call for backup as Christian ran to the back door and peered out into the wintry landscape.

The snowfall had ebbed once again and in the distance he saw somebody in a black coat moving among the trees. He raced from the kitchen and out the front door, gripping the long-handled flashlight in his hand.

She was out there and so was Brian Abbott. Christian circled the house, vaguely aware of Detective King behind him. As he drew closer to the trees, he heard a whacking sound. Then he spied Brian Abbott smashing a bat against a tree.

"Abbott!" he screamed.

The man paused midswing, his dark eyes connecting with Christian's. "Stay away." He turned to face Christian and wild laughter escaped him.

"Abbott, throw down the bat," Detective King called from behind Christian.

"I made them pay," Brian said, and laughed again. "I made them all pay. Andre and Matt, Gary and Scott. And your sweet Vanessa." His laughter filled the air.

A red fog filled Christian's head, a fog of despair coupled with an anger so rich it consumed him. With a cry of rage, he rushed Abbott.

He hit him in the midsection, tumbling them both backward onto the frozen, snowy ground. Detective King shouted, but Christian wasn't about to stop.

He wanted to pound in Brian's face. He wanted to take him by the throat and squeeze the life out of him.

I made them pay. I made them all pay. Brian's words echoed in every chamber of his heart, in all the recesses of his mind. Vanessa, his heart screamed.

Brian managed to gain his feet, the bat still in his hand. Christian tried to get up but lost his footing and fell on his back.

"Paint it red," Brian said, and raised the bat over his head.

"Time to wake up, honey."

Grandpa John sat on the piano bench and smiled at her. "Come on, doll. Time to wake up." He began to play the familiar, stimulating tune of "When the Saints Go Marching In."

She got up and sat next to him on the bench. Leaning into him, she smelled the scent of his cologne. Aramis. Grandpa John had always loved his Aramis.

He finished the song and then put an arm around her. "I've got to go now," he said softly.

"Take me with you," she said, and cuddled closer to his warmth.

He smiled, his eyes filled with the love that had sustained her through so many years. "I can't, baby girl. You have things to do, people to love and life to live."

"Grandpa John, I miss you so much," she said.

He smiled again. "There's no reason to miss me. I'm always with you in your heart." He got up from the piano bench and she wanted to weep.

"You get up now, girl. You've rested long enough." He walked toward a screen door and as he stepped out of it, it slammed with a resounding bang, which startled her.

Snow. It covered her. She brushed it from her face, disoriented as she forced herself to sit up. Where was she? Why was she in the snow? Sleepiness once again tugged at her, beckoning her to lie back down and close her eyes.

Sirens. She heard them in the distance and with that noise rushed back memory. Brian! She needed to run. She had to get up and escape.

She struggled to her feet as the sound of the sirens drew closer. They were coming for her. Help was on the way. It was only as she stood that a loud report came from the other side of the trees, the sound of a gunshot.

She stumbled in the direction of the sound and stopped

at the sight of Brian and Christian lying in the snow. Christian. Oh God, was he dead? Had Brian killed him?

"No!" The word ripped from her throat. She willed her feet to move, but she was frozen with grief, frozen with the cold.

And then he sat up. Christian rose and looked around. When he spied her he cried out. And a second later she was in his arms. He was crying and she was crying and the sound of the sirens was deafening.

He wrapped her in his coat and lifted her into his arms and carried her past Detective King, who had crouched down beside the lifeless body of Brian Abbott.

By the time they reached the house dozens of officers had arrived, along with an ambulance. Christian relinquished his hold on her only to give her to the care of the paramedics.

He climbed up into the back of the ambulance with her and told her how they'd found her, told her how much he loved her, and his presence, his words of love, warmed her more effectively than the blankets the paramedics covered her with.

"Johnny?" she asked.

"Is safe and sound at the police station with Detective King's partner," Christian said.

It was only then, with Christian sitting next to her and the knowledge that Johnny was safe, that she closed her eyes and gave in to the darkness that beckoned.

Tyler King returned to the police station just after ten. The snowstorm had finally passed, the bad guy was dead and he should be feeling the sense of a job well-done. But he was aware of the fact that it had been nothing but luck that had led them to Brian, nothing but luck that Vanessa Abbott hadn't either frozen to death in the woods or been beaten to death by her brother-in-law.

He'd missed something. He'd screwed up somehow and it would be a long time before he let go of this particular case. For the first time in weeks, he longed for sleep, but he still had work to do. He had a woman in the hospital who was eager to see her son.

He walked into the break room to see his partner, the irritating rookie, with a little boy's head in her lap. Johnny was sleeping, and for a moment Tyler stood and watched Jennifer stroking his hair as if to soothe him.

So the hard-ass Jennifer did have a heart. When she saw him in the doorway, she gently moved Johnny and got up from the leather sofa.

"What happened? Is Vanessa Abbott all right?" She stepped out into the hallway.

"She's suffering from hypothermia and a touch of frostbite, but she'll be fine. Brian Abbott is dead. I shot him."

"I wish I would have been there. I would have loved to plug the son of a bitch."

He motioned toward the sleeping boy. "Is he all right?"

A small smile curved her lips. "He beat me three games out of four in chess. He ate ten dollars' worth of vending machine food and he drew a picture of me that I'll probably frame and hang in my living room. Yeah, he's all right, not that I'm thrilled by getting stuck with babysitting duty."

Tyler stared at her for a long moment. She was probably going to drive him crazy before she was cut loose from his tutelage. She had a truck driver's mouth, a teenager's attitude and a penchant for popping chewing gum. And at the moment her eyes shone with a need for approval.

"You did more than babysit," he finally said. "You kept a little boy from being afraid when he didn't know where his mother was or if she'd be all right. You know what that makes you?"

She narrowed her eyes and took a step back, as if anticipating a blow. "What?"

Tyler smiled. "A good cop."

The snowstorm passed in the night and Vanessa awoke to the morning sun shining through the hospital windows. Christian was slouched in a chair next to the bed, his features relaxed in sleep. Johnny was on the sofa, snoring faintly between slightly parted lips.

Her heart swelled and unexpectedly tears filled her eyes as she thought of how close she had come to death, to never seeing Johnny grow up, to never knowing again the taste of Christian's lips on hers.

The doctors had been amazed how quickly she'd responded to treatment for the hypothermia and it looked as if she'd be released later this afternoon. That was fine with her. She was ready to go home with the men she loved by her side.

Men she loved. She thought of Grandpa John. There was no doubt in her mind that he had saved her life. He'd come to her from the afterlife to play the piano and wake her up. And if she hadn't awakened, she would have frozen to death.

Before Detective King had shown up at the hospital with Johnny, she'd told Christian everything that had happened from the moment the Brenners had left. She told him all that Brian had said to her, and once again related the story to the detective as Christian and Johnny waited in the hallway.

In turn, Christian had told her how they'd finally found her and how Alicia hadn't made any note of where she was and with whom.

But the most important thing that had come out of all this was that although Brian had wanted her to believe otherwise, it hadn't been Jim. Jim hadn't crawled out of his watery grave to torment her. Jim hadn't faked his death in order to kill anyone.

She turned her head to look at Christian once again, surprised to see him awake and gazing at her. "Hi," she said, noting the lines of worry still etched deep into his face.

"Hi, yourself," he replied, and reached for her hand. "How are you doing?"

"I'm doing great. I'm ready to go home and get on with my life."

He smiled. "Our life."

She nodded, her heart filled with so many emotions. First and foremost was love for him, but beneath that was a sadness.

"What's wrong?" he asked, as if able to sense her innermost thoughts.

"I was just thinking about Dan and Annette and Dana and the kids." She released a small sigh. "Dan and Annette have lost another son and I can't imagine what Dana is going through right now."

He squeezed her hand. "They'll get through it one day at a time. But my concern right now is for you." Tears shone in his eyes. "I can't tell you how scared I was that I'd lost you. I can't tell you how frightened I was that I'd never get to hold you in my arms again, that we'd never get our chance to share a future."

"Me, too," she whispered.

He got up from the chair and leaned over her. "And I can't tell you how much I want to marry you . . . to make you my wife forever."

She smiled. "What's stopping you?"

"For real? I mean, we can really plan, set a date?"

"Nothing would make me happier," she replied. He bent forward and kissed her forehead, then kissed her cheek and was about to take her mouth when a knock fell on the door.

He straightened up as Alicia walked through the door.

"I just had to come by and visit," she said.

Vanessa had a feeling the woman wasn't here to make amends for whatever role she might have played in the drama, but had come instead to feed her gossip monster.

"Alicia, I'm so glad to see you," she said. She motioned for Christian to help her out of bed. She stood, a bit unsteady on her feet, aware that she didn't make the most dignified figure clad only in the flowered hospital gown, with her hair wild.

"Christian, why don't you take Johnny out to the vending machine and get him a soda," she said. He looked at her curiously but asked no questions.

He motioned for Johnny to join him. "Come on, buddy, let's go get something to drink and maybe a snack."

Vanessa waited until they had left the room. Then she walked to where Alicia stood, the familiar hard gleam in the receptionist's blue eyes. She stopped when she was mere inches in front of her, so close she could smell her cloying perfume.

"I appreciate you coming," Vanessa said, her voice pleasant despite the cold, hard knot that formed in her chest. "I appreciate you coming because you being here saves me from doing this at the office." Before she was even aware of her own intention, she slapped Alicia across the cheek.

The blow stung her hand and brought with it a wealth of satisfaction. Alicia gasped and stumbled backward. "That's for not doing your job," Vanessa said. "That's for almost getting me killed."

"How dare you?" Alicia exclaimed.

"How dare I? If I were you, I'd start looking for another job, because I won't rest until you're fired from the Wallace Realty."

Alicia turned on her heels and ran from the room. Vanessa stared after her and she had a feeling she would never again walk away from a conflict that needed to be resolved.

Maybe it wasn't her best moment, but it had felt remarkably good. She should have confronted Alicia a long time ago.

She was standing by the window when Christian and Johnny returned, Johnny carrying a can of cola and a bag of chips. "Everything all right?" Christian asked.

He leaned over and kissed her forehead. Unconsciously she reached a hand up to rub the spot where his lips had touched.

"Don't worry, Christian," Johnny said. "She's not rubbing off your kiss. She's rubbing it in."

Vanessa laughed and she knew that happiness wasn't just out of her grasp, but rather it was in this room with her son and the strong handsome man who gazed at her with passion, with love. Happiness was in her hands and she grabbed it and pulled it straight into her heart.

Epilogue

Spring arrived early and brought with it many changes. Dan and Annette moved to a retirement community in Florida not long after Brian's death. Dana and her two girls went back East to live with Dana's mother and father, and Steve and Bethany separated. It seemed that Bethany's suspicions about her husband having an affair had proved true. Garrett had checked himself into rehab in an effort to finally get ahold of his life.

The biggest gift spring had brought was the discovery of Jim's body, putting to rest any doubts Vanessa might have had about his death.

She now snuggled deeper into the bed, her gaze going out the bedroom window, where the signs of spring were everywhere. Grandpa John had been right—she'd had things to do, people to love and life to live.

Just yesterday she and Christian had exchanged marriage vows in a small ceremony among friends. Johnny had given her away and after the ceremony he'd asked Christian if it was okay to call him Dad. Christian had

been so touched it had been several moments before he'd
been able to reply.

The attic room was no longer merely an art studio but
had become a place for Christian and Johnny to play
video games and practice football moves.

After the wedding, Johnny had gone to spend the night
with Scott and Eric, leaving Christian and Vanessa to
spend their wedding night alone.

And what a night it had been, she thought. The passion
that had fired to life between them on the first day they
had met had only grown stronger.

"Breakfast for my blushing bride," Christian said as he
entered the room carrying a tray. "We have microwave
bacon, microwave scrambled eggs, but I made the toast
from scratch."

She sat up as he placed the tray over her lap. "Hmm,
looks yummy," she said. But it was her husband who
looked yummy. Just looking at him, clad only in a pair of
boxers, made her heart race a little faster.

He sat next to her and those sexy, smoky eyes of his
narrowed. "You'd better stop looking at me that way or
I'm going to take that tray away and make wild, passion-
ate love to you."

She grinned and placed a hand on his sculpted chest.
"So, what's stopping you?" She laughed with sheer joy as
the breakfast tray hit the floor.

Turn the page for an excerpt
from Carla Cassidy's next novel,
coming from Signet Eclipse in March 2008.

He'd worked extra hard the last couple of days, sewing the clothes that would transform an ordinary woman into Kimono Kim. As he worked, he'd tried to keep his mind off that open window on the second floor of the doll shop. But [the thought of it tantalized him, excited him.

Soon, he thought. Soon he'd take Annalise and make her his final creative masterpiece. And just before he carried her out of her building, he'd set fire to the place.

Flames momentarily danced before his eyes, making it impossible for him to focus on the hand stitching he'd been doing.

A conflagration, that's what he wanted, a total fiery destruction of Blakely dolls. He could almost smell the smoke, hear the crackle and roar of the flames, feel the blistering heat on his face. He closed his eyes and lived in that moment of fire and soot and utter obliteration of the dolls that had ruined his life.

He finally opened his eyes and stared at the red and black silk he'd been stitching. Kimono Kim. That's who he was supposed to be thinking about.

He'd found Kim by accident. He'd been in his car stopped at a red light and had glanced at the driver of the car next to his. There she was. Her sleek black hair had glistened in the sunshine and her Asian features were absolutely stunning.

He'd followed her for the last three days, learning her routine and deciding how best to take her. She lived in an apartment with two roommates, worked as a dental assistant and was attending night classes at Maple Woods Community College. He had no doubt that he'd find a place to grab her. He'd have his Kimono Kim doll very, very soon.

The bulletin board displayed his genius, and he glanced over at it, smiling at the photos of the two life-sized dolls he'd created. His smile faded and a frown of dissatisfaction tugged at his features. What good was it to be a genius when nobody seemed to notice?

The news accounts of both the women's murders, in the newspaper and on television, had been sketchy. Nobody had even mentioned the intricate work that had been done by him on the clothing and makeup and hair.

"Someday I'll be famous," he'd told his mother one day when he was about ten years old.

She'd snorted with laughter, making him inwardly seethe. "You're nothing now, boy, and if you live to be a hundred, you'll always be nothing."

"Shut up," he now said aloud. "You shut up you old stupid, fat cow." It felt good to talk to her now in a way he never would have spoken to her when she'd been alive.

He glanced over to the chair, where a spill of lavender material awaited him. The Annalise doll was clad in a pretty lavender dress, and he'd already begun work on it. He wanted to be ready for her.

once again flames flickered in front of his eyes. His fingers tingled as he thought of wrapping them around Annalise's soft neck, then squeezing the life from her. As the flames subsided he saw in his mind the open window in her building. It was a sweet invitation to accomplish his ultimate goal.

Suddenly he needed to see the window in reality, not just in his mind. As if in a daze he got up and left his work behind.

Driven by an uncontrollable impulse his mind went blank and the blankness didn't pass until he found himself outside her building and staring up at the open window.

He climbed up the first five steps of the fire escape just to see if he could reach the window. His heart raced as he easily managed to grab on to the window ledge. He pushed the window with one hand and it rose easily without making a sound.

Maybe he'd just see if he could get inside. It was ridiculously easy to swing his leg from the fire escape through the open window and hoist himself up and over the sill.

He dropped to the floor behind a large stack of boxes, and for a moment he couldn't believe he was there. His exhilaration level was fever pitch. Standing perfectly still he listened, but could hear nothing but his own ragged, excited breathing.

He was just a flight of stairs away from her. He closed the window he'd come in through so that it was open a mere inch, enough for him to get a fingerhold to raise it back again and yet not enough to be visible from the street below.

He scooted out from behind the boxes, grateful for the moonlight that drifted in through the windows. The storage room was huge, but filled with enough boxes and old furniture to create an obstacle course.

He carefully maneuvered his way to the stairs. I'm not ready for her, he thought. It's not time for her yet. Still, his hand clutched the stair railing and he began to climb.

Impatient little snot. His mother's voice rang in his ears and halted him midstep.

He gripped the railing more tightly and willed the voice away. He climbed the stairs slowly, heart pounding in anticipation. When he reached the top he found himself in the small foyer, the door to her loft just ahead.

He imagined that he could smell her. The light floral scent she wore eddied in his head and made him half-dizzy. She would be sleeping now, lying in bed unaware of how close she was to immortality.

Stepping closer to the door he placed a hand on the wood. She was just on the other side. He could feel her life force warming the door.

He leaned his entire body against the door and closed his eyes. He could feel her. Her heat radiated through the wood, warming him and making him hard as a rock.

Take her now, a little voice whispered inside his head. *Open the door and take her right now.* He leaned back, breaking his contact with the only barrier that kept him from her.

His hand shook as he caressed the door and gripped the brass knob. Holding his breath he turned it, excitement sizzling through him as he realized it was unlocked.

He jerked his hand back and drew in several deep breaths in order to control his frenzied need. Not time, he reminded himself.

Slowly, without making a sound, like a shadow moving through the night, he backed away. Now he knew how easy it would be when he was ready. Now he knew he could take her without having to plan any further.

She didn't know it yet, but she was his . . . his beautiful doll.